MINE!

By

S. E. Robinson

MINE!

Text Copyright 2014 S. E. Robinson

This is a work of fiction. All the characters and events portrayed in this book are fictitious or are used fictitiously.

Edited by
Cassia L. Rainne
Erica K. Freeman

Cover Design by
Zel Scott

S. E. Robinson

This accomplishment is dedicated to the three Andreas of my life.

Andrea Cavanaugh, who taught me that the possibilities were endless
when pen hit paper.

Andrea Powell, who taught me that patience and understanding were
key elements to personal growth.

And

Andrea Robinson, whose undying love and never ending
encouragement and support helped me to realize my dream.
I love you, Mom.

MINE!

S. E. Robinson

MINE!

MINE!

"Sometimes, the demon we face is not *the reflection in the mirror."*
-- S. E. Robinson

MINE!

Prologue

It never ceased to amaze him that he could always find the perfect spot. The perfect perch, if you will. There he sat. A gentle rain danced lightly on his jet-black Yukon capturing glints of the full moon along its way. Series of beading raindrops conjoined to create small tributaries that raced to the bottom of his windshield. The street lighting had an eerie, yet romantic, aura as it illuminated East Franklin Avenue. It was whimsical and macabre at the same time. He listened to the raindrops. He swooned to the rhythm. Its melodic tone seemed to heighten his experience as he sat—and waited.

He looked down at his leather-clad hands. He could feel the strength within them as he flexed his fingers purposely, and almost violently clenched them into fists cracking every knuckle in the process. He grabbed the steering wheel as he sat in his vehicle strategically parked on Fourteenth Avenue South which ran perpendicular to East Franklin, acquiescing to the larger thorofare as Fourteenth came to a dead end. From this position, he could see the Santa Fe Villas Courtyard. It was an odd name for a housing complex in mid-town Minneapolis, but the residences were named more for its architectural design than its locale. The Villas were a series of townhomes—set in twos. She lived in 3-A, second archway on the right, the unit on the left. From where he sat, he would see her well. He glanced at his watch, a Tag Heuer, a handsome gift to himself. It was 11:30 p.m. In ninety minutes, she would be walking west on East Franklin, probably carrying her oversized purse and a bag of groceries. Yes, even at this hour. There was a 24-hour market down the street at the public transit stop at the corner of Fifteenth Avenue South and East Franklin. She would not have an umbrella, but she would be wearing a raincoat, probably her ancient Macintosh. At one o'clock, she would be traipsing home, seemingly without a care in the world—and he would be waiting.

He recalled the moment when he first saw her and knew. The moment when he knew that she would be next. He had been in Minneapolis nearly five months before on business. His business required that he travelled extensively, and he had been there for nearly three weeks. During that time he'd managed to do a great deal of "shopping," as it were, and when he saw her—just by chance, mind you—he'd known that she would be next.

He met her—well, not quite—he saw her at her place of employment. She was a nurse at the Hennepin Burn Center. She'd been attending to a young burn victim, and engrossed in her duties, she had scarcely noticed that he was there—but he'd noticed her. He'd seen how compassionate and understanding she was. She was attentive and endearing and the young victim, a girl no more than nine years old with third degree burns over twenty percent of her body, seemed to take to the young nurse and so was able to accept the treatment—even though she was experiencing a great deal of pain. The young nurse was in her late twenties and had striking features. She was not overly beautiful, but far from plain. Her skin was pale, but not peaked. She maintained herself well, though she did not exercise much—she had no gym memberships, but she ate very well— at least according to her discarded grocery receipts. He'd noticed how her dirty blonde hair had persistently crept in front of her face as she leaned over the child. He had noticed how well her slender, yet rather toned, body managed capably underneath her nurse's uniform. He had noticed all the potential she seemed to possess, and he'd known instantly. Just like with the others, he'd known right away—she would be next.

What he did not know was how long he would be in town, or when he would be back. So, just as his profession allowed, he was able to find out a great deal about her over the following few days. Enough to learn not only her name, her shopping habits, and about her associates, family and friends, but, also enough to become an expert on her travel habits and her daily routine. Enough to know what she would be carrying and what she would be wearing. After all, just like her, he too was very good at what he did. For even had she moved, changed jobs or even her residence, he would have been able to find her. No one ever escaped him. Ever.

He sat back into the comfortable leather seat and envisioned the dance. While others might categorize what he did as something different, something dirty, or something evil, he considered what he did as a dance. A devil's waltz, if you may. And just like a waltz, the steps were very deliberate. They had rhythm and purpose. They even had a certain grace and beauty to them, and he choreographed every move in his mind before he took the floor. He mentally rehearsed over and over, until every move was perfectly timed and every step was perfectly placed. And when the curtain was drawn—the waltz began.

He glanced at his watch again, his gorgeous watch. It was 12:57. He could hear the airbrakes on the Transit Bus squeal as it came to a stop and then, after a few moments, sigh as they released. Moments later he could see her walking slowly, carrying two bags of groceries up East Franklin. As expected, she had her oversized purse but she was wearing a black, three-quarter-length leather coat. An unexpected surprise. He had never seen that particular coat before, but that was okay. He liked surprises. Surprises always added something extra to the dance. He glanced at her and smiled.

Maestro, if you please . . .

MINE!

Chapter One

Minneapolis

"All right—all right, now. Let's get it together, folks!"

Lieutenant Brennan tried to bring the crowded room to order. It was 8 a.m. on Tuesday, April 20. The Minneapolis Police Central Command Post, which was set up very much like a modest telemarketing call center, normally accommodated twelve officers. There were twelve four-by-four desks placed strategically on the floor. They were each well spaced so as to not crowd one another and to give the normally assigned officers enough room to work comfortably. At the front of the room there was a blackboard and a whiteboard, both attached to the front wall. Just to the right of the boards there was some open space, while off to the left there was an easel with a large note pad, names scrawled across it in black permanent marker, just next to where Lieutenant Brennan stood. The lieutenant's office was off to the left. His office spanned two-thirds the length of the room, and windows stood where a wall would normally be. It allowed him to have a sort of fishbowl view of the floor. Adjacent to his office was a break room and civilian waiting area. It was comfortable and small, even cozy, but it served its purpose. In the rear of the room, behind the seven strangers, were twin elevators, the stairs that led one flight down to the main lobby, and the main entrance into the room.

"Can I have your attention, please?" Lt. Harold Brennan, normally a relatively soft-spoken man, raised his voice a bit. In the twilight of his career, with the grey hair and budding waistline to prove it, he wanted to cruise into retirement. However, sometimes life happens—and unfortunately this was one of those times.

"All right, everyone." He raised his voice a little more. "Quiet down!" he finally shouted. "There's a lot to do and very little time to do it." The room became quiet and the lieutenant continued.

"As you all know, state Representative Konetchy's daughter has been missing for three days. Ordinarily, that wouldn't raise any suspicions as Monica Konetchy is a very independent and strong-willed young lady." A small chuckle came from a few members of the crowd. "However, Representative Konetchy received a note in her mail this morning which leads us to believe that her daughter has been abducted. Jerry . . .?"

Brennan turned to a younger gentleman who was standing off to his left. Jerry Langdon, a sergeant in the Minneapolis Police Force and recent transfer from the Special Tactical Unit, called everyone's attention to an open area of wall. He motioned to Officer Soto, who was seated behind a computer with a projector. On the wall, before everyone, was a projection of the note. It was handwritten, not particularly neat, and apparently written in haste.

"This is the note. Lights, please?" Someone obliged, turning them off. Lieutenant Brennan pointed to the wall and began to read:

"To all that may be concerned. They lied to us and sent us to Iraq. We are dying in Iraq! And nobody seems to care. Well, I care. And until they pull us out of Iraq, I will keep this woman. Maybe then somebody will care."

"Now," the lieutenant motioned for the lights, "most of you know the routine when it comes to how we handle missing persons; and, let me state for the record that Monica Konetchy had not been reported missing. But with the emergence of this note, and the fact that Miss Konetchy has been unaccounted for, for the past two days, we are now officially considering this to be a kidnapping. And, as such, the FBI has been called in to head the investigation. The folks you see in the back are from the Behavioral Analysis Unit. They came here all the way from Quantico to lend us a hand with this little situation. The young lady with the intense look on her face is Supervisory Special Agent Constance Jordan, and she will run point on this investigation." Brennan motioned for Agent Jordan to come forward.

"I want to make this clear," he continued. "I have already pledged our complete cooperation to the Feds and to Downtown. I don't need any of that 'local authorities–FBI conflict, this is *our* turf' bullshit. We are all on one team, the same team, and I expect that we will conduct ourselves accordingly." At the front of the room Lieutenant Brennan gave Constance Jordan a weak smile—a "why me, why now?" type of smile. Somehow, she understood and returned it with a reassuring one.

"Ms. Jordan, . . ." he said to her softly and relinquished the floor.

Connie Jordan was the classic, native New Yorker. She had the accent, she had the attitude, she had the moxie. She was thirty-four years old, stood approximately five foot six, and had stark, black hair that almost looked blue when the sunlight caught it just right. Connie had strong features and was a very tough character, but she was not unreasonable. She was a sharp dresser, very professional in both appearance and demeanor. She did not beat around the bush.

"Good morning, ladies and gents," she began. "I want to thank Lieutenant Brennan for that brief introduction. The lieutenant and I have worked together in the past with great success. I must say that I expect that success to continue.

"As he stated, I am SSA Connie Jordan. I will introduce my team in a few moments, but first I'd like to get everyone up to speed with a little background on this case. Then, I'd like us to take a quick look at this note, and finally, with the help of the lieutenant, I want to go over a few housekeeping items.

"Now, as Lieutenant Brennan has stated, it appears that Monica Konetchy, the nineteen-year-old daughter of state Representative Susan Konetchy has been missing for three days—or at least that's the last time the state rep. spoke with her." Jordan paused for a moment, grabbed a small note pad from her jacket pocket, and read aloud, "Saturday, April 17, at approximately six-forty-five p.m." She turned back to the floor. "That's the last time the Rep. spoke with her daughter. Now, for anyone who has been following local politics and the associated social scene, you already know that Monica Konetchy is a bit of a wildflower. She tends to like the party scene and is not above disappearing for days at a time—and that's despite the fact that she has a full course load at U. of Minnesota.

"Monica Konetchy is five feet six, a hundred and twenty-seven pounds. She has sandy brown hair, pale skin, light freckles, and a dimple in each cheek. She has the tattoo of a rainbow at the base of her back just above her buttocks. She was last seen at about six-thirty on the night in question, leaving a local convenience store. We're not sure what she was wearing, but we'll get to that a little later. Reportedly, she was last seen right before the call to her mother, which was made from her cell. Thus far, she has not answered or returned any subsequent calls made to her phone. For the time being, we're running with the premise that Miss. Konetchy was abducted at the time of her last call, or shortly thereafter, and that's until the evidence directs us otherwise. Understood?"

Agent Jordan received a series of nods and grunts of confirmation from the room.

"Now," she said, turning to the wall, "looking at this note, we realize that it's not exactly a manifesto—but I'm sure we all get the point." She walked over to the wall before she continued. "Don't worry about the lights. I think we can all see this. Now, although the note wasn't signed, our kidnapper might have given us a couple of clues anyway. First, as you see here in the second sentence, he writes that 'they lied to *us* and sent *us* to Iraq.' That makes me think he's probably in the armed forces and might have already spent some time in Iraq. More than likely, he didn't enjoy his stay. Now, here and—here," she said, pointing to two statements. "Our kidnapper writes, 'Well, I care' and 'I will keep this woman.' This leads us to believe that this person is probably working alone.

"Now, at this point," Jordan said, turning to face the crowd." I want to introduce the rest of my team." She raised her hand and motioned to the back of the room. "The young man to the far left is Special Agent Jacob Lynch—he's our IT specialist." Agent Lynch moved forward and gave a small wave. A rather timid man, he stood at the average height of about five feet nine, and usually had very little to say. Somewhat plain to look at, Lynch had straight brown hair, and a slightly freckled complexion. He was a tad overweight.

"To his left," she continued, "is Special Agent Leisa Nance-Roberge. Agent Roberge handles all of our logistics, PR, and press conferences." Leisa Roberge stepped forward and nodded. She was very tall, standing at nearly six feet two inches. She carried strong features. She had long, brilliant, blonde hair, which she typically wore pinned up. She peered through ocean-blue eyes and displayed a magical and near-perfect smile. She was very dedicated to her job and to her team. She had a great deal of media savvy and knew how to put out fires. Leisa also had a very effective way of bringing persons of interest to the forefront using the media; she was the newest member to the team.

"Next up we have Agent Emiliano Torres and Agent Paul Andersen. Both are excellent crime scene experts." Emiliano Torres was a slight but sinewy man. He was very fluent with his movements;

years of training in classical music had had an impact on his mannerisms. He was one of the most astute crime scene analysis specialists in the Bureau.

Agent Andersen was also considered a crime scene expert. He was a tall, handsome man. While his looks often garnered attention, he preferred to be in the background. Relatively new to the team, Paul Andersen had shown special gifts from the beginning, especially in terms of getting into the mind of the unknown subjects or "unsubs." Some said his ability was almost psychic.

"Special Agent Terry Carter is a munitions expert and he's been with me the longest." said Jordan. Agent Carter was the second in command. He had been with Connie Jordan for eight years and they knew each other well. Carter, a Marine before he came over to the Bureau, was very regimented in his approach and an excellent interrogator. His manner of persuasion had proven most effective over the years. He stood a very imposing six feet four inches, wore a shaved head, and was chiseled from head to toe. When the man meant business—he meant business. There was very little room for compromise when Agent Carter was involved.

"Lastly, we have Dr. Eva Hermanski, who is both an M.D. and pathologist." Dr. Hermanski stepped forward. She gave a subtle nod and smiled at the crowded room. Dr. Hermanski was the oldest member of the team. She had a slight build with light, salt-and-pepper hair that made her appear slightly older than she was. Dr. Hermanski and her husband, Geoffrey, also a doctor, started their careers in the FBI together. They both left private practices to do so and found their second careers to be just as rewarding.

Agent Jordan continued, "At the risk of sounding brash, folks, I work with an excellent team. We are very good at what we do, and we have a very high success rate. However, our effectiveness goes only as far as our complete cooperation with each other. Every person in this room is essential to this investigation. We will need everyone to be at the top of their game if there is any hope of closing this case with a positive resolution. Understood?" She paused for a moment to see that everyone was on board. "Good. We're gonna split everyone up into four teams. Agents Lynch, Torres, Carter, and I will be team leaders.

"Lieutenant Brennan," she said, turning to him, "as we have discussed previously, I'll ask that you divvy up your personnel between the teams."

Brennan nodded.. Turning back to the rest of the room, Agent Jordan continued. "Once the teams are assigned, Jacob, I want you to take your team to the University of Minnesota and see what you can find there. Check Monica Konetchy's room, her class schedule, her whereabouts leading up to her disappearance. Talk to her roommate, her teachers, and classmates. Just learn what you can." Jacob nodded and started for Brennan.

"Emiliano," began Jordan, "I want you and your team to head over to that convenience store. I believe the location is written down here somewhere." She paused to look around. "I'm sure we have it, that address. Just see if there's anyone there you could talk to. Get in touch with whoever was working that night. See if you can track down any of the customers who might have been in the store at the time. Find out if they saw anything that might have seemed odd or out of order that night. Also check for any security footage that they might have. Let's see if there's any chance she was being followed. At the very least, let's try to find out what she was wearing that night."

"Terry?"

"Yes, ma'am!"

"I want you and your team to find out what you can about this note. Check into any military service personnel in the area who might have been deployed to Iraq and, of course, returned less than thrilled with the experience. Also, see if you can find out if there's anyone who had orders to return—but haven't. I wouldn't be surprised if we were dealing with a malcontent here. Oh, and have the note itself analyzed. Maybe this guy was clumsy enough to leave his DNA.

"You got it."

"Paul and Eva," she said turning to them. "You're both with me. We're going to talk to the state rep. I want to have a look at Monica's things at home. Maybe we can find something there. I also want to find out if this abduction has anything to do with the representative herself. We need to find out if she's pissed anyone off recently and whether or not this note is legit or simply a smokescreen for something else.

"Lastly, I recall rather distinctly that there were anti-war protests that took place in downtown Minneapolis back in '05 and '06. If memory serves, the protests were pretty tame without any major incidents. Lieutenant," she said turning back to Brennan, "could you please have your people look into those incidents to see if we can find anything or anyone there that might jump out at us?"

Brennan nodded.

"Then you have the floor, sir," she continued. "If you don't mind, I'd like you with me. We've worked well together in the past. No need to change up now."

"You'll get no complaints outta me," he replied. Agent Jordan started to make her way to the back of the room.

"All right, everyone listen up!" The lieutenant resumed lead of the floor, "I have your assignments right here." He started to call his first name, when Agent Jordan interrupted him.

"One more thing," she said, turning back to face the room. "No one, and I mean no one, is to talk to the press. Any and all statements must be approved and will be given by Agent Roberge. Any questions?"

A lot of heads shook, but no questions.

"Good. I'm sorry, Lieutenant. Please continue."

"No problem, Agent." The lieutenant raised his voice and began giving his assignments, "Harris, Boone, and Walczak! You're with Agent Lynch. Knox, Vernon, and Nolan! You're with Agent Torres. Reeves, Shugart, and Rodriguez . . ."

As the lieutenant continued to disseminate his personnel, Agent Jordan watched him work from afar. She had worked with Brennan on a couple of cases previously and found him to be a very competent, reliable leader and an excellent police officer. She knew that he was close to retirement, something like four months to go, and figured that a high profile case was probably the last thing that he needed right about now. In truth, it was the last thing any of them needed right about now. There was craziness happening all over the world, and Minneapolis had seen its share, but it had been rather tame, relatively speaking. However, this kind a business, with a state representative's daughter was bad news, not matter what "state" you were in.

Agent Jordan looked up when the lieutenant caught her attention. "Yes, Lieutenant?"

"Teams have been assigned," he replied. "Your move."

Jordan stepped a little further into the room. "All right, everyone you have your assignments. Check-in is every hour on the hour, but do not hesitate to call in if you find something of substance. We will reconvene here at . . ." She looked at her watch. It was 9:20 a.m. "At four p.m. At that time let's have some news, people. No news is bad news. We need good news on this one. Head out."

The teams wasted no time heading for the door. Jordan watched them leave. She believed that if they had any chance of a happy ending on this one they had to act fast. The first thing they had to determine was the validity of that note. She felt strongly that the

Rep. had some information that would help. She walked to the back of the room to gather her things. Agent Andersen and Dr. Hermanski met her there. Lieutenant Brennan followed shortly with two of his own: Officer Soto and Sergeant Langford.

"All right, guys," she said in a less formal tone. "Let's go take a run at the state rep. Although I know she keeps a place in St. Paul, her actual home isn't all that far from here in Richfield. Paul," she said turning to Agent Andersen. "Could you bring the truck around, please?"

Agent Andersen smiled, nodded, and headed out.

"Harry," she said turning back to the lieutenant. "Have you spoken with the Rep. at all about this?"

"No," he said as he shook his head. "I haven't. The brass downtown has really kept her under wraps, but I'm sure they realize that we're gonna have to speak to her at some point."

"Well, do me a favor, if you don't mind," she said almost apologetically. "Give your people downtown a heads-up and let them know we're heading out there. It's my understanding that we should find the Rep. at home on standby."

"Sure thing," Brennan replied as he began to scoot to the nearest telephone. "Just give me a minute," he said over his shoulder.

Agent Jordan got a brief glimpse of her team's faces. She tucked in her lower lip and gave them a brief nod and an accompanying sigh. Just as Lieutenant Brennan returned, Agent Andersen ducked his head into the room to inform them that the vehicle was ready and waiting. The team gathered their essentials and headed out. They had a date with a Minnesota state representative.

***

MINE!

Richfield, Minnesota, was a quiet, and conservative inner-ring suburb of Minneapolis. This quintessential suburban town of approximately forty thousand residents was nestled just south of Minneapolis with Edina to the west, the Minneapolis–St. Paul International Airport to the east and Bloomington to its south. It was a robust town, despite its population. It boasted several natural excursions such as Richfield Lake Park, Veteran's Memorial Park, and Wood Lake Park, which was also home to the Wood Lake Nature Center. Richfield was very unassuming, and was not a city that was often thought of when reminiscing about the state of Minnesota. It was not a place that made an effort to stick out in one's mind. Not much crime occurred there. Not a lot of national headlining news occurred there. It was a town that took life one day at a time. The residents were friendly and courteous and for the most part, they held a very neighborly attitude and approach to one another. Richfield was a peaceful place, yet close enough to Minneapolis and St. Paul to allow for some excitement, if one was starved for such a fix—which, for most residents in Richfield, was a very rare occasion.

Representative Konetchy's home was on West Seventieth Street, just across from Augsburg Park. It was a single, three-story home with colonial curb appeal—a red brick building with white shutters around all the windows. It even had an American flag protruding just over the front door. The home had a very "patriotic" feel to it and yet, it was not much different from any of the other homes in the area. It simply fit right in.

Agent Jordan's team arrived at the state representative's home in two vehicles. The Federal agents rode in the government issued 2008 black GMC Yukon, while the Minneapolis Police officers followed close behind in Lieutenant Brennan's sky blue 2002 Ford Crown Victoria. As they neared the Konetchy residence, they pulled up and parked behind two unmarked but very conspicuous vehicles—

one belonged to the sheriff of Richfield, the other to Minnesota State Security. On such an unassuming and quiet street, these vehicles signaled that something was definitely amiss in Richfield.

Agent Jordan stepped out of the front passenger seat of the Yukon. She took a deep breath and took a long deliberate look around the area. The location appeared quiet and serene. Every lawn was perfectly manicured; every hedge was perfectly trimmed. As her father used to say on Sunday mornings, as he made sure that he was appropriately dressed for Mass, "Every button buttoned, every hair in place." That was how Richfield appeared on this Tuesday morning in spring. So much for appearances, she thought to herself. She waited as her companions exited the vehicle before heading for the front door. Before Agent Andersen could raise his hand to knock, it swung wide open to reveal two young sheriff's deputies and a state security officer on the other side. The deputy closest to the door motioned for the team to enter. They were expected. Sheriff Cabell walked swiftly into the main foyer.

"Agent Jordan? Agent Jordan?"

"I'm Jordan," she replied in a rather stern voice.

"Hi," he said, rushing over to her with his right hand extended. "I'm Memphis Cabell." He began to shake her hand rather briskly. "I'm the sheriff here in Richfield. I'm really glad you're here. Even though we're pretty close to Minneapolis and St. Paul, we rarely see any big-town problems here. I can honestly tell you that on something like this, we could use all the help we could get."

Agent Jordan took a moment to look at the sheriff as she shook his hand. Sheriff Cabell was in his mid-to-late-forties, approximately five feet eleven, and weighed roughly 210 pounds. He had black hair with a little grey mixed in and a very acute jaw line. He was clean-shaven and wore designer eyeglasses. *Gucci*, Jordan thought. He looked to be in fairly good shape and could probably hold his own in a tussle. He also appeared to be a lifelong resident of the area, that is, if his accent was any indicator. He did not appear to be a country bumpkin or a clueless suburbanite although a first impression might lead one to think as much. He appeared to be a fairly capable man who was aware of his limitations. That meant that he was honest with himself as well as with others. Men like that were good to work with. It was the ones who lied to themselves, as well as others, that Jordan despised.

"Well, that's what we're here for, Sheriff," Jordan responded. "Is the Rep. available?"

"Uh, yes," he said almost bowing to Jordan at the same time. "She's right this way, in the sitting room."

Jordan took in her surroundings as they all headed for the sitting room. The foyer was very generous in size—roughly fifteen by fifteen feet. It was bigger than the living room in her apartment back east, she thought. The foyer had a marble floor that offered a white background with intertwining black and silver swirls. Opposite the front door there was a grand staircase that led to an upstairs walkway, which overlooked the foyer. The entry boasted a cathedral ceiling, which went all the way to the third story and from which a glorious crystal chandelier descended that both illuminated and dazzled at the same time. The formal dining room was off to the right of the foyer. With a quick glance, there appeared to be a cherry dining set with a table that could easily seat twelve, a magnificent china closet filled with fine china, a corner curio that housed miniature trinkets that the Rep. was famous for collecting, and a serving buffet along the far wall that displayed a sampling of exquisite silver serving trays and accompanying instruments. Brazilian cherry wood comprised the dining room floor. On either side of the main stairs there was a walkway, which led toward the back of the house where the kitchen and den were. Off to the left of the foyer was the formal living room, with the sitting or family room just beyond it. The living room, which was not much bigger than the foyer, was modestly furnished with a sofa, a love seat, and four antique-looking chairs. There were a couple of coffee tables and a few lamp stands, which held vintage lamps. There was a fireplace in this room, which appeared hardly used, and several portraits and pictures of the Konetchy family. Everything appeared to be perfectly placed throughout the room. Nothing was overdone.

As the team made its way to the sitting room, they came upon the Rep. who was sitting by a lit fireplace, with her husband, Ethan Konetchy, standing behind her and consoling her to the best of his ability. This room was much larger than the other rooms, and by the look of the furniture, the most used. There was seating for nearly twenty in this room. There were two doors that led to the outside of this multi-windowed room. One door led to the side of the house where there stood a detached three-car garage. The other door led directly onto the rear deck. There was yet another doorway in the rear of the room which granted access to the kitchen. Unlike the other rooms on the first floor of the house, the sitting room was carpeted from wall to wall—*Berber*, Jordan thought. *High end, too.* The furniture was much less formal and much more practical. The décor was simple and tasteful, and while there were photos of the Konetchys strategically placed throughout this room, they were of the candid and vacation-tourist variety as opposed to the professionally posed captures of the previous room.

"Representative Konetchy . . ." Jordan began.

The representative looked up and seemed scarcely aware that there were now strangers in her sitting room. Susan Konetchy was in her mid-sixties and approximately five years older than her husband. She was slightly overweight and always seemed to wear skirt suits that were somewhat out of trend. She had a plump, motherly visage and wore her hair pinned back into a bun like her mother and her grandmother used to do. She was very proper in her demeanor and her approach and, until now, there had never been even the slightest hint of scandal or impropriety where she was involved. While her mother was a homemaker, Susan Konetchy, formerly Susan Milbourne, began her career as a very successful attorney. She graduated from Yale School of Law with honors and began working at one of the biggest law firms in St. Paul almost immediately. Shortly thereafter, upon the urging of her colleagues and friends, she became a judge. She'd spent fifteen years on the bench before those same colleagues and friends urged her to run for the state house. Although she'd resisted, she'd honestly felt that she would not win such a high profile election, but she ran—and won—first time out. She was now serving her second term, having managed to maintain both her popularity and effectiveness. Connie Jordan did not know "the Rep." personally but she had always been impressed with how she handled herself.

"I'm Supervisory Special Agent Constance Jordan," she continued. "This is Lieutenant Harold Brennan from the Minneapolis PD and this is our team. We're here to do everything we possibly can to bring your daughter home safely." Jordan gracefully made her way to the Rep., kneeled down beside her, and took her hand.

"We need to ask you some questions to get as much information we possibly can about your daughter. Especially, with regard to the last week or so."

Susan Konetchy nodded as she unconsciously wiped a tear from her eye. "Whatever you need," she said in a slightly raspy voice, weary from all the crying. "We'll cooperate as much as we can," she looked up to her husband who nodded in agreement.

"Great," Jordan responded in an even softer voice. "While we talk, I'd like to have my team look at Monica's room. Is that okay?" The representative shrugged her shoulders and nodded.

Professor Konetchy stood upright and said, "I'll take you." He led the way back through the living room to the main stairs. Agent Andersen and Dr. Hermanski followed close behind along with one of the lieutenant's officers.

Agent Jordan walked over to the closest, unoccupied chair, picked it up, and sat it almost directly in front of the representative. She sat down and tried to catch the representative's attention. As she did so, she gave a small smile. "It's gonna be all right," she reassured the Rep. "We're gonna find Monica, and she will be all right."

The Rep. tried to return the smile but was unsuccessful. She did manage to compose herself, however, and was prepared to answer any questions. Jordan took notice of the indicators and began.

"First, let me ask you. Do you know of anyone who might want to cause you or your family any harm?"

The Rep. sank back into her chair and closed her eyes. She drew her lips into a bunch and sighed. She started shaking her head, leaned forward and looked at Jordan.

"No, I don't." She was confident in her answer. "My husband and I have been examining that thought ever since this morning and neither one of us can think of anyone who would want to do anything like this."

Her husband, Professor Ethan Konetchy, was an associate dean at the University of Minnesota. He worked at Appleby Hall in the University Counseling and Consulting Services Department. A doctor in psychology, he had worked for the university for nearly thirty years. He was well liked and well respected by both his students and his peers. His tenure not only allowed Monica to attend the university free of charge, but on occasion it, along with the Rep.'s position, afforded the younger Konetchy certain liberties which were not always wise. Especially, for someone who had such an inherently rebellious nature. Given the nature of both elder Konetchys' professions, Agent Jordan was not so eager to rule either of them out as a credible source for this situation.

"Had Monica given you any indication that she was having a problem with anyone? An old boyfriend maybe—or someone from school?"

The Rep. shook her head again. "Monica and I are not particularly close," she sighed. "She's closer to her father. But, I honestly believe that if she was in any kind of trouble," she leaned closer to Jordan, "any kind of *serious* trouble, we would know. She would've said something. But, I'm sure that nothing like that has ever come up. You can ask Ethan when he returns."

Jordan nodded and took a few notes.

"Representative, have you participated in any votes or committee discussions that someone could find controversial or volatile?"

"I serve on the Finance Committee, the Environmental Committee, and the Ways and Means Committee. The only thing on the table presently that comes close to being controversial is the budget hearings. The state has a huge deficit, as well as every other state in this country, and we're trying to find ways to close the gap. The House is at odds with the governor over cuts and spending. But, I'm not the head of any of these committees. I don't see how I would be singled out over, say Representative Trammell, who chairs both the Finance and the Ways and Means Committees. It just doesn't make any sense," she said, shaking her head again. "No sense at all."

"Were there any indicators that something like this might happen? Anything odd that you can think of? Strange phone calls, unsolicited emails, weird correspondence, either here or at the office?"

"There are always all of those things—it's the nature of my position. But there's nothing that stands out. Nothing that would lead me to believe that something like this could happen."

The representative looked at Agent Jordan with a soft, yet frustrated, look. Not that she was frustrated with the questions but that she was frustrated because she could not be of more assistance.

Jordan acknowledged the look and continued. "Have you had any problems with any of your staff members? Have you let anyone go recently? Could there be a disgruntled employee out there somewhere?"

"Not to my knowledge," the Rep. responded in a slightly more relaxed tone. "Quite frankly, I believe that I have one of the best staffs on the Hill. My team has been a cohesive unit almost since the very beginning. We have had only two staff members leave since I became state rep. One woman, Kathy Slagle, left to get married. She and her husband moved to Montana, I think. And Richard Rigney, one of my associate campaign managers, decided that he wanted to become a lobbyist. He's doing quite well. I don't think that there's any problem there."

Jordan continued to take notes as Lieutenant Brennan stepped in. "Representative," he began as he turned to Jordan. "If I may?"

The Rep. diverted her attention to the lieutenant.

"How well was Monica doing at the university?" he continued. "How were her grades? Was she getting along well with the faculty— and her classmates?"

The Rep. sank back into her seat again. "That, I do not know. Ethan would know better." She lowered her head. "You know, I have always realized that Monica and I weren't particularly close. Don't get me wrong, there isn't any tension or hostility between us. Just distance. What's unfortunate is that it takes an incident like this to show me how truly distant we had become."

Agent Jordan rose slightly from her seat and knelt at her side. She took the Rep.'s hand once again and spoke in her most reassuring tone.

"I realize that this is a very trying time for you. I can't imagine all of the images that have been scrolling through your mind since this morning, but I can tell you that I believe that we have a chance here. That means that we'll need you to be strong. Do you think that you can be strong for us?"

Representative Konetchy nodded with conviction.

"Good. What can you tell me about the note you received this morning? How did it get into your hands?"

Representative Konetchy gave a controlled sigh. "Today started like every other day," she began. "Ethan and I both got up at five and walked a half hour on our treadmills as we've done together every day for the last seven years. I took my shower while Ethan got the morning papers. Eliza, our housekeeper, started breakfast. Ethan took his shower and by six-forty-five we were at the table eating. While Ethan goes through the papers, I tend to read the mail. We have very early delivery here and Eliza usually has already retrieved it for me. I fingered through the envelopes and found this note. It wasn't in an envelope, it was handwritten—it was odd. I had to read it more than once before I could understand what it was trying to say. I dropped it and ran for the phone. Ethan, I guess he was taken aback by my behavior, picked up the note and read it. I tried to reach Monica but couldn't. Her cell phone went straight to voicemail. Ethan called someone down at the University, they tried to locate Monica and that's when we found out that she had been gone for a couple of days. My next call was to the sheriff."

She turned to Sheriff Cabell, who had been standing off to the side near the entrance of the room.

"Uh, yeah, that's right," he jumped in. "I sent a car 'round here right away, got on the horn to the University and got the same answers as the professor. Then I called Minneapolis PD and I guess they got the message on to you. I had one of my officers run this note over to the MPD, which is standard procedure 'cause we don't have a lab or anything like that 'round here. I knew this was a kidnapping case, so it was only a matter of time before the Feds got involved. And with the state rep. being involved and all—anyway, we got a call back from your people in downtown Minneapolis and pretty much waited for you all to get here."

"Let me ask you this," Agent Jordan resumed. "Have you notified anyone in your office yet?"

"No, not really," the representative replied. "They know that I'm not likely to make it into the office today, so they're holding my calls and rescheduling my meetings. But they don't know why."

"Good," Jordan concluded. "Let's keep it that way for the meantime. What can you tell me about your last conversation with your daughter?"

The Rep. managed a meager smile as she recalled the phone call. "That call came as a surprise, believe it or not. Like I said, Monica and I weren't particularly chatty, but we got along well enough. On that day, she called just to see how I was doing. Can you believe that?" She asked in almost amused amazement. "We hadn't spoken in about a week and a half, so I guess she thought we might touch base. She and Ethan talk much more than we do. She asked me about my day. She has a Saturday schedule and made it to her early class but her afternoon lecture was cancelled, so she had some free time on her hands. There was nothing really out of the ordinary beyond the actual fact that she called. She was fine. She sounded fine. I thought she was fine."

Tears began to swell in the corner of the Rep.'s eyes once again. Agent Jordan pulled a tissue from the dispenser on the coffee table just to her left and began to blot her eyes. "It's ok," she said, again reassuring the Rep. "We will find your daughter and she will be fine."

The Rep. took the tissues, continued to dry her eyes, and nodded ruefully.

Agent Jordan came to her feet and thought carefully for a moment. Nothing that she had learned so far had seemed particularly unreasonable. No damage control was necessary. At least, not so far. She needed to ask Professor Konetchy a few questions and wondered how her team was making out in Monica's room.

***

Professor Konetchy ushered the team into Monica's room; Agent Andersen was the first to enter. The first thing he noticed was the tidiness of the room.

"Did Monica always keep her room this clean?" Andersen asked the professor.

"No, not really," Professor Konetchy responded sheepishly. "Tidiness isn't one of Monica's strong points," he paused for a moment. "Or interests for that matter. No, Eliza has always kept her room neat. Since she's not here very often, it's much easier to do."

Andersen acknowledged the sentiment and stepped deeper into the room. It was a nice-sized, rectangular room that was positioned just off to the left of the main stairs once one reached the top. Inside the room, Monica's full-sized bed protruded from the right with the solid oak headboard up against the right wall. To the right of the bed was a matching nightstand that held a brass lamp and a few small collectable items. To the left of the bed was a very modern modular-type desk that had a few items on it: a desktop computer, a dictionary along with a few other assorted books, a couple of pens neatly placed, and two pictures of Monica and some friends. On the wall opposite the door was a dresser, flanked by two, over-sized colonial styled windows. There was a large mirror and vanity that were centrally located against the wall to the far left which was also flanked by posters of Robert Pattinson's "Edward" character to its left and Justin Timberlake to its right; both pieces of furniture were of the same design and strong oak construction as the bed and night stand. Along the wall beside the door was an oversized closet that one could scarcely miss. Twice the size of a normal closet, this one required the rest of that wall. Andersen noted that it would be of no surprise for Monica to have a great many clothes. Clothes for every season, clothes for every occasion however, her style only required that she wore certain select items. Most of which she had probably taken with her to school.

Agent Andersen moved toward Monica's desk. The other members of the team entered the room just behind. Officer Soto stood in the center of the room and took it in as Dr. Hermanski made her way over to Monica's vanity. Anderson picked up the two pictures. One was a photo of Monica snuggled up next to another young lady of about the same age. They both were wearing winter gear and there was the image of a mountain in the background. The photo was recent, and the frame appeared to be relatively new.

Professor Konetchy took note of Agent Andersen's interest in the photo. "That was taken last year," he began. "That's Monica with her best friend, Lori Adenhart. That was at the Indianhead Mountain Resort. Last year was the fiftieth anniversary of the resort and Monica always loved that place.

"The other photo," the professor motioned for Andersen to pick it up—he did. "That other photo is of Monica and a couple of her friends from high school. The boy on the left showing his tongue is Kyle Johnson. The boy kneeling down in front is Ian Buffington. There's Lori again just to Monica's left and that's Mahlia Carreon next to Lori. They were all really good kids. Kyle went to

Northwestern. Ian and Mahlia went out west to Cal, and Lori stayed here. She attends Minnesota with Monica."

"Is there any way we could get in contact with Lori?"

"Absolutely. I have all of her information downstairs. We tried calling her, you know. We thought that she might know where Monica was. But I understand she's in class until this afternoon. So, we're waiting to hear back from her as well."

"Good. As soon as you hear anything from her, it's imperative that we speak with her. In fact, I'm sure that as soon as she's available, Agent Jordan might want her brought in for questioning."

"Whatever you need," the professor said. "I'm sure Lori would be more than willing to help in any way possible."

Agent Andersen looked thoroughly through the young lady's desk. He leafed through every book and rifled through every drawer but did not identify any items that held any significance or even relevance.

"Is it safe to assume that Monica uses a laptop at school, and that's why this desktop is still here?"

"Correct," the professor replied.

"We might want to have our guys look at this. There could be something there—especially in her emails. We'll also need to find out if her laptop is still in her dorm room. If so, we're gonna want to look at that as well."

"Whatever you need, Agent."

Anderson nodded and then diverted his attention to Dr. Hermanski. He had hoped that she was faring better but suspected that she was not. He headed to the other side of the room. He passed Officer Soto who had begun to go through Monica's tower dresser before he moved on to her oversized closet. Both locations were filled with clothes but not much else.

"Have you got anything?" Agent Andersen asked the doctor.

"No," she replied looking up from the vanity. "There's some make-up here. Some grooming items, nail polish, mascara, and a very nice nail clipping set. An assortment of combs and brushes. Some perfume, nice but nothing too expensive. Just a lot of items that you would expect in a young lady's vanity. Nothing that screams out at me. Actually, nothing that even whispers."

Agent Anderson gave a small chuckle. He looked at the police officer who simply shrugged. They had nothing and began to make their way back downstairs.

As they descended the stairs, Agent Jordan, Lieutenant Brennan, and the other members of the team were awaiting them in the main foyer.

"Did you find anything?" Agent Jordan asked.

"Nothing that jumps out at you," Agent Andersen replied. "There is a desktop upstairs that she left behind. We're gonna want to go through that. She uses a laptop at school, so we'll need to look for that as well. But other than that, not too much to go on."

Agent Jordan nodded. She had hoped the other teams were faring better, but she hadn't heard from them as of yet. She glanced at her watch; it was a little past noon.

"Professor Konetchy," she said turning to him. "Do you mind if I ask you a couple of quick questions?"

"No, not at all, young lady," he replied.

Agent Jordan gave a quick smile and asked, "When was the last time you talked to Monica, and how did she seem to you?"

The professor reached the main floor. "I actually spoke with Monica the same day as Susan. We spoke just after her morning class. Her afternoon lecture had been cancelled—I believe her professor had a family issue at home of some sort, so she called to see if we could get together for lunch. I had appointments so I couldn't make it." The professor bowed his head and began to sob. Jordan gave him a moment to collect himself—he did, and continued. "I told her that I couldn't make it but suggested that she give her mother a call. She didn't exactly call Susan for lunch but she did wind up calling that evening. And that was the last time either of us spoke with her. She was her normal self. There didn't seem to be anything out of the ordinary."

Agent Jordan took a few notes and then nodded toward the professor; still nothing that seemed particularly unreasonable.

"Well," Jordan resumed her reassuring tone. "We all appreciate the time you've taken with us today." Representative Konetchy, Sheriff Cabell, his officer, and the Rep.'s security detail joined them in the main foyer.

"We might have more questions for you in the near future," Jordan continued. "I would urge you that if you can think of anything that could assist us, no matter how small or insignificant the detail might seem—please contact me." She handed the professor her business card. "My cell number is on there so you can call me anytime—for anything. Please don't think twice about it. Also," she stated in a slightly sterner tone, "it is very important that we keep this incident out of the media for now. Please do not speak to the press until we have something concrete. We're not sure what we're up against as of yet and oftentimes speaking with the media raises the stakes exponentially and unnecessarily."

The Konetchys gave affirming looks to each other, turned back to Agent Jordan and said, "We understand," almost in unison.

Agent Jordan turned to Sheriff Cabell. "Sheriff, we will be in touch. If something were to turn up on your end, I certainly hope that you will get in contact with us, forthwith."

"*Forthwith*," the sheriff said, smiling. "Ma'am, if that means 'right away,' then I will most certainly be in contact with you '*forthwith*' as soon as I hear anything!"

Jordan smiled. "In the meantime," she said turning towards the Konetchys, "the Minneapolis PD will send a surveillance crew out here to monitor your phone and computer lines." She glanced at Brennan, who gave his nod of approval. "We'll need to be vigilant in case Monica can find a way to get a message through to you."

"We understand," the professor responded.

"We're gonna have a car out here at all times until this is resolved," the sheriff added.

"Good." Jordan nodded, turned and led the team out of the house. She walked to the passenger side of the Yukon and took another long look around the neighborhood. She took another deep sigh and thought to herself *you never really know, do you?*

She got into the truck. Comfortably seated she checked her cell phone, hoping by chance that she had missed a call. Nothing. Apparently, the other teams had not fared much better, at least not yet. She could only hope that Monica Konetchy was still alive and kicking.

Chapter Two

At first, it sounded like a couple of voices. Garbled voices seemingly bickering back and forth. As she began to regain consciousness, very slowly at first but at an ever-increasing rate, she realized that the voices she heard weren't voices at all. They were one voice and that one voice was bickering with itself.

She was blindfolded so she couldn't see. Her mouth was duct taped, so she couldn't speak. But she could hear well enough, and what she heard was senseless.

"We're not the world police!" he proclaimed. Apparently, he was quite angry at something. "We're not their parents and they're not children! There was nothing there. *Nothing*! So why do I have to go back? Why should anyone have to go back? Especially, if they don't want to."

"But they need you," he continued, this time seemingly answering himself. "They can't do this without you. You're *too important*. The mission is *too important*.

"But they haven't seen what I've seen. They haven't heard what I've heard. They don't know what they're sending us into. They don't know what they're making us do. They don't know how they're changing us." His tone began to soften. "Turning us into something different—something evil. Monsters. That's what we're becoming. Monsters. Only monsters kill women and children. That's what we call them here, don't we? Monsters! Don't we call men who kill women and children 'monsters'?"

With that last statement, Monica Konetchy could tell that he was drawing closer. She could smell his rage as he knelt down beside here. Taking stock of what she could, she realized that she was laying on a hard surface, what seemed like a dirt or gravel floor. Her left side was very sore. She had no idea how long she had been laying on that side. Her hands were bound behind her and her legs were bound at the ankles. She felt a lot of stiffness and assumed that she had been bound for quite some time—the better part of three days to be exact.

"Hey," he said in barely a whisper. "Do you think I'm a monster?"

He gently removed the blindfold from her eyes. The room was dark with small streams of sunlight beaming in from several different locations. It made it difficult to see and the darkness required a great deal of time before her eyes could actually gain focus. Next, he removed the duct tape from her mouth, but did so in such a manner as to minimize her discomfort as much as possible.

He kneeled over her and asked her again. "Do you think that I'm a monster?"

Monica shook her head to clear the cobwebs a bit and took a good look at him. Her abductor appeared to be in his mid-to-late thirties. He was balding slightly with a receding hairline, and the remainder of his black hair was matted with sweat. He was unshaven and unkempt as if he had been roughing it in the wilderness for a month. His breath was poor, though his teeth looked relatively well cared for. She was unable to gauge his height because he was kneeling over. But he did appear thinner than she might have expected. He was clothed in army combat fatigues, but they looked loose and baggy on him. As if he had lost too much weight for the outfit to fit properly.

She craned her head back so she could look him directly in the eye, then spoke and managed to clear her throat at the same time. "No," she found it difficult to speak at first. "I don't think you're a monster. I don't know why I'm here, but I'm sure you must be a really nice man."

Monica Konetchy had mastered the art of getting into trouble. She had gotten into all sorts of trouble, on many levels, since she was a preteen. As a result of those endeavors, she was also extremely adept at getting out of trouble and defusing situations. Her lifelong vocation seemed to have provided her with the perfect training and experience for her present situation.

"How long have I been here?" she asked still slightly dazed.

"Well, I am *not* a monster," he reassured her without addressing her question. "I *don't* kill women and children, and I won't kill you. But something needed to be done. A statement needed to be made—and *I* needed to make it."

"What statement was that?" she asked, trying to follow his train of thought.

"That Iraq was a mistake. That we should not be there. That we should not go back there."

"Are you a soldier?"

He looked at her sternly for a moment. "Yes, I am a soldier. And I love my country," he declared. "But right is right, and wrong is wrong. And what we're doing in Iraq is wrong." He bowed his head sorrowfully and said, "What I've seen in Iraq is wrong."

He paused for a moment. He walked over to a table to retrieve something, which gave Monica an opportunity to take in her surroundings. In moments, she realized that she was in some kind of shed. There were containers and contraptions all around. She saw two lawn mowers, an assortment of hedge clippers, hoses, spouts, pipes, cans of paint, stain, and stain remover. There were two sets of windows, one on either side of the shed, but they were covered with some kind of not-so-clear plastic. There was an assortment of smells: old paint, kerosene, gasoline, spilled oil, and something else that she could not quite identify. There were three tables; the largest one was up against the far wall where most of the tools seemed to be. The second table was off to the right. It held an assortment of both large and small items. The third table was in the middle of the room. It appeared to have a weird, saw-like thing on it. The entire area was dusty and dirty. The dust particles in the air created a smoky, night club-like ambiance. The dankness of the room added to the feeling. Though the area was uncomfortable, it was not particularly frightening. The room appeared to be a normal work shed—not a torture chamber. There were no smears of blood on the walls or stains of dried blood pooled on the floor. There were no flecks of skin strewn about frivolously. Monica could see no meat hooks or any of the other detainment devices that she often saw in horror movies. Hell, she was bound by duct tape for Christ's sake. It doesn't get much more generic than that. From every indication, she had not been abducted by Ted Bundy's stepbrother, she thought. This area looked like a regular tool shed and considering everything that was mounted on the walls and hanging from the ceiling, there was probably every tool known to man here. At least that was what she believed. And that meant that there were more than enough items she could use to free herself.

The assailant returned from the largest table with something in his hands. Initially, Monica was unable to see what he was carrying and could feel the anxiety build inside her. But as he passed through a beam of light, she could see that he simply had a Diet Pepsi with a straw inserted inside. He knelt down beside her again.

"I'm not a monster. I'm not going to hurt you. You must be really thirsty."

Monica leaned back and nodded.

"Here," he sat the bottle down momentarily. "Let me help you up." The assailant reached down and helped Monica into a seated position. He propped her up against a standing tool chest, reached for the soda and brought the straw to her lips. Monica began to sip slowly but consistently. She had not realized how thirsty she was. She hated Diet Pepsi, but it was wet and it was cold. As she drank the soda she took the opportunity to really look at her assailant's face. *He's probably younger than he looks* she thought. At first, she thought he might have been in his mid-to-late thirties, but now she wasn't so sure. It was his eyes. There was a wildness and slight insanity in his eyes, but she thought there was actually something else there, too. His eyes looked weary. Like they had seen things that they were probably too young, too innocent, to see. But she was also able to see something that she could recognize in those brown eyes. Rebellion. She knew rebellion. She knew it rather well as a matter of fact. It was something that she could definitely relate to and possibly use to her advantage.

"You've been here three days," he finally answered reservedly. "You've been pretty much out of it the whole time. I guess the stuff I made to knock you out was really strong. It wasn't supposed to last so long. This is the first time you've been awake for more than 5 minutes." He knelt down beside her again.

"Are you hungry, Monica?" he said in a whispered tone. She jerked back completely surprised that he knew her name. "It's okay," he tried to reassure her. "I looked at your ID. I know who you are and where you live. I know you're a student. I even left a note at your home for your parents."

"Did you," she began to ask. "Did you see my parents?"

"No," he sighed wistfully. "I simply slid a note into their mail. I didn't see them, and they didn't see me. I'm sure that they're worried sick about you, but you'll be okay. Once everybody understands what we're doing is wrong everything will be okay."

He quickly stood up and took a step back. "I'll make you something to eat," he said briskly. As he turned to head out the door, Monica called after him. "Wait," she said. "I know you're not a monster. Tell me your name." He turned to her and gave her a very serious look. "It's only fair," she said. "You know my name. I should know yours." He gave the request some serious thought. "Drake," he responded. "Call me Drake."

S. E. Robinson

"Well Drake, I am very glad to meet you. Although, not so much like this." Drake moved his head from side to side as if he was sizing up her comment. "But I am very hungry," she continued, "and I would really like something to eat."

Drake smiled, took another step back, turned and made his way out of the shed and toward the house. Monica was unsure of what Drake had to eat, so she had to move fast. From what she could tell, he was not aware of whom her parents were. She believed that the longer he was unaware, the safer she would be. She tried to get to her feet.

As best she could, she brought her bound legs to the front of her and began to push up against the tool chest to her back. In her first couple of attempts, her legs simply slid out in front of her. However, by the fourth attempt, she was able to gain enough traction to manage her way up the tool chest in order to stand. She took a moment to catch her breath. She looked around the room, able to now see it from standing eye level for the first time. Carefully, she hopped over to the door and peeked through a plastic covered window to see the rear of a three-story home that was approximately forty feet away, separated by a grassy yard and a paved driveway. There were two cars in the driveway, an abandoned old Pontiac from the seventies, and an old SUV, which was parked closest to the shed. Although she tried, she could not see clearly into the house. But she could see that he wasn't returning immediately. She turned to face the shed. She caught sight of the miter saw in the center of the room and hopped over to it. There were a few loose saw blades lying about. She bent down, and with her chin maneuvered one of the blades to the edge of the table. She turned around to grasp the blade with her hands. She gave a small yelp as she nicked her right thumb as she picked it up. She managed to position the blade so that it was upright with the teeth facing toward her back and began to cut herself free.

Chapter Three

Agent Jordan sat in the front of the Minneapolis Police Department Central Command Post looking on as the various teams returned from their various assignments. Out in the field, she received no significant calls prior to this debriefing. No significant findings, no one that came forward, no true shreds of evidence. Thus far, it was as if Monica Konetchy had simply vanished into thin air. Jordan was not discouraged, however. There really did not seem to be a mastermind at work here. The hastily written note was evidence of that. There had been no demands for money and no demands of the parents. There had not been anything to indicate that Monica Konetchy was specifically targeted. However, until proven otherwise, it would be irresponsible to believe otherwise. There was a much greater chance that she was targeted as opposed to simply being a victim of circumstance. That angle must be played until it was played out. Until then, the team must continue working from every angle. However, from where they stood right now, the pickings were slim with regard to both evidence and facts.

"Let's get it together, people!" Lieutenant Brennan gained the room's attention. "Each team leader will have a chance to fill everyone else in. Let's get it together, so we can see what we have and determine what we need to do next." He turned to Jordan. "Connie?"

Jordan stood up and addressed the room. "Let's dive right in, folks," she said. "Jacob, what do we have?"

Agent Lynch came to the front of the room. "Well," he began timidly, "we were assigned the University, the dorm room, classmates, and instructors. There wasn't anything of any significance to be found there. No strange mail. No strange emails. No conflicts with classmates or faculty. She had had an incident first semester with regard to a public disturbance, but other than that, not much of anything at all. The IT boys here have her desktop but nothing yet. I was able to get her login password for her laptop from her roommate, and nothing. Like I said, no strange emails. IT will dig deeper but I wouldn't hold my breath.

"We did manage to talk to Lori Adenhart, Monica's best friend. She didn't have too much to tell us. She said there was a kid that was interested in Monica, a fellow student named . . ." he looked down at his notes, "Bradley Thompson," he continued. "She told us that Thompson had a little issue with understanding the word 'no.' Monica really didn't want to be bothered with him. He seemed to be a little infatuated with the idea of dating a state rep.'s daughter, but according to Lori, the kid was really harmless."

"Did you manage to speak with the Thompson kid?" Jordan inquired.

"Not yet," Lynch said. "But we were able to ascertain that he was not in school or even in the area during the time of the abduction. According to school records, he had permission to miss a few days in order to attend his older sister's wedding with his family. She got married in St. Croix, so it's highly unlikely he's our guy. Besides, according to Lori, whenever he got out of place, it was nothing for Monica to snap him back into reality."

"Okay," Jordan sighed. "Good enough." She looked around the room. "Torres, what do you have?"

He began talking while on his way to the front of the room. "My team had the convenience store and the surrounding area. The clerk that was on duty on the night in question wasn't there—we had to track him down at his other job but he really didn't have anything to give us. However, we were able to get the surveillance footage for that night, and it showed Monica entering the store at about six-thirty. She milled around for about ten minutes before making her purchases and leaving the store. She must've dialed her mother during her walk back, probably right before she was snatched. From the video, we were able to get a decent description of what she was wearing that night. We had to guesstimate the colors a little bit because the tape's in black and white but, according to those who were at the store that evening, we did ok. From what we could gather, Monica was wearing a pink and white, striped knit sweater that wasn't particularly thick. She was wearing faded blue jeans and a pair of pink and white Nike tennis shoes. That's the best description we have so far. Now, the convenience store is about a half mile from campus, which makes it about a five-to-ten-minute walk. From what we learned, most of the kids walk there to get their cigarettes and beer. We have some street teams canvassing the area between the school and the store just on the off chance that someone saw something."

Torres turned to Jordan and shrugged. That was all he had. She smiled back at him. It was better than nothing. She nodded and he began to make his way back to his seat. Without uttering a word, Terry Carter made his way to the front of the room.

"Good afternoon, team!" The military training was unmistakable.

"Good afternoon," replied the floor unanimously and instinctively.

"My team worked to track down the origins of the note. The unsub tried to play it smart, so there were no fingerprints found on the note. The paper is of the cheap variety. It could have been bought from any of the local dollar or stationery stores, or even any of the chain pharmacies. There was also nothing unique or special about the ink. All we have is a really bad note on really common paper. I made a call to my guys down in Washington and from what I was able to get, there have been a few recalls of army squads ordered back to the Middle

East. The squads were issued orders to go to Afghanistan. I have yet to find out if there have been any no-shows. But as soon as I know, you will know."

"Thank you, Terry." Agent Jordan moved back to the front of the room and an officer came rushing in from downstairs.

"Lieutenant!" she said loudly as she entered the room. "Lieutenant," she called again as she rushed over to his side. Upon reaching the senior officer, she leaned forward and spoke softly into his ear. Brennan stared at Jordan as she spoke. Jordan took that as a cue and made her way over to them. The rest of the floor began to murmur as everyone wondered what the excitement was about. He filled her in. Abruptly, Jordan forced her way out of the room with the lieutenant and the notifying officer quickly on her heels. She turned to Agent Nance-Roberge on her way out the door, pointed, and said, "Come with me." The agent hopped up and joined the caravan. The four of them hurriedly made their way down the steps and out to the front of the building where they found state Representative Susan Konetchy and her husband, Professor Ethan Konetchy, alongside their attorney, Warren Westerberg of Westerberg, Rowe & Holbert, a founding partner of a prestigious midtown Minneapolis law firm and one of the most successful and high profile attorneys in the region, holding a press conference with regard to their missing daughter.

They were standing on the first landing of steps in front of the Minneapolis Police Administration Building, roughly five feet above everyone else. There was a clamor of news reporters and media jostling back and forth in order to gain the best position. There were four camera crews, one for each of the major news stations in the area. There were folks with microphones, hand-held digital recorders, and notepads, each one of them eager to catch every word, every expression, every nuance of the press conference. Any actual facts that were shared were simply icing on the cake to these hungry reporters.

Immediately, Agent Jordan was filled with anger and disdain. She specifically asked the Konetchys to refrain from holding any press conferences until the time was right and more facts were in. This would do nothing but increase the risk of danger for their daughter. This was absolutely the wrong thing to do at this time. Jordan moved closer so she could hear.

"Representative! Representative!" The clamoring was cacophony to Jordan's ears. "State Representative!" Mr. Westerberg pointed to an eager young lady in the front. "State Representative, I'm Melodee Maddux from the Daily Post. Have you spoken to your daughter at all since she was abducted?"

"No," Rep. Konetchy replied, trying her best to stay composed. "We haven't heard a word from her since Saturday."

"So you have no idea if she's okay?"

"No. Not at this moment. This is why we're making this plea. We're trying to reach out to anyone who might have seen her or spoken to her on the night she was taken. Anyone who can let us know where to find her or if she's okay."

"State Representative!" The attorney pointed to an older gentleman towards the back. "State Representative, what more can you tell us about this note? Have there been any ransom demands? What do they want?"

"There's nothing more I can say about the note. The note itself has been handed over to the authorities. Who, I might add, are working very hard on this case for us. There have been no ransom demands, and we have absolutely no idea what it is that they want."

Warren Westerberg, who stood tall and thin with his six-foot-two, 195-pound frame, was seventy-three years old but easily looked twenty years younger. He wore very expensive suits, as he could afford to, but he was never overdressed. He had thinning grey hair, which looked silver in the sunlight. Over the years, Westerberg had gained a great deal of respect in his profession and in the community. While he never shied away from the cameras, he was never one to seek media attention. He was, however, very adept at manipulating it to his advantage. A ploy he certainly hoped to accomplish here today.

"Just to reiterate," Westerberg said as he stepped forward. "We're looking for anyone who might have any information with regard to the abduction of Monica Konetchy, the only daughter of Professor Ethan Konetchy and state Representative Susan Konetchy. Monica is nineteen years old, approximately five feet six inches tall, approximately 120 to 130 pounds. She's got sandy brown hair. Her only true identifying mark is a tattoo she has on her back just above her buttocks. It's a rather small rainbow. If anyone has seen Monica or has knowledge of her whereabouts please contact the authorities immediately. Dial nine-one-one. Please share what you know. Every little detail is welcome at this point.

"Thank you so much for your time. We will conclude this press conference and promise to keep you posted of any future developments as they occur. Again, thank you." Westerberg turned his clients away for the clamor and headed toward the entrance of the building. Jordan was able to catch a weary yet almost shameful glance from the Rep. as she walked by. Jordan, Brennan, Roberge, and the officer followed the threesome into the building.

Inside, Jordan opened her mouth as if to speak and was quickly cut off by Westerberg. "Agent, before you begin, let me state that this conference was my idea. I have had some experience with abductions in the past and in each case, appealing to the public has always proved fruitful."

Jordan gave Westerberg a sharp look and retorted with a tempered tone, "Appeals to the public are delicate and carefully designed. They normally require a modicum of accurate information and some background with regard to the source of the abduction. To this point, we have very little of either and you have even less than that." Turning to the Konetchys, she said, "The reason I insisted that you wait before talking to the press was that we wanted to try and ascertain the motives behind the abduction—first. As of right now, we have no clue. And, if by chance this abduction was simply by random and the abductor didn't know who Monica actually was, he could very well panic, kill her, and dispose of her before we have a chance to catch him. The last thing we wanted to do was to put this person into panic mode. This little stunt might very well have done that."

Though Connie Jordan did her very best to disguise her disappointment and disgust, she was livid. It was the first day of the investigation and already unnecessary risks had been taken. Risks accumulate, and the more there are, the greater the chance that things could go wrong. In order to find anyone who had been kidnapped and subsequently bring them home safely—things needed to go right. She shook her head and turned away. She motioned to Roberge who approached quickly.

"See if you can get a full copy of that press conference. We only managed to catch the tail end of it. Once you get it and review it, let me know what you can do to minimize the damage."

"Gotcha," replied Roberge.

"Go," Jordan ordered. Agent Roberge spun around and left.

Representative Konetchy approached Jordan. "Agent Jordan," she began. "We're not trying to make things any harder than they already are. I know you told us not to speak to the media. But according to Walter, he thought it was best to get as many people looking for Monica as early as possible. It seemed like the right thing to do at the time. But now I understand," she paused. "Now, I see the mistake we might have made. Please," she began to sob. "Just tell us what we need to do. We'll do it. We'll do whatever you need us to do."

S. E. Robinson

Connie Jordan took a deliberate look at the Rep. as she dried her tears. The initial damage had been done. Now, it was just a matter of assessing how much. Jordan effortlessly went from feeling disgust to empathy and concern. She reached out to the Rep., grabbed her by her shoulders, and drew her near. She whispered as she spoke. "These are very difficult times, Representative. I know this more than most because this is what I do for a living. It can be very difficult to know what to do and what not to do during a time like this. I need you to understand that we know what we're doing. If we make a request of you, it's for a good reason. We want to bring your daughter back safe and sound just as much as you do. Please understand that. Okay?"

Jordan leaned back to look the representative in her eyes. Jordan nodded and asked again. "Okay?"

The Rep. nodded and turned to her husband, who quickly swallowed her up into his waiting arms. Jordan turned to the attorney.

"Mr. Westerberg, we will keep you and your clients posted with regard to any future developments. But, in the meantime, please keep them home. We need to know that someone will be there at all times. The monitoring equipment we have set up at their home is useless if neither of them is there to receive any phone calls."

Westerberg nodded reluctantly but understood. Just beyond Westerberg, Jordan could see Terry Carter bolting down the stairs taking them two at a time. Jordan quickly trotted away from the Konetchys to catch Carter before he got too close.

"What's up?" she said as they met.

"We might have a hit," he said panting slightly. "A couple of the uniforms we've got canvassing the area between the convenience store and the university have two people who claim to have seen Monica get taken. They said that there's a guy who's been selling bootleg movies and video games from the back of a cargo van. The witnesses believe that Monica might have been looking at his collection when she was taken."

"Where are these witnesses now?" Jordan asked hurriedly.

"They're on location."

"Well let's get there as soon as possible. Have someone bring a truck around."

"Already done. The Yukon is parked out back."

Jordan turned and motioned to Brennan. Brennan, who had been imploring the Konetchys to stay homebound, sent them on their way and quickly made his way over to Agent Jordan.

"We might have a couple witnesses," she said as soon as he was in earshot. "Get your team together and follow us. We're moving out in three minutes. Wait," she paused for a moment. "My purse."

"Already taken care of," Carter said, and winked.

Brennan grabbed his cell phone and called his office upstairs. He asked for Officer Soto and Sergeant Langdon to meet him at his car ASAP. Once the call was completed he, Agent Jordan, and Agent Carter bolted across the expansive marble floor lobby of the Police Administration building headed for the employee parking lot at the rear of the building. This was their first real hit, and they needed to get to these witnesses while the information was still fresh.

Chapter Four

The team hastily headed for the intersection of Sixteenth Avenue South and Sixth Street South, where uniformed patrol officers were waiting with the two potential witnesses. The intersection was just west of the southernmost portion of the campus. Their destination was just up the street from the Riverside Apartments, just down the street from Vinnie's Supper Club, and directly across the street from Cedar Riverside Community School. It was also one street east of Dressler's Deli, the popular convenience store that most of the college students frequented in order to purchase their sundries.

Upon arrival, Jordan could see the two uniformed officers talking to the witnesses. The taller officer, who appeared to be doing most of the talking, had been directing most of his attention to a well-polished, stately woman who looked to be in her early to mid-fifties. She was thinly built and warmly dressed. She had brilliant, auburn hair, even at her age, which was well cared for and crept out from underneath a shearling cuff hat. The hat perfectly matched her shearling, three-quarter-length fur coat. She was sporting a pair of Foster Grant sunglasses, reminiscent of Raquel Welch, and, at the moment, appeared to be completely enraptured by whatever the officer was saying. The other witness was much younger. He appeared to be in his early-to-mid twenties and could very well have been a student himself. He was underdressed for the season in a dark grey Aeropostale T-shirt, Dockers multi-pocket, khaki shorts and flip-flops. Apparently, he had been walking his dog when the officers approached because he had his miniature Doberman Pinscher in tow, which appeared fed up with the conversation because it constantly pulled against the leash, hoping to lead its master away from the officers. The Yukon pulled over to where the party was standing with

Lieutenant Brennan's Crown Victoria close behind. They exited their vehicles and approached.

"Good afternoon, Lieutenant." The taller, talkative officer was the first to speak. "Officer Gharrity," he continued, "along with Officer Tooley from the Third Precinct, sir." He made a small gesture toward his partner, who in turn gave a nod.

Officer Tooley was the older of the two officers. He was in his early forties and had been on the force since he was nineteen years old. Although Officer Tooley did not have any official designations, he was often used to break in new recruits. Gharrity had only been in uniform for about four months and Tooley was showing him the ropes, as it were. Tooley had seen more than his share of recruits come and go. Some could handle it—others could not. Gharrity seemed to be handling things, and himself, rather well. Tooley always took pride in polishing good officers. He suspected that Gharrity was going to be a very good officer.

"Good afternoon, officers," Brennan responded.

"Lieutenant, we have Therese Triplett and Chad Lillard. They both live down the street in the Riverside apartments. They both claim to have seen what could have been the kidnapping of Monica Konetchy. Ms. Triplett here was just arriving home from a trip into the city. She had just been dropped off by a friend and had started to walk around a little bit before going in. She states she saw a van parked right over there . . ." The officer pointed to an area across the street and up the block a little way. "It's a vehicle that she's seen several times before."

"We both have," Lillard interjected.

"Tell us about it," Jordan said, stepping in.

"Well, it's this big, blue . . ."

"Bluish-green," Ms. Triplett interrupted.

"Or bluish-green cargo van. This guy comes up here a couple times a week and parks right over there." He pointed to the same spot that Officer Gharrity had indicated. "The kids from the college come through, they know the van, they knock on the doors, the guy opens the doors and you can see all these CDs and DVDs and video games he sells at street prices."

"Have you ever bought anything from him?" Jordan asked quickly.

"Well . . ." Lillard was very hesitant about his response.

"Look, Mr. Lillard," Jordan interjected. "We're with the FBI, not the U.S. Marshal's Office. At this juncture, we couldn't care less about what you bought or did not buy from this guy. I'd just like to know if you got a good look at him. Now, if you did buy from him, you had to have gotten a good look at him. Do you remember what he looks like?"

Still hesitant, Lillard looked sheepishly at Ms. Triplett, then at the two interviewing officers before turning back to Jordan.

"Yes," he surrendered. "I remember what he looks like. I've bought some games for my Xbox from him. I can tell you what he looks like."

"Good. Do you know his name?"

"No, I don't know his name." He answered without hesitation. "I just called him 'hey guy.' I didn't really need his name."

"No problem, but we will need that description. Now, please tell us what you both saw Saturday night."

"Well," Ms. Triplett began, "I had just returned from visiting friends in the city. It was a little warm, so after my gentleman friend dropped me off, I thought that I might take a nice little walk before turning in. I started up the walkway, going that way." She pointed west towards where the van would have been parked. "I saw a young lady looking into the back of the van as I have seen so many college kids do. I didn't pay it too much mind at the time so I looked away. But when I looked back the girl was gone, the van doors had been shut and it hastily pulled away. Now, I've seen than van many times in the past and I've never seen it speed away like that before. It was very odd."

"Did you see the young lady actually get into the van?" Lieutenant Brennan asked.

"No. I didn't," she responded almost nonchalantly. "But she was just gone. I would have at least seen her walking away and she wasn't. She was just gone."

Jordan turned to Agent Carter and saw him taking notes. She nodded and turned to Mr. Lillard who took the cue.

"I was out walking my dog. I usually walk him between six and seven on the weekends. I passed the van on the way out and it was just sitting there. On my way back, I was actually walking behind the young lady that was taken."

"Really?" Carter interjected..

"Yeah, she was about forty or fifty feet ahead of me. She had a small plastic grocery bag and she was talking on her cell phone. She really didn't seem to be paying attention to much of anything, but when she looked up she saw the van and she walked over there. My dog held me up a few minutes." Lillard motioned sheepishly towards the pet. "So, I didn't really see what happened next. But as I was cleaning up, I heard a kind of a bang, which drew my attention back to the van. It was like the back doors were slammed shut or something and then the van peeled out, which you don't really expect from a piece of junk like that. After that, I didn't see the girl anymore. It's just like she said," he stated pointing toward Ms. Triplett. "We should have at least seen her walking away. She had to have been in that van."

"That van," Jordan spoke. "What can you tell us about that van?"

"It was a blue . . ."

"Bluish-green!" Ms. Triplett insisted.

"Or bluish-green cargo van. It was pretty banged up. Not like it's been in an accident or anything like that, but like it's been used for years. You know, like a used truck that's been sold fifty times over the years."

"It was an older van?" Brennan inquired.

"Yeah," Lillard answered. "It was from the eighties easy. It was dirty and real grubby on the inside. But because all of the CDs and stuff were in that plastic, I don't think anybody really cared."

"Econoline!" Ms. Triplett shouted.

"Pardon?" Jordan said, turning to the ambitious socialite.

"The van had 'Econoline' written on the side of it."

Mildly confused, Jordan turned to Carter.

"Econolines were made by Ford," Brennan offered. "We can track down all of the Econolines that are registered to area residents. It might point us in the right direction."

Jordan turned back to the witnesses. "If you don't mind, I'd like to have these officers take you downtown so we can formalize your statements. Additionally, Mr. Lillard, we'd like you to speak with a sketch artist so we can get a look at this mobile street vendor. I'd like to put a face on our hustler."

Both witnesses shrugged in resignation.

"Can I take my dog back first?"

"Sure. These officers will see you back to your apartments and then escort you downtown." Jordan looked at the officers expectantly as both nodded in confirmation.

She turned back to her team. "We've got to find this van. It's possible that he's ditched it already, which actually might make it easier to find. If this is our guy, he's not a professional by any stretch of the imagination. We should be able to find something in that van if we can get to it soon enough.

"Harry," she said turning to him. "Give your office a call. Let's get the word out that we're looking for an older, blue or 'bluish-green' Ford Econoline that's really raggedy on the inside. Let's get your guys moving on this as soon as possible. The sooner we can identify our perp, the sooner we'll find Monica Konetchy."

Chapter Five

Willard Drake IV had had more than his fair share of challenges throughout his life. His mother left his biological father when he was two years old, so he never really got to know him. She remarried and subsequently left his stepfather when Drake was six years old—but this time, she left without her young son. Thus, leaving poor Willie—or "Drake" as his platoon comrades called him—to be raised by a man who could not buy a clue when it came to raising kids, not even a free one. It was not that his stepfather, Larry Robert Howard, had been a particularly cruel or abusive man. That was not the case—far from it. It was also certainly not the case that Mr. Howard doted on Drake with an abundance of love and affection, because good ol' Larry "Bob" had been a little short on both. It was simply a case of insufficient and substandard parenting skills. Howard had left school in the fifth grade and had never had much of an interest in scholastics. As such, he'd been incapable of helping Drake with any of his schoolwork. He and Drake never participated in any school related activities. He couldn't even afford any of the afterschool or summer activities that Drake had become interested in. He'd seen no need to allow Drake to stray very far from home, which limited Drake's childhood experiences and circle of friends. As a result, the boy became a reluctant loner as early as grade school.

Howard had worked in construction as a general laborer. He'd only been able to get work as he found it—which, during Drake's childhood, was few and far between, so the cupboard was often bare. Amenities and extras were fleeting dreams. Drake held no ill will toward his stepfather. As the years went by and he grew older, he came to realize that Howard had simply been unprepared to be a single father, and without any extended family on either side, there'd really been no one to turn to for assistance or even advice. Whenever Drake thought of it, which was often, he thought it was a wonder that he managed to turn out as well as he did, given the circumstances.

Still, Howard had had certain redeeming qualities. He'd showed Drake how to hunt. He'd showed Drake how to fend for himself and survive should he be placed in an impossible situation. Howard had also been very good with his hands—able to fix or modify almost anything—and he'd always been more than willing to show Drake everything he could do. In that respect, Drake could consider Howard to have been a good father. Howard had been willing to spend time with him and shared with him what knowledge he did have. He'd been willing to have Drake by his side.

Drake also credited Howard for having instilled in him a sense of patriotic pride and a strong desire to serve his country. Howard had been unable to join the service—his limitations and lack of elementary education had restricted him—but he'd constantly expressed his patriotism and insisted that Drake become a soldier when he came of age. When Drake neared the end of high school, having been left back one grade, he felt strongly that college was not really an option. So, upon graduation a few years before, he enlisted in the army and he had been a military man ever since. Basic training went well, and for the first four years Drake found a home in the armed services. He found the discipline and structure he so badly yearned for, and he was able to see the world; something he thought he would never be able to do. He met new people and actually attained some friends. But as the war in the Middle East lingered on, Drake and his company were deployed as support to some of the forces that were already there. It was during this time in Iraq that Drake began to see things differently. He began to feel things differently. A storm of conflict began to stir inside his head and he grew increasingly agitated by the state of affairs with regard to his career choice. Death was all around him. He could see it.

He could feel it. He could smell it. He could taste it. He had not experienced death on a personal level before. People had abandoned him sure—insert "mom" here—but that was not the same as dealing with so much death. He witnessed the death of friends. He witnessed the death of associates. He witnessed the death of enemy soldiers. All of which he could cope with on one level or another. After all, this was war, and these things happened in war. But it was the deaths of the civilians that really ate at him. It was the deaths of innocent men, women, and children that he could not reconcile. Yes, he was the first to agree that not all civilians were innocent, but there was a great many that were and that was what he had the most difficulty with. There was no mechanism in his psyche that allowed him to justify the death of these innocent civilians. Hence, he began to crack.

After two uninterrupted tours in Iraq, Drake was more than thrilled when his company was allowed to return home. As far as he was concerned, he had seen enough. He had experienced enough. He had done enough. He needed time to gather himself and needed time to reconcile all that he had been through. He needed time to put things into perspective and time to decide what to do with his future. Through one of his contacts in the army, he was able to tie into a pipeline of bootleg CDs, DVDs, and video games. He figured that the kids at the university would jump at the opportunity to buy his stuff at discount prices. It allowed him to get quick money above the stipend he had been receiving from the army. It was easy money, and it paid his bills.

Despite the time off, Drake had two more years to serve in the army, so it came as no surprise when he was recalled to go to Afghanistan. He knew that his turn was coming. He had learned of others who had been deployed, and he just *knew* that, sooner or later, the letter would arrive with his new set of orders. The problem was, of course, that he did not want to return. After it became clear that there were no weapons of mass destruction in Iraq and that overthrowing the government was the chief concern of this country—*and* after he became acutely aware of all the atrocities that needed to occur in order for that to happen—Drake's patriotism turned from pride to confusion to disdain. He now saw his country as a meddler, as an entity that was only interested in achieving its own agenda, and that anyone or anything that got in the way was anti-American and hence an enemy to its "noble" cause.

Even before he'd returned home, Drake decided that he was no longer going to participate in such folly. He decided that should they try to recall him and send him back to the Middle East, he would make a statement. He would tell everyone about the things that were taking place over there and that we, as a nation, needed to pull our troops out of the Middle East—that we needed to focus our attention on the things that were taking place right here within our own borders instead of sending our folks overseas to die, or worse yet, to kill innocent men, women, and children.

So when Drake received the letter that he knew inevitably would arrive, he knew what he had to do. He had everything already planned. He would park at his usual spot. He would wait for someone to approach his van *alone*. He would take his sickening sauce, a concoction that he created from various chemicals he had in his tool shed, dab some of it with one of his oily shop rags and expose it to his "target" by smothering him, or *her*, with it. He would effectively acquire his quarry and head back to the family homestead. That was how he bagged Monica Konetchy. She was easy, almost too easy. It was almost as if she was *meant* to be his target. She was so engrossed with his black market CD collection that she was completely unaware when he approached her from within the van and applied his sauce. She became violently ill almost immediately, which made her relatively easy to acquire. Once she finally passed out, it was all smooth sailing from there. He took her back, bound her securely, and waited for her to wake. In the meantime, he was able to rifle through her things and find her identification. He was pleasantly surprised to learn that she was from the area. Richfield was fairly close. That allowed him to write his note and deliver it personally. Using the Postal Service was unnecessary, so it kept things relatively simple. Things really could not have worked out any better.

Drake was actually taking the time to cook for Monica. She had not eaten anything for a few days so he was planning a full meal for her. He bought some rotisserie chicken from a nearby Boston Market, baked a potato in the microwave, and had corn boiling on the stove. Regardless of what anyone thought of him, he was not a monster and he wanted people to know that Monica was treated well during her stay.

Drake had been monitoring the news reports over a couple of days and was surprised that there had been no news of Monica's abduction. They had to have seen his note by now, he thought. Surely, she had loving and caring parents. At least someone from home should be concerned. With that big beautiful house they had in Richfield, there had to be someone who wanted Monica back home safely. As he started to prepare a plate of food for her, Drake turned on his satellite radio, which was pre-tuned to the region's all-news station. As he did so, he caught the tail end of the Konetchy press conference. He heard Warren Westerberg give a brief description of Monica and appeal to the public for her safe return. For the first time since her abduction, Drake learned that Monica was the daughter of a state representative and while, for all his intents and purposes, this news could be construed as divine intervention, Drake became extremely perturbed. For now he believed that because Monica was who she was, the authorities would stop at nothing to reclaim her. This meant that Drake now became public enemy number one. He was now expendable, and whatever statement he wanted to make was now irrelevant. Sooner or later, they were going to find him. Sooner or later, they would make him pay. He had to get on the move. He had to get out of there as soon as possible. As he looked out of the kitchen window at the rear tool shed, he could see shadowy movement inside. A wave of panic overcame him. He bolted out of the kitchen, across the rear yard, and toward the shed.

Inside the shed, Monica Konetchy was working feverishly to saw herself free from her binds. She did not know what Drake's story was, nor did she care. She simply wanted to be out of that shed and back home where she was safe and sound. The saw blade in her hands was at a very awkward angle, which made moving quickly, difficult. She had already nicked her thumb, and she wanted to keep the collateral damage to a minimum. She cut steadily and with some persistence she was able to free her hands. She hopped back over to the door to peer towards the house—still no sign of Drake. She hopped away from the door and back to the area where she found herself originally. It was the only area in the shed with enough floor space to crouch down and cut the tape that bound her ankles. While on the floor she thought she heard heavy footsteps outside. She was unsure, but did not want to chance it, so before she was finished freeing her ankles she folded her legs and arms behind her and held still. She was sweating heavily from all of the awkward, frantic movements. She was stiff and sore from lying on the hard, cold floor and she was hungry. She did not know how or when she used the bathroom last, but she started to recognize the other smell as the odor of stale urine, which began to rise above all of the other "fragrances" she was presently being exposed to. She could only assume that during her brief bouts of consciousness he made some arrangements for her to relieve herself. She did not even want to imagine how that took place.

As her last thought fleeted away, Monica was certain she heard Drake approaching. She steeled herself and he burst into the tool shed. The door flung wide, so hard and fast that it slammed up against the wall and bounced back with such a force that Drake had to raise his arms to protect himself. He looked very sternly at Monica and asked, "What are you doing in here?"

Before she could answer he started to look very slowly around the room.

"What am I doing?" she responded almost indignantly. "What in the hell could I be doing? You got me all tied up over here. Now, if you want," she said suggestively. "You can untie me and . . ."

"Shut up!" he shouted. He continued to look around very slowly. As he did so, Monica took the opportunity to resume sawing her ankles free while his attention was diverted. As she continued to watch him closely, she could see that his attention was intently focused on something across the room. She followed his gazed and softly gasped. He was staring at the duct tape that she had cut loose from her hands and casually tossed to the floor. Drake turned his gaze back to her.

"Lemme see your hands!" he demanded.

"What are you talking about?" she retorted. "My hands are taped behind me. You should know. You taped them there."

"Lemme see 'em!" he started to make his way over to her. Monica had nearly finished cutting her ankles free. She reversed the saw blade and gripped the end of it firmly.

"Come here," Drake said and bent down to grab her by the shoulders.

Monica lurched back, which took Drake by surprise, and with one fluid movement she came around with her right hand, her saw-blade hand, and cut Drake along the left side of his face, from his temple to his chin. He jumped back and screamed. Monica reached down to her ankles and with newfound strength ripped the tape free of her ankles. She jumped to her feet and had to take a moment as she became dizzy from the head rush, which had been enhanced by the lack of nourishment. Drake took a moment to compose himself. His face was stinging, and the blood was flowing from his wound. He looked around to find an appropriate weapon only to realize that Monica had managed to get herself completely free. He positioned himself between her and the door. Monica approached with blade in hand. She swung at his face again, but this time he was able to avoid contact. He rushed at Monica attempting to grab her. He managed to hoist her up into a frenzied bear hug. He reached for her right hand and squeezed her wrist so hard that she dropped the blade. Monica screamed and tried to claw at his open wound. Drake let loose a subdued cry so as not to be heard, but the pain was incredible. He utilized some of his army training and applied a restraint move that often left an adversary unconscious but relatively unharmed. Monica kicked and scratched in defiance but finally succumbed to the move. Slowly, she fell limp into Drake's arms. He looked at her almost apologetically. She had blood all over her, his blood. But he believed that she was relatively unharmed. He had hoped that physical violence would not be necessary, but he really did not anticipate that she would be who she was, nor that she would be so resourceful. He needed to get her out of there, and he needed to do so fast.

He gathered Monica up into his arms and started to make his way out of the shed. He moved toward the front of the house where his van was parked before he suddenly stopped. People knew that van and it was only a matter of time before the authorities would stop him in it. There was also the chance that some of his neighbors would be out and about. Surely they would see his blood-covered captive, and that would raise concerns that he really needed to avoid. He quickly diverted his attention to the old International that his stepfather used to drive. It was a little beat up but Drake always kept it running. It was very reliable, and it would need to come to the rescue once more. He made his way over to the truck and opened the back door. He laid Monica down on the back seat, hurried back into the shed, and snatched up an old wool blanket to lay across her. He took one last look around the shed and shook his head at the sight of all the blood. He retrieved the first aid kit that he kept by the main table and worked as fast as he could to clean and patch his facial wound. At some point, he thought, he would need to see a doctor about his face, but that would have to wait. Right now he had to get far away from this place as fast as he could. It took a few minutes, but once he finished bandaging his wound he snatched up the first aid kit and made his way to the vehicle. He got behind the wheel of the International and cranked it up. It started on the first try. Old faithful, he thought to himself. He backed out of the driveway and onto the street. He was unsure of exactly where he was headed, but for right now it didn't matter. He simply needed to get away. He threw the truck into drive and pulled away.

***

Back at MPD Central Command Post, it was nearly 6:30 p.m. and the investigation was in full swing. The task force assembled to find Monica Konetchy and bring her home safely managed to document complete statements from the two witnesses. Chad Lillard had given a fairly good description of the mobile street vendor to a skilled police sketch artist, and copies of the unsub had already been forwarded to the other MPD districts and university police. Agent Jordan believed that since this guy was a street vendor, it might actually help to identify him sooner than later. Street vendors of illegal wares were few and far between in Minneapolis, which she knew would make the job a little easier. There had been reports, especially from the university police, of other students buying from this vendor but, as of yet, no one could identify him or knew where he lived. Additionally, since it became clear that Monica was abducted on her way back from the store, she had been missing for the entire three days. A lot of things can happen in three days. She could be in need of medical attention. The team had to be completely prepared for every contingency when they found her—and Connie Jordan was determined to find her. Agent Carter had received his list of area servicemen who had been recalled to the Middle East. He did not yet have a list of the personnel who had gone AWOL, but he was crosschecking his list against the list of persons that had registered an older model Ford Econoline in the area. No hits as of yet, but the process was moving along. Jordan's team had been running all day and while there was still plenty of work that needed to be done, it was time for a break. She pulled Lieutenant Brennan over to the side.

"Lieutenant, I'm thinking we need to take a moment to grab something to eat. I don't know about your guys but we really haven't had moment to take a breath. And I wouldn't exactly call what we had to eat for lunch *food*."

Brennan chuckled. Taco Bell had never been his definition of authentic Mexican food, either.

"Why don't you let your guys go for the night," Jordan continued. "And we can get a fresh start in the morning. I know my guys could do with a decent meal." She paused for a moment and smiled. "You should join us."

Brennan took a moment to consider it. He lived alone on the northern side of Minneapolis. He'd been married once, but at this point in his life he was divorced longer than he had been married. It had been twenty-six years since Mona left him. And while it was a little rough to deal with at first, the last twenty-four years had been pretty smooth. You never really knew how crazy your life had been until that craziness leaves you and your eyes began to see clearly through the haze.

"Sure," he responded. "I enjoy a good meal as much as the next guy."

"Good," she said with a genuine smile. "You pick the place and the meal is on me."

"Well, that's a deal!" He returned her smile. She nodded and turned to gather her team and her things. Brennan called the room to attention.

"Folks, if I could have a minute, please!" Everyone looked up. "As you all can see, the second shift has arrived. I've brought the shift commander up to speed with regard to where are and what we're doing. If anything jumps off tonight, I've been assured that Agent Jordan and I will be contacted promptly. So, until then, we can knock off for the night. I expect to see my team here bright and early at eight-thirty tomorrow morning. Keep your cell phones on. If I need you, I'll call you. We're all on call until the moment we get Monica Konetchy home safely and we've got this son of a bitch in cuffs. Understood? Good. See you in the morning."

Lieutenant Brennan's team gathered their things and began to file out of the command center. The lieutenant made his way over to his relieving watch commander to share a few more final words before departing with the FBI agents. Jordan watched Brennan finish up, completely unaware that Agent Nance-Roberge was approaching from her right side.

"Hey, Connie."

Jordan turned to her in a bit of a start. She smiled, "You startled me, Leisa."

"Sorry about that. I didn't mean to."

Both ladies chuckled a bit. "No problem. What's up?"

"I was able to get a copy of the press conference from earlier today. There's not too much to do with regard to damage control. They put her name and description out there and made it clear that Monica was the Rep.'s daughter. The conference started airing on various outlets at five o'clock. So it's out there. If our guy didn't know who Monica was when he grabbed her, he sure as hell knows who she is now. If he watches any of the area television stations, or just listens to the radio, he's *got* to know who she is now. Give it another hour or so, and this will be national news, if it's not already. The Konetchys didn't give up much of anything in terms of what we have—they really don't know anything. So, I'm working on a way where we can use this to our advantage. I've got a couple of ideas, but nothing that I am completely comfortable with yet. I'll run it by you when I come up with something I like."

Jordan took a moment to digest what she just heard. Not exactly terrible news, but it was far from good. She turned back to Leisa, sighed and nodded. If there was a way to flip this, Leisa was the person to find it.

"So where are we eating?" Leisa asked with a wry smile. She was a tall, shapely woman who did a fabulous job maintaining her figure. But when she was ready to eat, she could put the men on the team to shame. And she did so with such elegance and grace. Jordan smiled.

"I don't know yet," she said nodding her head in Brennan's direction. "I'm letting Harry pick the spot. When he gets through over there, he'll lead the way."

"That sounds good to me." The other team members began to gather at the back of the center. All were more than ready for a hearty meal. Brennan slowly made his way over to the group.

"So what's it going to be, Lieutenant?" Jordan asked in a tone a little louder than her usual.

"Well, I'm a seafood man, myself. Whaddaya say to McCormick and Schmick's on Ninth Street South?"

Brennan and Jordan both could see a few heads nod in approval. Jordan turned back to Brennan and said "McCormick and Schmick's it is. Lieutenant, if you could be so kind as to lead the way." Jordan motioned toward the stairs and the rest of the team parted to allow Brennan a path through. He headed out of the building and the FBI's Behavioral Analysis Unit, a hungry Behavioral Analysis Unit, followed close behind.

***

He took a moment to glance at his Tag Heuer. It was 7:53 p.m. Tonight would be the night—the night for his one-man show. Tonight, he would be the leading man, the headliner, the closing act, the choreographer and spotlight performer. Tonight, like so many other nights in the past, he would conduct his symphony and make his music—make his magic. He would allow his light to shine, and gloriously, he would take his place among the stars. Tonight he would perform his "Devil's Waltz." He would perform the carefully choreographed ballet to perfection and afterwards bask in the glow of his masterful performance. As usual, in the hours preceding his performance, he found himself growing increasingly anxious. The butterflies in his stomach had begun a ballet of their own, which would grow increasingly more frantic as the opening curtain drew nigh. He smiled. He knew tonight would be an exciting night, a thrilling night, an exhilarating night. He could already hear the orchestra in the pit tuning their instruments.

He glanced at his lovely watch again. The curtain would rise in five hours.

Chapter Six

It was 12:45 a.m. He was already inside her home, hiding in a shadowy spot between the front window and the fireplace. The drapes were drawn, and since this particular spot was not in the line of sight upon entering the home, he knew that she would not immediately notice him. Access into her home was smooth and easy. Unbeknownst to her, he had been here three times before. He'd had to assess the ease of access, get a strong understanding of the layout, and carefully plan all of his moves in order to make this as quick and as effective as possible.

She had a lovely home. Modest. Not too big. Only about 1,100 square feet, but he was sure that it was more than enough to suit her needs. It was a two-bedroom townhome. She had been living here, alone, for five and half years and was able to make her purchase when these units were practically brand new. She was able to buy in at a very reasonable price and at last check these units had not been affected by any manner of violent crime.

He took a moment to take in his surroundings once more. She had an ample living room, which was neatly furnished. There was an inviting cream colored, leather sofa, which sat almost in the center of the room opposite the fireplace separated by a long cherry-wood coffee table with eight tinted, rectangular glass panes on top. An incense holder, a crystal candy dish, and an assortment of magazines and books were strewn strategically across it. There was a matching leather easy chair with an ottoman off to the left of the sofa and positioned in the very front of the house underneath the bay window. It was perpendicular to the sofa and fireplace and faced the coffee table. There was a standing overhead lamp next to the chair, which was perfectly situated for reading. Just to the right of the fireplace was a wall unit, which held an assortment of books, magazines, small figurines, and miscellaneous items. The room was fully carpeted in beige, which appeared hardly ever used.

Just beyond the living room was a cozy dining area. This small area had hardwood floors and a small circular dinette set with a glass tabletop supported by a wrought iron base with seating for two. There was a small baker's rack against the long wall that held a spattering of items: a few cooking magazines, clipped coupons, small cooking and baking utensils, and in the wine rack portion of the piece, four bottles—one Chardonnay, one Pinot Grigio, and two Zinfandels—one white and one red. To the rear was the kitchen. It was fairly modern and boasted all of the newest and trendiest items that could be found at the time these units were built six years ago. It had stainless steel appliances, including a range with a matching companion overhead microwave/hood unit. It had the side-by-side refrigerator with the drawer freezer at the bottom of the unit. It even had the matching dishwasher, which she hardly ever used. She had an abundance of paper products—paper plates, paper cups, paper towels, and plastic utensils, which she preferred and used for almost every meal. In truth, she disliked doing the dishes, even with the machine. There was a pair of sliding French doors that led to a rear deck. The deck was small, only about four by eight feet, but there was a set of steps that led down to a small patch of grass that was more than likely billed as the rear yard by those who constructed and sold these units. Unfortunately, for the unsuspecting lady of the house, that deck and those doors were the weakest points of the home and the perfect place to gain entrance.

Upstairs were the two bedrooms. She had a modest sized guestroom that was completely furnished but rarely used, accompanied by an even less frequently used guest bathroom. She spent most of her time in the master. Like the living room, the master bedroom was ample in size. It held her queen size, four-poster bed that she had always adorned with some kind of flower print. There was a mahogany clothes dresser, which held the only television in the house, a 32-inch plasma. There was a large wall closet with sliding doors that ran nearly the full length of one wall, sparsely populated, as she did not have many clothes beyond her nurse's uniforms. There was a generous master bath. It had two sinks, one that she never used, a jetted garden tub, and separate shower. The counter between the sinks held myriad personal grooming items, many of which one would expect from a lovely young lady that took the time and care to address her appearance. It was an upstairs that, if things went as planned on this night, she would never see again.

The home held no surprises. It was well suited for her needs and tastes and was perfect for the duty that he had to perform on this night. He appreciated that there was good space between the furniture. He would need the room. He was sure that she would put up a considerable fight but the ample space should allow him to conduct his business with relative ease. He smiled to himself. It was nights like this that he lived for.

Everything was in order. He was wearing a hazardous materials protective jump suit and Kevlar gloves. He wore protective goggles and had his face completely covered. He could not afford to leave any evidence behind or track any with him. This was going to be a messy night and he made sure that he was adequately prepared.

He glanced at his watch. It was 1:03. She should be arriving momentarily. He pressed his back up against the wall. He would not see her enter but he would hear her. He closed his eyes and awaited the curtain call. Eight minutes later, he heard the key in the door. Once the tumblers released, she entered her home and flicked the switch just to her right, which turned on the light in the dining area. She was visibly tired but apparently upbeat. She was humming something he did not recognize and cared even less about. She had one small bag of groceries, which she promptly sat on the kitchen counter. She walked over to the dinette set and rested her oversized purse on it. She started for the living room and stopped just before entering to hang her coat on a wall rack that was mounted just at the border between the living and dining rooms. She looked around the living room and whirled back to the kitchen to put her groceries away. He stood in complete silence and watched her. He watched as she almost gracefully attended to her groceries. She appeared to be a very self-assured and confident woman. She looked completely comfortable with herself and her life and appeared to be without a care in the world. He watched her as she put the last of the groceries away, folded the paper bag, and placed it into a cupboard where she stored them. She turned to face the front of the house. She placed her right hand on her hip and leaned up against the cabinet with her left. She started tapping her fingers against the cabinet as if she was deciding what she should do next. He was aware that she would be off from work for the next two days, so she was probably trying to determine what she should do with the rest of the night since she was able to sleep late the next morning. She stood up straight and loosened the top two buttons of her nurse's uniform. She began to mosey toward the living room. She reached the coffee table and leafed through a few of the magazines looking for anything that might grab her attention. She found a *Vanity Fair* that caught her eye. Its cover story had something to do with Rosie O'Donnell coming back to daytime television. She considered it for a moment, gave a little sideways nod, and picked it up. As she flipped through the pages, she slowly headed for her reading chair. Without ever looking up from the magazine, she slowly turned to be seated and in doing so, turned her back to him. In just that instant, he had her. His left arm came across her left shoulder and his hand covered her mouth. Completely shocked she stood motionless for a moment. Her mind wasn't quite processing what was happening. He drew her close to him and began to whisper into her ear.

"Don't try to scream," he whispered. "No one will hear you." He knew that her neighbors on both sides were out of town. The residents to the left in 5-B were away on vacation. They liked to travel to Arizona in the spring. And the college kids that sublet the unit to her right in 1-A had gone to Florida for spring break. They indeed had the night to themselves.

She tried to wriggle herself free to no avail. She tried to bite his hand through the glove and was actually able to catch the meaty part of his palm, but she didn't break the protection of the glove. She only managed to hurt her teeth and gums and instead of letting go, he grunted and squeezed his hand tighter over her mouth.

"Ah ah ah," he said as he raised his right hand and brought a sharp, fully extended folding knife to her neck. "Don't be a naughty girl."

She could feel the three-inch blade against her skin. It cut her slightly as a result of all her movement. Despite her fright, she stood as still as possible.

"That's better," he continued his whispered tone. "Do you know what I want you to do for me?" he asked calmly.

She started to shake her head, but very slowly so as not to encourage the blade any more than she already had. She began to cry, and he could see the tears as they pooled against his left hand. A reservoir of tears. He nearly smiled at the thought.

"I want you to dance with me," he said. "Will you do that? Will you dance with me?

"Here . . ." he pulled the blade away from her neck which allowed her to nod slightly. Then with his left arm across her left shoulder and still covering her mouth, he wrapped his right arm around her right shoulder, almost as if to hug her from behind, and slowly, following his lead, the two of them began to sway into the open area of the living room floor. They moved to the rhythm of whatever imaginary music being conducted in his head. They swayed. They twirled. They danced.

She hoped to catch him off guard. She was unable to see his face, but if she could sense that he had grown too relaxed, perhaps she could find a moment to break free. They continued to move around the living room. They were circling the sofa and coffee table. She thought that if she could break away as they cleared the coffee table on the way to the fireplace then perhaps she could grab a poker and possibly defend herself enough to escape. They continued to dance. He began to hum to himself—something she did not recognize. He was somewhere in his own little world. As they moved back around the sofa, back around the coffee table and neared the fireplace, she took her chance. She raised her right leg and kicked back against his right knee as hard as she could. Shocked back into reality, he released her and limped backwards.

"Bitch!" he cried as he winced in pain.

He lunged at her. She quickly grabbed the poker from the fireplace. As she turned, she got to truly see her attacker for the first time. He was dressed as if he worked in a quarantined environment. He was in a grayish, one-piece HAZMAT suit, which covered him from head to toe. There was nothing about this man that was recognizable. She whirled to strike him with all the might she could muster and missed. He ducked, evading the poker completely. The force of the swing forced her to follow through entirely too much, leaving her completely vulnerable to his advance. He grabbed her up again and forced her to drop the poker. He pulled her close again, forced his hand over her mouth and from behind angrily whispered into her ear, spewing spit along with his words.

"You should not have done that! You clearly do not know who you are fucking with," he growled. "But it doesn't matter. You're done, bitch. Say good night."

He took the blade, still in his right hand, brought it up to her neck just below her left ear and cut from left to right. As the blood began to spurt from her neck, he pushed her down to the floor and quickly stepped back to avoid being exposed. Even though he was dressed for the occasion, he wanted to keep the possibility of leaving evidence to a minimum. He stood back and watched as the blood and the life of the young woman flowed from her wound. Using both hands, she frantically tried to stop the bleeding. She pressed her hands against the wound but was unsuccessful with every attempt. She gasped desperately for air, but every breath seemed less successful than the last. After a few moments, as the blood reduced from a gush to a trickle, taking the remainder of her strength along with it, he looked at her intently as her body twitched involuntarily trying to hold onto the memory of the free movement that it once took for granted.

During her final moments, as he tried to absorb every sensation, every nuance, every morsel of the experience, something he had not seen before caught his eye. Something shiny. Something that managed to glisten, even as it was being enveloped in her blood. It was a pendant that she was wearing around her neck. He peered closer and realized that it was a silver Aesculapius. It was the small figure of a sword with wings intertwined with two snakes that twisted around the sword to where they faced each other at the top. Seeing that it was the symbol for the medical professions, he thought, *That's right. She's a nurse.* There seemed to be a great deal of detail in the charm. The wings were very well defined, wraught with attention to the minutiae. It appeared, even from this distance, that the feathers held particular detail as well. The dual snakes were just as impressive. The eyes, the fangs, the scales and even the forked tongues were meticulously etched as to give brilliance even to such a small piece of jewelry. This was no ordinary pendant, and regardless of the material, he surmised that it must have cost a pretty penny just from the craftsmanship alone. He reached for the necklace, paused, and then decided against it.

During this current active streak, he had killed six women. This young lady made seven. No two women were the same. They had absolutely nothing in common and each victim was completely oblivious of the others. Each manner of death was different. Each waltz occurred to a different tune. That was how he managed to stay ahead of the authorities. There was nothing to tie any of his murders together: there was no way to connect them. The fact that they had been committed by one man had yet to dawn on anyone, so he was able to stay well below the radar.. One of the most essential elements of his method was that he did not take souvenirs. He always thought that it was absolutely ludicrous to take something from a victim or crime scene. In the end, it always led to the complete downfall of his peers because there were always those souvenirs to confirm a killer's identity. It always baffled him, and he knew better. He knew that in order to keep his identity safe he had to minimize his connections with victims. This meant forgoing any and all souvenirs. It was a no-brainer as far as he was concerned, a matter of common sense.

He took a step back and assessed his work. She was dead, he was sure of that. The dance occurred fairly close to script so he was pleased with his performance. It did not last as long as he would have liked, but that was okay. He took a look at his person, and although he had been sprayed with some of her blood, the exposure was kept to a minimum. He walked over to the drawn drapery on the opposite side of the front window from where he had hidden and retrieved his "clean-up kit." Inside this bag was the set of clothes he had worn when he arrived, various chemicals that he used to cleanse himself and the area he had designated to make his change, and it also included the appropriate accelerants that he would use to dispose of his jumpsuit. He took all of his items upstairs into her rarely used guest bathroom. He then slowly and methodically undressed, taking care not to touch anything in the room. He carefully placed his suit, his gloves, and his goggles into separate plastic bags and then into his kit. He got dressed in his civilian clothes, donned a pair of latex gloves, retrieved his cleaning materials, and began to thoroughly clean the bathroom. When this chore was completed, the bathroom would be spotless. There would not be a shred of evidence to indicate that he was ever there.

On his way back downstairs he took another look at his work. He smiled. He was always proud of a job well done. He thought again about the pendant and paused. He was very tempted but he knew better. It would be best to just leave it behind. He turned and headed for the front door. He turned off the dining room light as he prepared to leave. He decided to walk straight out the front door without even locking it behind him. He knew she was off the next couple of days and, because she was primarily a loner, no one would think to start looking for her until Sunday when she was due to return to work. So she could lie there and marinate in her own blood for the next couple of days and no one would know a thing. He smiled again and casually walked out the front door.

He walked over to his vehicle, which was parked on Fourteenth Avenue South. He tossed his bag into the back and started his truck. He closed his eyes and took a deep breath. The rush from such an evening did not subside quickly. He could still feel the adrenalin rushing through his veins. He could still feel his heartbeat pounding like a jackhammer. This night was glorious and like any other event that could cause such a natural euphoria, he wanted to hold onto this high for as long as possible. He wanted to savor the moment and relive the experience for as long as he could.

He pulled his truck out onto Fourteenth and made a right onto East Franklin. First things were first. He headed over to the Tenth Avenue Bridge, where on a chilly night like tonight, he would find a few homeless people burning a barrel to keep warm. Along the way, however, he could not help but bask in the glow of his glory. It started to rain again but he was completely oblivious because his mind was solely focused on the events that had just transpired. In his mind's eye, he could see all of the events as they occurred, as if he was a spectator rather than participant. From the moment she walked through the door, to the unpacking of the groceries, to the choosing of leisure reading, to the abduction, the waltz, and the kill. Even the clean up afterwards held a certain amount of ecstasy for him. Everything was so well conceived, so completely well planned. And the execution—the execution was flawless. He was good, and he knew it. When he was ready to retire—and he knew that one day *he would*—there was no way that he would be caught. He would retire as one of the greatest serial killers of all time—that no one would ever know about. That thought made him smile again.

As he pulled up to the Tenth Avenue Bridge, he could see a couple of guys around a burning barrel. He had hoped it would be idle. He reconsidered his original disposal plan and decided to drive a little further and toss his bag into the Mississippi. While he preferred to burn the items, he would simply open all of the plastic bags in his "kit" and let the river wash away any shreds of evidence that might have been found. Nature could be quite handy sometimes. As he pulled away, it was the first time he realized it was raining. He turned on his wipers, drove a few hundred feet and pulled over. He hopped out, reached into his bag and opened all of his carefully packaged items and reclosed the bag. He walked down to the banks of the Mississippi and tossed the bag in. He stood and watched as it began to drift away while sinking at the same time. Even on the outside chance that someone would retrieve that bag, any DNA or prints that were on those items were gone now. He was free and clear.

He got back into the truck. His mind was still on that pendant. He was completely fascinated by it. It held his attention for entirely too long and he was unable to let it go. He started to drive. Once again, he wanted to relive the experience. He always enjoyed his post-*muerte* drive. It was like having a cigarette after sex. It allowed him to keep his high for as long as he possibly could. It allowed him to re-examine the night's events. It allowed him to uncover any mistakes he might have made. It allowed him to think of ways to improve his process for the next time. He drove through the glistening streets of Minneapolis for forty minutes, awash in his feeling of accomplishment but all the while he was nagged at the same time. That pendant. That damned pendant. It was not like he had never seen an Aesculapius before. Truthfully, those medical charms were a dime a dozen. But he had never seen one quite like that before and what made it worse was that this pendant called to *him*. It beckoned him and he found himself slowly acquiescing to its call. He was growing weaker to its will and suddenly, before he even realized it, he found himself heading back towards the Santa Fe Villas.

In his mind, he began to justify his actions. Since he had not taken any souvenirs from any other victim, there was still no way to connect her with the others. Worst-case scenario? The authorities would simply to try to tie this victim to the others that had missing items, none of which could be tied to him. He would have to find a secure and discreet place for the item, though. Some place where no one could find it, but, at the same time, would grant him easy access any time he desired to see it—hold it. He was sure that such a place existed. Taking a souvenir this one time should not upset the apple cart. It should not upset the apple cart at all.

He parked his vehicle back on Fourteenth Avenue South. It was pushing 3 a.m., and there was hardly a soul on the road. He trotted across East Franklin, mindful of any potential witnesses—but there were none to be seen. He made his way through the arch and up the three steps that led to unit 3-A, but before he opened the door he caught sight of something that made his blood run cold. Affixed to the door, just above eye level, was his victim's pendant. The object he had been nearly obsessing over for the past hour was pinned to the door with a note attached. Along with the pendant were three words that were clearly written in the blood of his victim.

They read simply:

"SHE WAS MINE!"

He fell backward down the steps, as if he had been dealt a blow to his midsection by a mythological giant. He could hardly breathe. From the ground he stared at the note. He stared at it as if it was written in a foreign language, yet he could somehow understand exactly what it said. He understood all too well. From the crown of his head to the soles of his feet, a feeling of dread began to wash over his body. It sought to consume him, completely relieving him of his sanity and sense of being. It started raining harder, but he hardly noticed. He could have just as easily been in the middle of a desert—it made little difference. He was completely oblivious to his surroundings. Still trying to catch his breath, he scrambled to his feet and clumsily ran back to his vehicle. He had trouble with the fob while trying to unlock it. Instead, he depressed the panic button, which set off the truck's alarm. If no one had been paying attention to him previously, he'd get some attention now, he thought. It took him a moment to silence the alarm again. He managed to do so and unlock the truck at the same time. He jumped into the truck and sat there a moment. For the first time that he could remember, he was truly and utterly frightened. He had to piece together what had just happened. He had to evaluate the situation in its totality and explore all of the ramifications that might occur. The first thing he needed to do, however, was to get the hell out of there. He started his truck and headed back to his hotel, blowing every light possible along the way. Frantically, he began to examine his situation aloud.

"What the fuck is going on?" he started. "I mean, what the fuck!" He banged on the dash with his right hand. "Someone saw me? Someone knows? How the fuck is that possible? How the fuck does anybody know? How in the fuck did they know I was coming back?"

He started to get a real sick feeling in his stomach. He pulled his truck over and opened the door just in time as he began to vomit out onto the street. He heaved several times even after he was empty. He tried to compose himself but was having extreme difficulty doing so. His world had just turned upside down and it was all over a damned pendant. The pendant, he froze at the thought. He needed to go back and grab that pendant and the note before it caught anyone's attention. He wheeled the truck around and sped back to the Villas. This time he pulled up alongside the Villas on East Franklin Street. He left the truck running and darted back to her unit. Before he completely reached her door he could see that the note was gone. The fucking note was gone. He could feel all of the strength drain from his limbs. He had barely enough strength to stand, let alone walk back to his vehicle. It was clear that somebody was fucking with him. He was smack down in the middle of something and he had no idea of what. Not a mutherfucking clue. He pitifully made his way back to his truck and hopped in. Once again he needed a moment to gather himself. However, this time when he pulled away from the Santa Fe Villas, he pulled away for good.

By 4:30 a.m., he was making his way through the hotel lobby on his way back to his room. On the elevator, Paul Andersen did everything he could to keep himself together. His limbs were weak but his mind kept racing into several different directions. He tried to recall if he had seen or done anything tonight that was out of the ordinary. "Who could this person be?" he whispered to himself. "What the hell is going on?" He got off on the fourteenth floor and made his way to room 1410. Still fumbling, it took him several moments to properly use his key card. He stumbled into the room and collapsed onto the bed. After a few moments, he sat up and began to peel away the wet clothes from his body. Slowly but deliberately he made his way to the bathroom for a shower. For several minutes he let the water beat against the crown of his head. For several minutes he just stood there and tried to come to grips with the reality of his situation. What it came down to was simple. Someone knew. Someone knew where he was tonight. Someone knew what he was doing tonight. Someone had seen his handiwork—firsthand. And someone knew him well enough to know that he would be back for that damned pendant. In an instant, his triumphant evening had become a living nightmare that was beyond his imagination.

He finished his shower. He was unable to wash away his despair or fear as he did his sweat and odor. This time he gently laid back into bed. His mind continued to race, and there was nothing he could do to stop it. He had to get himself together. He had to find a way to see this thing through while still maintaining his focus. There was still a job he had to do in the morning. There was still a kidnapped girl out there that he wanted to bring home safely. But there were just so many questions that he needed to answer. He had hoped that a couple hours of sleep would allow his mind to take a break—even if only he could manage just a short nap. He was wrong. Paul Andersen would get no sleep on this night.

Chapter Seven

It was 8:30 a.m., Thursday, April 23, and the local authorities participating in the frantic search for Monica Konetchy were abuzz with excitement. The scene in the Minneapolis Police Central Command Post office was bedlam as Minneapolis police officers and FBI agents alike scrambled to gather their necessities as they prepared to head to the scene of an overnight house fire. This particular fire location was of great interest to these investigators as an older, bluish-green van that had been so strongly sought after in connection with this kidnapping was parked in front of the residence. By far, this was the best news yet, and it required everyone to get hopping.

Naturally, everyone was excited. Everyone save Agent Paul Andersen. This was not to say that Paul was not excited or even thrilled at the prospect of this development—he was. Despite his extracurricular activities, Paul was very concerned about his job. He enjoyed what he did and he had grown very good at it. He wanted Monica Konetchy home, safe and sound, just as much as the next person and he was willing to do everything possible to see that through.

No, the reason for Paul's less than enthusiastic demeanor had a great deal to do with last night. He was still reeling from last night—still coming to terms with last night. Still wondering what in the hell *happened*. A night that started so wonderfully right ended so terribly wrong. A night that turned into a nightmare and, as a result, had etched caution and worry into his newly fragile psyche. Paul was now in a place where he must be wary of, and question, everything and everyone around him. There was someone somewhere out here that knew a hell of a lot about him—too much about him. Paul was in a lost place where reality simply did not seem *real* anymore. He gathered his things and made his way out to bring the truck around.

It took just over twenty minutes for Jordan, Andersen, Carter, and Torres to reach their destination. They arrived at a white, three-story, wooden house located in the northeastern area of Minneapolis. Originally constructed in the Victorian style, the single home had several double pane windows and a green, shingled roof. It was a large, older house. It had an open wraparound porch that might have been inviting many years ago and a substantial front lawn that extended along both sides of the house and led to an even larger yard in the rear. Up by the front of the house there was a good mix of flowers and hedges that had apparently been neglected and left to fend for themselves this early spring. Though not in complete disrepair, the house had not been well cared for. However, it was not to a point where a little tender loving care would not have helped return the home back to its once impressive splendor. Just off to the left of the house was a driveway that led to a two-car garage. Alongside the garage, roughly twenty feet to its right, was a wooden shed that was roughly ten by twenty feet in size. To the naked eye, it appeared to have been constructed by hand and with considerable skill. Fortunately, that rear shed also appeared to have made it through the night relatively unscathed.

Their prize was in front of the house. Parked right in front of the home was a dirty, blue—not bluish-green—1983 Ford Econoline Cargo van; a vehicle that was registered to none other than William Drake. Mr. Drake was a private first class in the U.S. Army who had received orders to return to the Middle East, but had failed to report. Once the team got word of the fire and learned that a van resembling the description of the vehicle they had been searching for was parked out front, a patrol car was immediately dispatched to run the plates. Once the query came back with a name, Agent Carter ran it by his people in Washington and was able to confirm Drake's military record and current orders. William Drake was ordered to report for duty on Tuesday the twenty-first. Now, forty-eight hours later, he was officially AWOL. This was their guy. Now, they had to find out if he was the *right* guy. They needed to find Drake, and they needed to find out if he had any connection with the kidnapping of Monica Konetchy.

The fire at the Howard homestead was extinguished overnight and the preliminary investigation had already been completed. There was water throughout the scene, much of it pooled in the lawn areas around the home. There was endless debris, especially in the rear of the home where most of the fire damage occurred. Presumably, that was where the kitchen was. There was smoke damage everywhere, and the roof in the rear of the house had collapsed into the rear yard. Fortunately, neither the blaze nor the subsequent fire department activity affected the adjacent properties.

On this morning, the fire marshal, Lucinda Brantley, resumed her investigation with the assistance of daylight. Jordan pulled her notepad out from her bag to glance at her notes. She skimmed the page until she found what she was looking for. The vehicles snaked through the remaining fire department apparatus, pulled just past the house a bit and parked across the street. While Agents Torres and Andersen began to survey the area, Jordan, Brennan, and Carter gathered at the front hood of Jordan's vehicle.

"Harry," Jordan began, brushing the hair from her face so she could see. She had to raise her voice a bit to be heard above the diesel engines of the fire apparatus. "I want you and your guys to get that van out of here as soon as possible. We need to get it processed."

"We don't have a warrant," Brennan replied in a matter-of-fact tone.

"I know," Jordan said shaking her head. "You made that call to the ADA's office, correct?"

"Yep. Before we left. I hate to tell you this, but it could take a while to get here."

"I know, I know," she said slightly flustered.

Jordan stood completely erect and closed her eyes for a moment. She opened them and looked around the scene. There were still three fire department vehicles parked at the scene. She barely glanced at the midsized water truck, the fire marshal's brightly colored red and white Denali, or the Emergency Medical Vehicle which were all parked in a random fashion in the middle of the street before her eyes rested upon the van. She needed to get her clutches on that van. Jordan was certain the vehicle was doused with water at some point during the night, and she wanted that van out of here before they risked the chance of losing any more of the evidence it could possibly provide. Her gaze slowly took her past the van and to the rear of the home where she could see the fire marshal surveying the rear of the property and working on her Panasonic Toughbook..

"Hang tight for a moment," she said and hastily began to trot towards Fire Marshal Lieutenant Brantley.

"Lieutenant Brantley!" She began to call out as soon as she felt she was within earshot. "Lieutenant Brantley!" The lieutenant raised her head at the sound of her name and gazed toward Jordan.

"Excuse me!" The lieutenant cried out as Jordan continued to approach her. "This is a sealed scene. You're not supposed to be here." Jordan managed to reach her. "You're not supposed to be here, miss," she repeated. "Don't you see all the yellow tape?"

"Yes, I do, and I don't mean to interrupt you," Jordan said slightly winded. She took a moment to catch her breath, reached inside of her jacket to retrieve and show the fire marshal her credentials. "I'm SSA Connie Jordan with the FBI." Brantley was not overly impressed. "Look, I know you're busy and you've got your job to do. I don't want to get in your way. I'm here working with the MPD on the kidnapping case of Monica Konetchy." Lieutenant Brantley rocked backward slightly, now showing a modicum of interest. "We believe strongly that the person who lives here might have been involved in her kidnapping."

"Really?"

"Yes."

"Well okay, what can I do for you?"

"Well, for starters, can you give me any idea as to what happened here?"

Brantley gave a small frown but saw no harm in sharing what she had. "Well," she started slowly, "from the looks of things so far, it looks like a typical kitchen fire. It looks as if someone left some food cooking on the stove, it burned out and eventually spread into the rest of the kitchen. There was no one home, so no one was hurt. No signs of any foul play or anything like that, just negligence."

Jordan processed the information. "Is there any way to know who or how many people were here at the time?"

"No," Brantley shook her head. "There's no way to know that."

Jordan took another moment. "Look," she started frankly. "We have a warrant on the way, but we're not sure when it'll get here. We believe that that van parked out front . . ." Jordan stopped, turned and pointed, "is connected to the abduction and I'd like to get that thing out of here and move it to downtown where it could be processed. Now, I can't really touch it without the warrant. But . . ." Jordan turned back to the lieutenant and continued with her straightest face possible. "But if that van is in any way impeding your investigation I'm sure the MPD would be more than happy to move it out of the way for you."

S. E. Robinson

Brantley took a moment to look at Jordan. She leaned slightly to her left to look past Jordan and at the van. She straightened back and looked at Jordan again.

"You know," she started. "There's always a chance of a flare-up in one of these old houses. There is a lot of old wood here, and I suspect that there still might be some smoldering taking place. We're gonna have to get some heavy equipment up here to sift through this stuff to make sure this fire is completely out. That van is gonna have to be moved in order to allow enough access.

"Officer!" Brantley called to a uniformed officer who had been standing in the front of the house. The officer jogged over to the ladies. "Officer, could you please have that van out front removed? I might need to get a front-end loader in here to sift through this debris."

The officer turned to Agent Jordan who spoke quickly, "Officer, Lieutenant Brennan is out front. I'm sure that he can make all of the appropriate arrangements. In the meantime, please make sure that this location remains secure. We're waiting for a warrant to search the premises in its entirety."

The officer nodded and made his way back to his post. Jordan turned back to Brantley.

"Thank you," she spoke softly. "Thank you very much."

"No problem," Brantley responded. "Just get that son of a bitch."

Jordan smiled. She liked the lieutenant. She trotted backwards a few steps before turning and heading back toward her team. Brantley took a moment to look after Jordan, and smiled. She thought momentarily of all the responsibility that Jordan must have, shook her head and returned her gaze back to the rear of the house.

Upon returning to Brennan and Carter, Jordan informed them that it was all right to take the van. Brennan got on his cell and gave the order to have the van transported directly to the police impound lot. There, a forensics team would go over the truck methodically and thoroughly to glean every possible shred of evidence they could from the vehicle. With any luck they would be able to put Monica Konetchy in the van. If they could do that, then they would be sure that Drake was their guy.

Milling around in the street, many of the area residents, Drake's long time neighbors, were taking in the action. They stood and watched and talked and watched, most of who did so in disbelief. After all, theirs was a quiet and old neighborhood with history and significance. The loss of any of these homes was a loss to the community. Most of these neighbors held no ill will toward Drake, or toward his father when he was alive. It was simply sad to see someone's property, a neighbor's property, suffer so much damage. Jordan caught notice of these neighbors and turned to Brennan and Carter.

"Gentlemen," she began, capturing their attention. "Take a look around. Let's get a canvass going. We've got several neighbors out here and we need to talk to them. Maybe they know something. Maybe, they've seen Monica and haven't even realized it. Let's get to them while we've got them."

Both men agreed. Brennan called a few of his officers over and ordered them to corral the spectating neighbors, and Carter passed on the assignments to Andersen and Torres. Both parties fanned out and began their interviews.

The canvassing took about two hours to complete. None of the neighbors saw Drake with Monica. They had, in fact, never seen Drake with any woman. There were no complaints about Drake. No strange behaviors or antisocial activity to speak of. They were able to confirm that he sold bootleg items. For some of the neighbors, he even took orders. They confirmed that he was in the military but no one knew if he had grown dissatisfied with the service. The one bit of information that was deemed most important was the description of Drake's missing SUV. With the van parked out front, if Drake was on the move, he had to be driving something else. The neighbors were able to confirm that Drake had three vehicles: the cargo van; the Catalina, which was still parked in the rear of the house; and an older red and white International truck, which was nowhere to be found. Through Central Dispatch, Brennan called for an all points bulletin on Drake and his vehicle. Assuming he left before the fire started last night, Drake had more than enough time to get out of Minneapolis, and he could be headed anywhere.

As Brennan continued along his train of thought, he was distracted by Lieutenant Brantley, running from the rear of the house and yelling for Jordan along the way.

"Agent Jordan!" she screamed as she stopped in the middle of the street. She fell to her knees and gathered her arms to her chest. She was panting heavily and was clearly shaken. Jordan and the others rushed toward the woman. The officer posted at the front of the house was the first to reach her. He placed his arms around her and tried to comfort her. By the time Jordan reached her, she could barely speak above a whisper.

"The shed." She struggled with her words. Jordan knelt at her side. "The shed," she repeated. "There's blood everywhere."

Jordan whipped her head around to gaze at the rear of the house. She turned to the officer. "Get her out of here."

She jumped up and started for the shed. Brennan and Carter were close behind.

"What about the warrant?" Brennan asked.

"Forget the warrant for now. I want to have a look. There could be a body back there. And if this doesn't count as exigent circumstances, then I don't know what does."

MINE!

The three of them carefully navigated their way to the shed through all of the charred and, in some pockets, still smoldering debris. With her weapon drawn and each person properly positioned, Carter slowly opened the door. Taking care to remain outside of the shed, the three of them gazed inward and were greeted by a bloody scene. Items were tossed about. Canisters were overturned. Even in an area such as this, where one would expect a certain level of disorganization to be present, it was clear that a struggle had taken place.

Without entering the shed, Carter slowly closed the door and the three of them backed away. Jordan turned to Brennan. "There's a lot of blood, but not enough to think that somebody bled out. We need a forensics team out here—like yesterday."

Carter interjected, "I saw a couple of strands of duct tape on the floor. If this is where he kept her, it looks like Monica might have gotten loose and put up a pretty decent fight."

"Yeah," Brennan agreed. "But I'm concerned about that blood. I sure as hell hope it isn't hers."

"Harry," Jordan resumed. "Check again on that warrant. We're losing precious time here. We really need to know what we're looking for. Clearly someone was wounded here. We need to find out who."

As the three made their way back to their vehicles, they continued their speculation. Jordan glanced over at Lieutenant Brantley who appeared to be recovering from the unexpected surprise she had just experienced. Agent Torres, who had been participating in the neighborhood canvassing, caught her attention and came running up to Jordan with an odd look on his face that seemed to express both excitement and trepidation at the same time.

"We got him!" he exclaimed. He almost could not contain himself.

"What does that mean?" Jordan asked.

"It means that we got him," Torres huffed as he came to a stop. "This fool is in downtown Minneapolis. He's standing in the middle of Twelfth Street South in front of the convention center screaming at the top of his lungs."

"You gotta be fucking kiddin' me," Brennan uttered as he stepped away from the group to receive a call that came over his handheld radio. It was an officer's request for assistance with regard to a disturbance on the highway. The location was Twelfth Street South between Second Avenue South and Third Avenue South, right in front of the Minneapolis Convention Center.

"And you're sure that this is our guy?" Jordan asked.

"From the description I got, and the shit he's reported to be screaming about, he's our guy."

"And what about Monica? Any signs of her?" Jordan inquired further.

"No. No signs of anyone else in the report I got. But, I sure wouldn't mind asking him personally," Torres replied.

"I know that's right," Carter added.

"Let's get a move on," Jordan ordered. "Harry, let's make sure that this scene is secured and ready for when your forensics team gets here."

"Gotcha."

"Emiliano," she said turning back to him. "I want you to stay behind and wait for the warrant. Once the forensics team gets here and completes its investigation, I want you to go in and do your thing. On the odd chance that he took Monica somewhere before he decided to do his little sideshow downtown, I need to know if there are any indications of where that 'somewhere' might be."

"No problem."

Jordan turned to the others. "Now, let's get our asses downtown before somebody with an itchy trigger finger decides to scratch."

Chapter Eight

By the time Agent Jordan and her team arrived on location, the area was already swarming with Minneapolis's finest. Every available officer, which included members of the Special Tactical Unit and two negotiators from the Hostage Crisis and Control Unit, were present. The team abandoned their vehicles midway along Third Avenue South and walked the remainder of the way to Twelfth. In the middle of Twelfth, William Drake was screaming and ranting like a lunatic. Parked behind him, and just in front of the convention center, was his vehicle. From her present position, it did not appear to Jordan than anyone else was in the vehicle. However, she did allow for the possibility that Monica might be lying down in the rear.

Jordan took a look around and could see that the STU was already in place. She could hear a voice coming from one of the patrol car's PA system. She saw the officer who was doing the speaking but did not know him. She turned to Brennan.

"That's Stan Fanovich," he answered before she could ask. "He's from the Hostage Crisis and Control Unit. He's probably our best negotiator."

Lt. Stanley Fanovich was the department's lead negotiator. Fanovich was a shade taller than five-eleven. He was fairly fit for being in his mid-fifties, weighing roughly 200 pounds. He had thinning and graying hair that he still managed to part on the left side. He was wearing one of his customary grey pinstriped suits but without the jacket as it was strewn across the back seat of his unmarked cruiser, which was also parked back on Third. He was a charismatic person and intellectually, he was very quick. He had always been adept at understanding the totality of a situation and using newly received information to his advantage. He was very good at his job and loved doing it. He felt extremely fortunately to have found what he considered his true calling. For ten minutes, he had been attempting to reach a meeting of the minds with Drake, but so far had been unsuccessful. Fanovich did not have all of the background on Drake as of yet, but the reports were steadily streaming in. Jordan, Brennan, Carter, and Andersen made their way over to the patrol car beside which Fanovich was standing.

"Stan!" Brennan called out to him.

Fanovich turned toward the voice and was pleasantly surprised to see Brennan approaching. The two worked together a few times in the past—the last time being about four years before. A mother had intended to kill her newborn and subsequently commit suicide by jumping off the Dartmouth Bridge. It was cold that night—the morning of February 8. He would never forget it. While he handled the negotiation, Brennan and his squad handled all of the logistical responsibilities. Fanovich recalled that he tried to reason with that woman for four and a half hours—Marisol Lopez was her name. He could remember it like it was yesterday. It was almost three in the morning before they were able to finally talk her down. It was wet and nasty that night. It was colder than a witch's tit too but, if he could recall correctly, Brennan had hung in there the entire time. Even as the shifts changed, Brennan stayed—and because there was no change in leadership or philosophy midstream, it allowed Fanovich to become completely comfortable with his logistical support during the entire negotiation. Sometimes, especially with some of the more difficult cases, the logistical support was just as important as the negotiation itself. And when the conditions were as bad as they'd been on that night, and the subject, fraught with grief and despair, had an infant she wanted to toss off a highway and into the Mississippi—sometimes that support was the only thing a negotiator had to keep it together. Fanovich would always appreciate and respect Brennan for that night.

S. E. Robinson

"Harry, what's going on?" Fanovich tried to smile, but the current circumstances made it a little tough. He glanced at Brennan's companions.

"Stan, the man." Brennan made his way over to Fanovich's side. "This is SSA Connie Jordan. That's Agent Carter, and he's Agent Andersen." They joined Fanovich, and the entire party crouched down beside the driver's side of the squad car.

"FBI?" Fanovich was a little puzzled. "Already? I mean, I just got here."

"Hold on, Stan." Brennan raised his hand.. "It's not like that." Brennan paused. "Well, not exactly like that," he continued cautiously. "See, we're working the Konetchy kid kidnapping case."

"Okay," Fanovich said, thinking carefully. "I know a little bit about that, but . . .?" Fanovich shrugged and awaited the connection.

"Well, we think that Mr. Drake there is our guy."

"Really?" Fanovich tilted his head to the side as if to accentuate his surprise. "No shit."

"Yeah," Brennan said acknowledging the gesture. "We've got witnesses that put our perp in a van that fits the description of a vehicle we just found parked in front of a fire location. Both the vehicle and the house belong to our guy there. To make matters worse, there's a tool shed in the back that has a whole bunch of blood in it." Brennan glanced back at Drake who continued to rail in the middle of the street. "Probably came from that wound on his face—at least that's what I'm hoping. Besides, he's military and currently AWOL, which fits the profile we're working with currently."

Fanovich took a moment to process the information. He needed to find a way to use his newly acquired information. He thought for a moment more, stood, and raised the mic to his mouth.

"William Drake!"

Drake, in the meantime, had been rambling incessantly about how the system was corrupt. He raged against the war in Iraq. He vented against the incursion in Afghanistan. He decried the fact that, as an American, his voice was never really heard. He needed everyone to see that things were awry and that he would never go back to war.

"William Drake!" Fanovich tried again. This time he seemed to gain Drake's attention who stopped yelling and looked over into Fanovich's direction.

"Mr. Drake," he began. "Listen to me. I want to hear you. I want to understand everything that you have to say. But, I need to know some things first. Is that okay?"

Drake stood still for a moment as if he was unsure of the request.

"Is that okay?" Fanovich repeated.

"*What?*" Drake shouted back. "What do you want?"

"First, tell me, are you hurt?"

Everyone could see the bandage on the left side of his face. It was bloodstained and needed addressing. Drake slowly raised his hand to his face and touched the bandage. For the past several minutes, he had forgotten it was there.

"No!" he screamed back. "I'm not hurt!" His volume started to wane a bit. "This is just a scratch!"

"Good!" Fanovich conceded. "What about Monica? Is *she* hurt?"

Drake stood startled for a moment, as if he was completely blindsided by the question. In an instant, however, his surprise turned to defiance. "I knew it! I *knew* it!" he cried. "All you really care about is *the precious daughter of a US senator!!!* You don't give a damn about me!"

"Drake," Fanovich used his trademark soothing tone. "Drake, that's not true. I don't know about anybody else, but I care about you.

I care about *you*. Understand? And I care about everything that you have to say. And because I'm the one who's in charge out here today, what I care about is all that matters. But, it's like I said. I need to learn some things first. Like making sure that you both are okay. I can see that your face is hurt from here. That might need some medical attention. I need to know if we're gonna need a doctor while we try to talk things through."

Drake took a moment to consider Fanovich's words. Despite his apparent reluctance they seemed to make a sort of sense.

"I'm okay," he responded. He gave a quick glance to his truck and said, "Monica's okay, too."

"Did you see that?" Jordan whispered to her crouching colleagues.

"Yeah, I saw it," Carter responded.

"I saw it, too," Andersen added.

"Saw what?" Brennan asked feeling a little left out of the loop.

"That truck," Andersen spoke in a hushed tone. "When Drake responded about Monica, he looked over at his truck. Monica's in that truck."

Jordan squeezed up next to Fanovich, who crouched down next to her. "Do you know if he has any weapons on him?" she asked.

Fanovich shook his head. "We haven't seen any, but we don't want to take any chances, which is why we haven't rushed him yet." Fanovich stood again and continued.

"Drake. Now, the next thing I need to know is whether or not you have any weapons."

Drake took a moment. "What if I did?"

"Well, if you did, we'd like to see you toss any weapons you might have on the ground in front of you. We don't want to have any mistakes out here today. If you have any weapons, just toss them out front there. Right there on the ground so we can see. That way, we can have a civilized and respectable conversation without the worry of anyone getting hurt."

Drake took a step back. He stared at Fanovich and then slyly glanced over at his truck. Andersen caught this second glance. He leaned over to Jordan, said, "I'll be back," and started to stealthily move away from the team. Brennan and Jordan followed after him with their gaze.

"Where's he going?" Brennan asked. Jordan shook her head and shrugged slowly in response.

Andersen hoped that Lieutenant Fanovich could keep Drake distracted long enough to allow him to get to that truck. If his suspicions were right, he would find Monica there. As Connie had been saying all along, Drake had given no evidence that he was some kind of mastermind. He did not demand money; he simply wanted to be heard. Andersen figured that Drake probably caught wind of the Rep.'s press conference and for the first time realized who he abducted. In his panic, he tried to flee, but, somehow, some way, wound up here.

As he moved away from his team, Andersen took the opportunity to get a good look of the layout. Drake's vehicle was parked on the south side of Twelfth Street South directly in front of the convention center. There were police vehicles parked across the street from the convention center and at either end of the street to deny access from both Second Ave South and Third. As such, Drake was covered on three sides by the authorities. The vehicle the team was standing next to was directly in front of Drake, so he was relatively unaware of what was going on around him. While most of the officers attained positions by which they could key in on Drake, there was enough periphery movement to allow Andersen to make his way around, crouching down behind the vehicles without attracting any particular attention. He moved east along Twelfth until it intersected with Third· and then moved along Third until he was able to make his way to the convention center side of the street. From this position, he was roughly forty feet away from Drake's parked truck.

He looked back, hoping to find Carter or Jordan in the crowd and realized that they both had been looking directly at him. He nodded to affirm his position, and Carter nodded back.

"Do you see him?" Jordan asked.

"Yeah, I got him."

"He's gonna try to get to that truck." Jordan looked back at Drake who appeared to be responding well to Fanovich's conversation. "Drake doesn't have a clue."

"No, he doesn't," Carter agreed. "But to be honest, there are so many officers out here, there's no way that he can keep track of everyone. He's in panic mode right now. There's no way in hell that you're gonna convince me that this . . . " Carter looked around as if to emphasize the point, "was all a part of his master plan."

Jordan chuckled ever so slightly. It would actually be funny if it weren't so sad, she thought. She turned to Brennan.

"Your guy is gonna have to keep Drake talking. My guy is over by his truck. If we can keep him distracted well enough, we'll be able to learn whether or not Monica is in that vehicle."

Brennan started to stand, but paused as the negotiator held up his hand to stop him.

"Drake," he continued, "listen, I understand what it's like not to be heard. Not to be *listened* to. The most important thing that I do in this job is communicate. But people fail to understand that communicating doesn't just mean talking. Communication also means listening. It means understanding. It means sharing ideas, concepts, and principles. It's a whole helluva lot more than just talking. And I get that. I understand that. I can't tell you how many times I've wished folks would listen to me when I'm trying to share stuff with them. I get it. I really do, and I really want an opportunity to communicate with you. I want to hear everything that you have to say, and I want to give you the opportunity to say it. But in order to do that we've got to bring this to an end. I'm gonna need you to tone this down a little bit, son. I'm gonna need you to bring this to a close, so we can get together and have that chat."

Drake listened intently to the lieutenant's words. He was not completely sure whether the officer could be trusted, but at this point he was tired. He was tired of yelling. He was tired of screaming. He was tired of the whole damn thing. This was *not* what he wanted. This was *not* part of the plan. But he was extremely fearful that things would only get worse. Of all the people in Minnesota that he could have snatched, why in the world did he have to snatch *her?*

As Drake weighed his options, Andersen decided to make his move—but before he could get started, he hesitated. He suddenly found himself incapable of moving. He could not help but wonder how this, Drake's current situation, mirrored his own. Here he was, about to make a move against Drake, a man who had absolutely no knowledge that Andersen even existed. Here he was, about to make a move that would take Drake by complete surprise and throw him for yet another unexpected loop. Andersen knew all too well what it was like to have well laid plans obliterated by the arrival of an unknown variable. The pit in his stomach began to resurface. Despite the cool temperature, beads of sweat began to form at the top of his forehead and his bone-chilling feeling of dread sought to stop by to revisit its old friend. Andersen turned his back to lean up against the car beside which he was kneeling. He had to take a moment to reclaim himself. He closed his eyes and mumbled, "Not now, damn it." He held his hands in front of him to see that they were trembling involuntarily. This was neither the place nor the time, he told himself. With the back of his right hand he shakily wiped the sweat from his brow, turned back around to face the International, and steadied himself for the task at hand.

After regaining his composure, he crouched down as low as he could and slunk his way along the sidewalk until he was able to reach the truck. He reached the passenger side front door first. He reached up to try the handle and found it locked. Still crouching, he felt for the window and found that it was partially down—he would have to stand to reach inside the truck. Peeking over the hood, he could see that Drake's attention was still completely directed away from him and toward Fanovich. Again, he was able to catch Carter's eye.

"He's at the truck," Carter whispered, quickly turning to Jordan. "Look. If Monica is there, once we get her to safety, we can just take this joker down."

Brennan, who had been kneeling nearby, heard Carter's assessment and tugged at Fanovich's pant leg. He stood up and whispered a few words into his colleague's ear. Fanovich nodded and Brennan began to move away and back into the pool of officers, reaching for his radio along the way.

Andersen stood up slowly and saw that there was just enough room to ease his arm through the open window and unlock the door. He glanced into the back of the vehicle and could see Monica sprawled across the rear seat—but, he couldn't tell whether or not she was breathing. He reached in through the window and fumbled around for the door lock. After a few moments, he managed to grab it and, with some effort, unlocked the door. He immediately knelt down beside the vehicle again and reached for the handle. Again he tried to open the door.

After speaking with Fanovich, Brennan requested that only officers with rubber bullets be prepared to fire. If Monica was found in Drake's truck and Andersen could get her out safely, they could end this thing swiftly. It was not as if Drake were standing there waving a gun around. There had been no signs of any weapons to this point. If he were truly unarmed, it would be an easy takedown.

Fanovich attempted to keep Drake calm and collected. If he could, he wanted to bring Drake in without a single shot being fired. However, he was well aware of the seriousness of the situation. If the Rep.'s daughter were in that truck, and that agent could get her out of the line of fire, this was going to be out of his hands quickly.

"Drake," he continued. "Why don't you come on in? All you need to do is lie down on the ground with your hands out in front of you and we can call this a day. How 'bout it, son?"

Drake took a moment to think. He started to pace back and forth and began to hold a conversation with himself. He was tired, he was hungry and he was frustrated to all hell. There was no good way out of this situation and he knew it. Nothing had worked out as he had planned. He had not accomplished what he wanted to accomplish. He had not made the statement he wanted to make. Now, the most important thing he could do was to get out of this situation alive. He paused for a moment and turned his gaze back to Fanovich, who had been standing, taut, awaiting his response. This was over. He knew it. Everyone around him knew it. Without saying a word he slowly began to raise his hands.

Andersen tried the door handle once more and again found the door difficult to open. Apparently, it was jammed in some way. He needed to pull with some extra effort in order to open it. He heaved and the door gave way but not without a loud protestation. The door banged as it pulled wide. Quickly, Andersen reached in to unlock the rear door and immediately tried to retrieve Monica.

Drake nearly had his arms fully extended when he heard the familiar sound. That passenger side front door had made that banging noise for years. It was the result of an auto accident that had left some damage on the passenger side, which his stepfather had attempted to fix but with only moderate success. Drake spun and faced his truck. "No!" he yelled as he began to run for his vehicle.

Upon seeing Drake turn and head for the truck, Fanovich immediately transmitted *"Hold your fire!"* through the cruiser's PA system. Drake's vehicle was still in the line of fire and although he felt sure that the snipers could take him out, he did not want to take that risk.

Anderson looked up through the window on the driver's side of the truck and he could see Drake barreling towards the vehicle. He felt for Monica's pulse and was relieved to find one. She was unconscious, but her pulse felt strong. He tried to arouse Monica but she barely managed to stir. He grabbed at her and tried to pull her out of the vehicle but surmised that he would not have Monica free and clear before Drake would reach the vehicle. He carefully placed Monica back down on the seat and swiftly made his way round the front of the vehicle with his weapon drawn and pointed directly at Drake.

"Hold it right there!" he commanded. Drake halted as quickly as he could. "Get on the ground! Do you hear me? Get down on the ground, NOW!"

"Okay, okay!" Drake dropped down to his knees. "Just don't shoot me. Please!"

"Hands out in front!" Andersen ignored the request. "Move it—*move it*!" Andersen left no room for disambiguation. "You make any sudden moves and it's good night. Do you hear me?"

"I hear you, I hear you." Drake stretched out onto the ground just a few feet away from Andersen, who then promptly pinned him to the ground, placing his knee in the center of Drake's back. By this time Andersen had been joined by a couple of the officers who were standing nearby and were more than eager to take Drake into custody. Once he felt that Drake was secured, he rushed back to the vehicle to attend to Monica. Hastily, but carefully, he pulled Monica out of the back seat. He dropped down to his knees and cradled her head in the nook of his left arm and tried again to rouse her.

"Miss Konetchy," he said to her as he stroked the left side of her face with his right hand. "Miss Konetchy!" he said again, this time a little louder—no response. He looked up and caught the attention of one of the nearby officers. "Get the EMTs over here right away." The officer nodded, turned, and headed for the nearest paramedics. "Miss Konetchy," he returned his attention to the young lady. She began to stir, but was not quite there. Andersen continued to stroke her and call her name until she finally opened her eyes. He looked down at her until her vacant stare came into focus. He smiled and began to speak.

"Hello, Miss Konetchy. My name is Paul Andersen, and I'm with the FBI. It's all over now. You're safe. Are you hurt? Can you talk?"

Monica tried to speak but could only muster a raspy and weak, "I'm okay. He didn't really—hurt me."

"Well, we've got him now. You don't have to worry about him anymore." He looked up to check on the status of the EMTs who were just arriving.

"We'll take over now, sir," the closest medic spoke.

Andersen turned back to Monica before releasing her to the paramedics. He smiled at her again and began to rise. She weakly grabbed for his arm and pulled him back to her. He lowered his ear to minimize her effort. But instead of words, Monica Konetchy offered a slight kiss upon his left cheek. Andersen turned to look at her and could see a tear streaming down the left side of her face. He tenderly wiped the tear away and softly said, "You're okay now. These men are going to take good care of you. You're gonna be just fine." He smiled once more, stood, and allowed the EMTs access to their patient.

Paul took a few steps back and finally became cognizant of all the action that was taking place around him. Drake, handcuffed and with the assistance of three officers, was being placed into the rear of a holding van, apparently against his wishes. Other officers, under the direction of Lieutenant Brennan, were preparing to leave the scene to return to their previous assignments. Off to his right, only about twenty feet away, stood Connie Jordan and Terry Carter, both of whom were wearing peculiar smiles on their faces.

"What?" Paul smiled sheepishly.

"I don't know," Connie smiled as she and Carter approached him. "I just don't know what to say."

Carter shook his head. "Kid," he began. "I always knew you had it in ya. You did real good, kid. You got the girl out safe and you took this joker down without firing a single shot. That's a good day's work if you ask me. A damned good day."

"What you did today was impressive, Paul." Connie chimed in. "It was effective and it was clean—very impressive."

Paul simply stood and shared the moment with his two colleagues. After a few minutes, Brennan joined the group.

"Andersen!" he started. The adrenalin was clearly still rushing through his veins. "You got one big set of balls on you, son. That was one helluva stunt you pulled there. I still can't believe it." He turned to the others. "We're about done here if you wanna pull out. There's gonna be a forensics team left behind to process this scene, and we're gonna need to get that truck down to the pound, but as for us—we're good to go."

Jordan took a quick look at her team, smiled at Andersen, and turned back to the lieutenant. "I think we are good to go, Harry. Let's get the hell outta here."

"Sounds fine by me," Brennan responded. He turned and led the way as the team headed back to their vehicles. Though the walk took mere minutes to complete, it seemed to take nearly an eternity to Paul Andersen. It seemed to him that everyone was moving in slow motion. He could still see officers running from here to there. He could see the paramedics who had Monica on a stretcher making their way back to their vehicle. While he was sure that they were rushing to do so, it appeared as if everyone was moving through water. Even the helicopters that flew overhead seemed to be moving unnaturally slow. Additionally, Paul could hear so many different sounds and smell so many different scents. It was as if all of his senses had become extraordinarily heightened in the aftermath of this event. He was being bombarded by everything, all at the same time, and while all of these sensations were new, they were also quite frightening at the same time. It was if he had been he had been seguéd into a different reality without either his knowledge or his permission. Everything was so surreal. He started to question the soundness of his sanity. It was not until they reached the Yukon that everything seemed to return slowly back to normal. At the vehicle, Jordan stopped Andersen from climbing into his customary driver's seat.

"You know what, Paul?" she began, almost amused with herself. "I've got the drive back. Just sit back and enjoy the ride. You've earned it today, my friend." Not willing to argue with his supervisor, Paul tossed the keys to Connie, made his way around to the passenger side of the truck and hopped in—needing a few moments to get comfortable in the unfamiliar seat. Carter eased into the back just behind Andersen, reached forward and grabbed Paul by his left shoulder. He squeezed and shook Paul briefly, as if to accentuate the job well done. Jordan made all of the necessary adjustments with regard to the position of the seat, the steering wheel, both side view mirrors, as well as the rear view. She started the Yukon and fell in line behind Brennan's vehicle as he led the way back to the Central Command post.

Along the forty-minute drive, Andersen was able to enjoy the ride without applying the requisite concentration that was necessary whenever he was assigned to drive—which was nearly all of the time. For the first time, Andersen was able to see the city of Minneapolis for the beautiful and magnificent city that it truly was. He was able to see how clean and neat the city was. He was able to appreciate all of the magnificent architecture and even the newness that the city seemed to emit despite some of its older structures. During the rain on the previous night, the city glistened against the backdrop of the opaque sky while the lighted buildings glimmered to accentuate the effect. Its beauty was a sight to behold, but at the time that beauty had been lost to Andersen, self-absorbed as he was with the tumultuous situation that he begrudgingly found himself in. On this day and at this moment, he was able to see the city in the daylight, really for the first time. He was able to see this wonderful city, a city he had visited many times in the past, in a way that he had never seen it before. But despite all of its outward splendor and the warming brilliance that this sometimes frigid metropolis radiated, he could not help but wonder about all of the hidden demons that found refuge in the darker corners of this otherwise illuminated locale.

Paul found his mind drifting inward. He could feel the despair creeping along the tributaries that carried his blood. The sensation in his fingertips, a spiny tingling that one would expect from the prickling of a thousand tiny needles, shook his spirit to the bone. He began to feel ill to the point where he could feel his heartbeat reverberate throughout his entire body. He leaned his head against the window. Carter and Jordan were holding a pleasant conversation, but the words held little meaning to him. It was as if they were miles away instead of mere inches. They had no idea, not the faintest clue, of the hell he had found himself in. Balancing his job with his personal life was delicate enough. Being able to deal with this current situation would take considerable skill. He could only hope that his tormentor was as discreet as he was. Somehow, Paul believed that he was.

Somehow, Paul believed that this was a duel that was meant to be shared by two. Paul shivered. This was still too much to take.

He continued to stare vacantly out the window and began to stir only when he recognized some of the buildings as they neared their destination. Andersen sat upright in the seat and shook away all of the cobwebs. Somehow, some way, he was going to see his way through his situation. He was going to find whoever it was that was taunting him and resolve this situation to his own satisfaction—which meant resolving it for good.

Jordan followed Brennan's vehicle around the back of the building and into the employee parking lot. After the vehicles were parked and both parties began to mosey back to the building, Andersen was still in a somewhat otherworldly place. He was there, but not quite. He felt the weight of the world on his shoulders and he had no idea how to remove it. Despite the gravity of the situation, Andersen was not discouraged, however. He, more than anyone, was well aware of his abilities. He would see this nightmare through and bring it to an end, one way or another. He followed his colleagues into the rear entrance of the building.

Chapter Nine

"Here he is!" someone declared as Paul Andersen followed Agents Connie Jordan and Terry Carter into the Minneapolis Central Command Post. The room was abundant with people: the remainder of the B.A.U., several members of Minneapolis' finest, and even a few members of the local media. The clamor was almost deafening. Lieutenant Brennan, who had already arrived at the CCP, began to make the appropriate arrangements to have the unnecessary personnel removed. However, he was having difficulty doing so as everyone present, elated with the safe recovery of Monica Konetchy and impressed with the remarkable way it had occurred, was too animated to pay their supervisor the requisite attention.

Andersen, completely uncomfortable with all of this newfound attention, could hardly make his way into the room as he was mobbed—at some points by two and three at a time—by the various people who were all too eager to congratulate him on a job well done. Apparently, this type of news travelled fast in the big city. Already he could hear murmurs of "hero" and "commendation" being thrown about. Neither of which he had any interest in. He was paid to do a job, and he took a great deal of pride in doing his job well. That was more than enough recognition than he required. All of *this* was unnecessary.

"Okay, folks! Okay!" He could just barely hear Brennan at the front of the room. "Everyone, please! Let the man have some room, he needs to be able to breathe. Whether you realize it or not, we've all had a long and tiring day, and I'm sure that Agent Andersen simply wants to take a load off at this point."

Brennan gave it a moment. "All right, everyone, that's enough! Now, let's settle down."

Finally, the room came to order. A small path was cleared to allow Carter, Jordan, and Andersen to join Brennan at the front of the room. Once Brennan felt comfortable that he had everyone's attention, he continued.

"All right, everybody. Now, as I'm sure you all know by now, we've found Monica Konetchy!" A roar erupted from the floor. "From the last report I received, she's doing well. She's a little dehydrated and needs to get some nourishment into her system, but the girl is okay. I understand that the Rep. and the Professor are down at the hospital and the whole family is doing fine.

"As for our perp, William Drake, we've got his ass cooling off in Central Booking and that's all because of this young man right here!" Brennan walked up behind Andersen, placed both hands on his shoulders and shook him with excitement. Another roar came from the exuberant crowd and even the often stoic Andersen was incapable of containing a bashful grin. He bowed his head as if to hide it, but the smile managed its way through. He was clearly embarrassed.

"Lemme tell you folks," Brennan continued. "This young man, right here, was able to detain our perp and rescue his prisoner without firing off a single shot. Not one shot! This was a good day, folks. It doesn't get any better'n this!"

The crowd roared again and gave Andersen a standing ovation. A few started to make their way to the front of the room to congratulate him when Jordan moved to take the floor.

"If I may, people!" With a wave of her hand she quickly controlled the room. "We have a few things that we need to do before we can call this a wrap. There are a couple of loose ends that need to be tied up and the sooner we nail things down, the sooner we can call this a night.

"First," she said half turning to Brennan. "We need to iron out all of the jurisdictional issues with regard to Drake's arrest—local or

114

federal. Lieutenant, I'll have Leisa cover that with you. Speaking of Leisa, we'll also need to draft a press release for the media. Leisa," she directed her attention to Agent Nance-Roberge. "You might want to coordinate with the Konetchys on that. If we could do a joint thing, I think that that would be best."

Leisa stood for a moment. "If I may . . .?" Jordan nodded.

"Just to let everyone know," Leisa continued. "I've been in touch with both the media and police headquarters and they are all ready to give a press conference. The police chief's press secretary has already scheduled a conference to be held here, downstairs in about thirty minutes."

Jordan was slightly surprised, but not overly so. Sometimes it was simply very hard to do things in a mannerly and orderly fashion without the influence of outside forces. Resigned to the reality of the situation, Jordan reclaimed the floor.

"Well, there you have it." She simply shook her head. "Paul," she said turning to him. "You're the man of the hour, my friend. Don't be surprised if you garner a great deal of attention over the next couple of weeks, starting with today. You'll be standing right there when we address the media—soooo, I hope you've packed one of your good ties."

The crowd released a chorus of chuckles this time and the humble smile tried to recapture Paul's face. This time, however, he was able to contain it.

"While we still have a few minutes, we'll need to make a comprehensive report. So, let's get all the information we have together: including the analysis of the Drake home and let's put this one to bed, folks. Hey," she paused for a moment. "I just want to say great job, everybody! I had a good feeling about this one from the start. You can't always be sure, but I'm glad we came out of this one with a win. This was a *good* win."

Jordan accompanied her last statement with an affirming nod. She, as well as anyone, was acutely aware that this abduction could have ended in any number of ways—most of them bad. Brennan was right; this could not have ended any better than it had. For that, she was most grateful.

The crowd, which was still exceedingly excited, continued to paw its way up to Paul who could do nothing more than submit to the wishes of his "fans". It was such a hectic and energetic atmosphere that no one noticed when the mail delivery person arrived to forward the mail. Working her way in between everyone, she placed the various items on the desks of the corresponding officers. After dropping off Lieutenant Brennan's mail in the inbox on his desk, her customary last stop, she had one letter left to deliver. In a very nondescript, full-sized manila envelope, she had a letter addressed to Agent Andersen. Slowly, and with a great deal of persistence, she made her way through the crowd. From everyone trying to gain his attention, it was relatively easy for her to identify him. After a matter of a few minutes, she was finally able to reach the agent. She handed him the envelope and he took it almost unconsciously. Shortly thereafter, the crowd began to disperse, each person returning to his or her various assignments. The few reporters that had managed to gain access were politely escorted from the floor, most of who were quite satisfied with their "inside" information, and made their way downstairs to prepare for the upcoming press conference. Most importantly for Paul, the need for him to be the center of attention began to ebb. For that, he was most grateful.

The team members turned their attention from Paul and toward the task at hand. They had very little time to put together a sensible presentation for the media. Fortunately for Jordan, however, it was not as difficult as it could have been. According to the report she had just received, Leisa Nance-Roberge had done an effective job of collecting and collating all of the information, for just this type of a situation. Agent Roberge always liked to keep what she called a running press release. It was a real time report that could be presented at any given moment of an investigation, which gave the most current and pertinent information to be disseminated to the public without compromising the investigation. It always gave her something to report *that made sense* in the event that a news conference was staged with short notice and without an appropriate amount of time to prepare fully. It was a practice that Jordan had grown to appreciate more and more over time.

"This is great," she noted leaning toward Roberge. "Let's go with it. I'll see you downstairs in a few." Roberge smiled and started to head downstairs to assess the logistics of the presentation. Jordan turned back to the once manic room and gave a small sigh. There was still worked to be done, but the hard part was over. Now, she could breathe again.

In time, normalcy began to claim the Minneapolis Central Command Post. Paul made his way to the back of the room where he was able to find a degree of solitude, relatively speaking. He found an empty desk, sat, and tried to collect himself. The range of emotions he'd experienced over the last couple of days was so far apart that they did not seem to belong in the same spectrum. Paul raised his arm to wipe the sweat from his brow. He wanted to relax, but with the impending press conference, he knew that it was probably only a matter of minutes before he was right back out there in the middle of that infernal spotlight all over again.

He looked around the room and caught the attention of Agent Jordan. They both smiled. Jordan mouthed, "Are you going down?" apparently, referring to the media circus that was bound to take place outside. Paul responded, mouthing, "Do I have a choice?" and smiled. Jordan shook her head and Paul acknowledged with a faux grimace.

Paul looked around the room again and noticed that folks were starting to make their way downstairs. Most of the Behavioral Analysis Unit had already descended. Paul decided that he should make his move as well before he realized that he was still holding the piece of mail. Finally, the letter caught his full attention and his mind began to wander. It seemed highly irregular that he would receive any mail here—now. He took a moment to look at the letter. It had a typewritten label in the center of the envelope, which simply read "Agent Andersen." There was no return address, no cancelled stamp or metered postage. There was no indication that this letter was mailed at all—there was no address under his name. He turned the envelope over and noted that nothing was written on the back either. He noted that the envelope had been glued shut and nothing more. Frowning, Paul slowly slid his finger underneath the sealed flap of the envelope and steadily worked it along the edge. It took him a moment, but he managed to open the envelope with almost no tearing at all.

Once opened, Paul held the open end of the envelope up to his nose and smelled. He thought he caught a whiff of something familiar, but it was gone in an instant. He peered inside, his eyebrows nearly touching as his brow burrowed down onto his eyes. He took the envelope and turned it upside down in order to jettison its contents, if there were any, onto the desk. As he did so, a small slip of paper, approximately one inch high and three inches long flitted its way out of the envelope and down onto the desk. Paul sat back with puzzled indignation and murmured, "What the hell?" softly underneath his breath. He picked up what initially appeared to be a blank piece of paper, turned it over, and released it as if it had caught fire. Paul sat motionless and just stared at the paper on the desk. All at once, it seemed as if the muscles in his body began to seize, making it impossible for him to move. He could feel the sweat begin to surface at the top of his brow and he had an ever-increasing urge to scream, "*What the fuck!*" at the top of his lungs.

Slowly, he managed to steal his glare away from the small slip of paper and methodically began to scan the room. He looked at every single person in order to determine if anyone was paying him any attention whatsoever. He felt that if he could discern even the slightest hint of interest in him with regard to the slip of paper, he would have someone he could consider a person of interest. However, as he scanned the room and went from person to person and from face to face, there did not seem to be anyone who was even remotely interested in his reaction to his mail.

Reluctantly, Paul turned his gazed back to the note. He read it again. *1118 Union St., Clarksville, Tenn. 4/21/2006.* That was all it said. It was typed, probably a computer printout that had been cut down to size. It gave not even the slightest clue as to its origin. One line: an address and a date. Innocuous enough on the surface, but overwhelmingly profound to Agent Andersen. On April 21, nearly four years ago to the day, Agent Andersen had the privilege of visiting 1118 Union St. in Clarksville, Tennessee. He visited and stayed just long enough to kill Maureen Foster, a second-grade teacher who had just begun what appeared to be a promising career in the Clarksville School District. He killed Maureen by injecting a small amount of air into her blood stream. Initially, it appeared that she had died from natural causes—a heart attack. Eventually, an air embolism was properly diagnosed as the cause of death. However, no one ever came to the realization that it had been murder. Maureen Foster was Paul's second victim. She was someone he had studied for six months before killing her. In his mind, there was no way that anyone could know that he was the cause of her death. Paul's stomach began to turn. He felt as if he could vomit at any moment with very little prompting. He bowed his head forward and fought to keep from being ill. He closed his eyes as tightly as he could and opened them again. He took several deep breaths and mentally began to focus on calming himself.

Paul stared down at the note again and as he did so, the initial wave of sickness that threatened to overtake him started to convert to anger. He suddenly and almost uncontrollably became angry at himself, angry at his current situation. How could he have been so careless? Where did he make a mistake? How many mistakes had he made? What could he have done wrong? He could not conceive of how he could have possibly wound up in his present situation. He was so consumed with his now swelling self-loathing that he could not hear Agent Jordan as she was trying to gain his attention.

"Paul!" she called his name for the fourth time. "Are you with us?"

Quizzically, he looked up. "Hunh?" He snapped back into the here and now. "I'm sorry," he said as he tried to shake out the cobwebs. "What's going on?"

Jordan shook her head. "Some people's kids," she marveled. "It's time, Paul. Let's go."

Finally comprehending her meaning, Paul shook his head again, just to make sure that all of the loose parts were back in place, and hopped up to join Agent Jordan, Lieutenant Brennan, and Agent Carter as they started to make their way out of the room and down the stairs. Paul did his best to compose himself along the way. He made sure that his clothes were as tidy as possible and prepared himself for the unexpected.

***

Of all of the things that Jordan considered silly at these types of press conferences, the ritual of positioning was the most derisive. Everything was always staged for maximum impact. It seemed so ridiculous to her. The police chief had already arrived in full blues. He was accompanied by the deputy chief and the chief inspector who presided over Lieutenant Brennan's department. They too were in full uniform. The mayor was present, as was her chief of staff and press secretary. For the moment, the press secretary was running the show. She was giving commands as to who should stand where; who will talk and when; as well as informing the media of which topics would be covered and which definitely would not. In Jordan's mind, the press secretary had everything in complete control. After a few staunch commands, she made her way over to Jordan.

"Good evening, Agent Jordan. I must congratulate you and your team on a job well done." She was very polite and proper in her manner and tone.

"Well, thank you." Jordan responded without really knowing what else to say.

"If you don't mind," said the press secretary, getting straight to the point. "When we begin, I'd like you to stand over here." First she pointed then she laid her hands onto Jordan's shoulders and directed her to the exact place she initially indicated. "And now where could I find . . .?" the press secretary looked about. "Agent Andersen."

Jordan turned and identified Paul for the woman who seemed very committed to doing everything just right. "That's Agent Andersen right there."

"Oh, I see." She rushed over to Paul, placed her hands on his shoulders and utilized, what appeared to be a well-rehearsed technique, in order to position him where she wanted him to be, just to the left of Jordan.

Jordan turned to him and said, "I almost feel like a marionette."

"Yeah, I know what you mean," Paul responded.

"Hey," she began with a certain thoughtfulness in her tone. "Paul, are you okay?"

"Yeah, I'm fine," he said, relaxed but reserved. "It's just been a crazy day and it doesn't seem like it's ever going to end."

"Oh, I know that feeling." Jordan gave a contented sigh. "At least it's almost over now. Let's just tuck it in for a few minutes and hopefully, we'll be able to get out of here unscathed."

Paul chuckled at the notion and they both turned their attention back to the front to face the media. Once again, the steps in front of the police administration building were mobbed with media. This time the occasion was to announce and celebrate the safe return of Monica Konetchy and to report the capture of William Drake, her abductor. As the mayor's press secretary began, by explaining how and why the Konetchys were not present and informing everyone that the Konetchys would present their own statement at a later date, *after* their daughter made it home safe and sound, Paul was giving the conference his utmost attention. But not long after the mayor began to talk, Paul's mind began to wander.

The bigwigs continued to clamor about the heroics of the day and how a justice system that works is a justice system that benefits all Americans. With his mind's eye, Paul sought to find the hidden clue that could uncover the nature of the nightmare that lurked in the darkest corners of his own psyche. Mentally he retraced all of his murders, all the way back to the beginning—all the way back to when all of this began. It was in his hometown of Tulsa, Oklahoma. Paul attended college in Norman as a student at the University of Oklahoma. While he excelled in practically every venture he participated in, he came to realize that he had another calling. A higher calling, as it were. He came to realize that he had skills: gifts, that allowed him to ascend to a higher place, a higher plane. A place that most human beings never realized even existed. These gifts came to him gradually over the years, however he had not uncovered them—until the day he met *her*.

Her name had been Nomi Greenfield. She'd been seventeen at the time. She'd been at the peak of her naiveté, and the first time Paul laid eyes on her, inexplicably he knew that she would be his first. She'd been lovely—very lovely, with strawberry blonde hair so long it'd tickled the top of her waistline every time a small breeze passed through. She'd had long features: long legs, a very long and slender frame, and an appropriately, proportionally long neck. Her face was oval and almost came to a point at her chin. Paul hadn't really known Nomi. He had seen her around Tulsa—a popular girl. They had even exchanged words on a few occasions, but they certainly never qualified as friends. As far as Paul had been concerned, they hadn't really rated as acquaintances either, but Paul knew from the first time that he saw her that they would be inextricably linked, forever.

Over a matter of months, while he was finishing up his senior year and during the time he was going through the application process for the Bureau, Paul began to learn whatever he could about Nomi. He began to study her. He began to learn her habits and her tendencies. He studied the things that she did and how she did them. He did this always from afar and completely without her knowledge. He often wondered how, at times, he would be the center of everyone's attention and yet when he needed to be, he could be almost completely invisible—in plain view—another one of his gifts, he'd always assumed. Through his research, Paul had been able to learn Nomi's routine. Where she worked, where she went to school—nearby at Oral Roberts U., which classes she took, who her friends were, which movies she liked, even the route she liked to take when she walked her shih tzu, Brittani, every morning and every evening.

Learning those things had always come so natural for Paul. It was innate. It was as if he had a second sense for it. It was precisely that sense that allowed him to become such a proficient profiler. However, as keen and reliable as that sense had been, it had not foreseen any of the demons that had come to haunt him now.

On November 11, 2005, shortly after 9 p.m., as Nomi was just leaving her work study shift at the school library, Paul, using chloroform, managed to subdue Nomi without incident. She'd never seen him coming. He approached and took her from behind. He took her away from her family, her place in society, the rest of her life. After being abducted on her way home from work, Nomi Nicole Greenfield was never seen or heard from again. They searched for her for months. It was a massive manhunt that bore no conclusion. By Paul's account, there were folks still looking for Nomi, five years later. They would never find her. Of this, he was sure.

The press conference continued; now the police chief was talking. If Paul remembered correctly, Leisa would be next. He continued to reflect on Nomi. He could not help but wonder if all of his current troubles had started then. He quickly dismissed the notion. He simply could not accept that his nemesis could have knowledge of everything he had done. That just was not possible. He did not give a damn how good he was—he could not know everything. Paul literally shook the idea out of his head. Jordan shot him a quick glance, which he caught out of the corner his eye. He quickly gathered himself and mentally transported himself to the here and now.

The press conference continued for another forty minutes. The mayor spoke, followed by the police chief; the inspector, head of the Central Command Post; Agent Leisa Nance-Roberge; and back to the mayor's press secretary. Many questions were asked. Only a few were answered with any real substance. The information of any true importance was that of the safe return of Monica Konetchy and the capture of William Drake. Everything else was fluff. The Minneapolis

Brass knew it, the investigators knew it, and, of course, the media knew it—but the fluff was proffered just as well.

The reporting of the actual take down was the *coup de grace,* however. Paul's heroics would not go unstated as the media clamored for a retelling of the course of events that led to the eventual capture and recovery. While the reporters had his name and wanted to hear from him, Leisa Nance-Roberge quickly intercepted all inquiries aimed at Paul and handled them with the conciseness and grace that she'd mastered in her career, along the way. For his sake, Paul did not have to utter a word, and when the festivities finally concluded, he was the first to make his way back into the Command Center and away from the vultures. He made his way back to the desk he had previously occupied, leaned back into the chair, and closed his eyes.

Agent Jordan, after lingering a bit at the press conference to answer a few of the leftover questions, made her way upstairs a few minutes later. Paul was sitting with his head back. She walked over, reached out with her right hand, and touched his forehead. Instinctively, he opened his eyes and jerked upright.

"Just checking," Jordan offered. "I wanted to make sure that you weren't coming down with a fever or anything."

Paul shook that off. "No," he said, regaining his relaxed posture. "I wish it was that simple." He stood up. "I'll be okay. I don't know how or why, but this case got to me a bit. But I'm cool."

"I hope so." Jordan looked at him closely. "Because we need you, my friend." Jordan playfully bumped her shoulder into his chest. "Besides, we'll be able to get outta here and head home tonight. That's gotta make you feel good."

Paul looked at her with a gratitude and relief she had never seen before. "You have no idea how badly I want to go home," he said. "Just to be back in my own bed." He managed a small smile. Jordan returned his smile and then looked to find Lieutenant Brennan.

They had some finishing up to do and she wanted to have everything concluded and done so she and her team could go back to Quantico. Once, she caught sight of the lieutenant, she quickly made her way over to him and they both left the floor for the privacy of his office.

Over the next hour, the phone calls that needed to be made were made. The reports that needed to be written were written. The goodbyes that needed to be said were said. State Representative Konetchy called into the command center and spoke with both the lieutenant and Agent Jordan, thanking them for the safe return of her daughter. Though she did not speak with him personally, she also wanted to extend a heartfelt thanks to Agent Andersen that came not only from her, but from her husband and daughter as well. Agent Jordan assured the Rep. that she would pass on the message, which she did.

Twenty minutes later, the B.A.U. team made its way out of the Minneapolis Command Center and back to the Minneapolis-Saint Paul Airport where their jet waited, warmed and ready, to take them back home to Virginia. For Paul, he could not get home soon enough. After easing himself into a window seat, he reached down into his pocket and retrieved the slip of paper he had nonchalantly slid into his pocket earlier. He read the address again. This time there was no emotional reaction. This time, there was only the sense of determination. He balled up the slip of paper and tossed it into a nearby wastebasket. He turned to look out of the window by which he was sitting, closed his eyes, and even to his own surprise, managed to get a little bit of sleep on the trip back home.

S. E. Robinson

Chapter Ten

Connie Jordan was seated comfortably in the seat closest to the pilot's cockpit with her back nestled right up against the wall. For some odd reason she always preferred that seat. She presumed it was for the vantage point but she also found an almost perverse pleasure in feeling the droning of the plane's engines reverberate through her body as she could do while seated in this seat—it had a massaging effect. It allowed her to relax both going to and coming from an assignment. On this flight home, the massage, coupled with the knowledge of a successful assignment, was especially therapeutic.

She looked around the plane and gazed upon the people on her team. Though she rarely admitted it, she was very proud to not only be the leader of such a team, but to simply be a part of it. She never spared a compliment and was very vocal with respect to her respect for her colleagues, but she has never really expanded upon all of the various feelings she harbored with regard to them. Each was a unique individual, who brought his or her own distinct qualities to the team. However, as a unit, they were the perfect pieces that made a complete whole. They worked well together. They got along well with each other. There have been no issues of stepping on another's toes. There were no instances of disrespect. In Jordan's experience, this was by far the best and most effective unit she had had the pleasure of working with—hands down.

Jordan snuggled up against the back of her seat and took a look around the passenger area of the plane. This jet, the B.A.U.'s primary mode of transportation when they had to fly across the country on a moment's notice, was a late model that was cozy, practical, and could safely serve twenty passengers. It had modern conveniences, two small tables that separated the front seating area from the rear seating area, a small kitchenette, and even a wet bar that was filled with only non-alcoholic beverages. The plane had a very accommodating interior with its richly beige motif, including the carpeting, the leather seating, and the wall coverings. There was not an over abundance of creativity with regard to décor, but it was pleasant and non-distracting which did more than just get the job done. Jordan sat in a double seat positioned up against the cockpit, which sat opposite to double seats facing her. To her left, across the center aisle, was yet another set of double seats, situated in exactly the same fashion. Up against the back of seats opposite Jordan were the backs of another set of seats that faced the rear of the plane. The four remaining sets of seats, situated beyond the tables, faced forward and allowed Jordan to steal looks at her colleagues as they drifted off into their own separate worlds on the trip back home.

Leisa, completely engrossed and apparently oblivious to her surroundings, was seated at one of the tables with a collection of papers strewn about her as she made sure that all of her facts were in order and that all of the reports were accurate. Leisa Nance-Roberge had a tenacity that Jordan could not help but admire. She was probably the most completely thorough person that Jordan had ever worked with. She made sure that all the I's were dotted and that all the T's were crossed—literally. She could discern facts like no one's business and could identify false information with an exactitude that bordered obsession. Jordan appreciated Leisa on many levels, not the least of which was the professionalism she brought to her job and to the team.

Terry Carter, who was also seated alone, was reading and taking notes, his usual practice during these flights to and from assignments. Terry loved to read non-fiction. His mind was like a sponge that absorbed information at an almost unnatural rate. Terry was always driven to feed his ever-hungering mind and he did so voraciously. Additionally, Terry seemed adept at getting his hands on articles and information that were not necessarily available for public scrutiny. He never had anything that was necessarily "top secret" or anything, but his reading material was definitely not anything that one was able to find at a local newsstand or a neighborhood public library. Whatever he managed to get his hands on, however, always kept him current with the latest interrogation techniques and trials. He was also always up to date with the latest firearms and ammunition advances: how these items were rated; what they were used for; and what group, military or otherwise, appeared to have access to them. Whenever the B.A.U. was assigned to a case that had militaristic or terroristic implications to it, Terry managed to shine like a strobe light in the dead of night. He was a hell of an ally and he loved his country. Jordan smiled. She did not know what she would do without him. They managed to create a bond that simply was not easily broken. "Hell or high water," was what he would tell her. She believed it with all of her heart.

Eva and Jacob were seated together, chatting and smiling, as was their custom on most flights: "The Odd Couple," as they were affectionately called. Together, they were the oldest and the youngest members of the team, respectively. They were almost inseparable between assignments. They shared a certain kind of kinship that one does not often find between persons that were born and raised from two completely divergent generations. However, despite the nearly twenty-five-year difference, they had been drawn to each other almost since day one. Jordan suspected that part of the reason might be that Jacob reminded Eva of her oldest son, Anthony. Anthony Hermanski was a med intern at County General Hospital back in Tempe, Arizona, where Eva was from. Anthony had a homely, nondistinct look about him, very similar to Jacob. He was intelligent and approachable, just like Jacob, and they both happened to share a few of the same interests—especially, with regard to computers and their ever-advancing capabilities. Eva took to Jacob almost immediately, and her motherly approach had allowed Jacob to grow into himself as he grew more comfortable with the team and his abilities as a profiler. Eva's expertise as a doctor was valuable enough, but what she did for Jacob was invaluable, both to him and to the team.

Jordan turned her gaze to Emiliano Torres who was relaxing, eyes closed, headphones in place and iPod blasting away. Torres needed his music to help him unwind. He had been studying to become a classical pianist before he came to the Bureau. More than likely, he was probably listening to and thoroughly enjoying either Chopin or Debussy, his two favorites. Debussy was normally his preference for the trip home. But he usually listened to Chopin to prepare. Classical music was such an integral part of Torres's routine, Jordan believed that the discipline required to become an accomplished pianist, which Torres reportedly was, helped him become a proficient profiler. The attention to detail that Torres applied to crime scenes was extraordinary. He was able to glean information that even the best analysts missed. However, the thing about him that fascinated Jordan the most was the way in which he moved during his investigations. He approached a crime scene in such a graceful manner that it was almost as if he was performing a piano sonata as he worked. It was mesmerizing to see him work. It was a pleasure to see him work. Above all else, no one could argue with his results. He was damned good; there was no question about that. He was a very thoughtful and reserved personality, but he could sometimes be full of energy, given the circumstances. Again Jordan smiled. Thinking about Torres made her smile.

Lastly, Jordan's gaze fell upon Paul Andersen, the hero of the day, the man of the hour. Paul was sitting in the last row of seats and to Jordan's far left. Seated diagonally opposite to where Jordan was seated, he was leaning up against the window and, though at first he appeared to be simply staring off into space, Jordan realized he was actually drifting off to sleep. As with Emiliano, Paul was an excellent crime scene analyst. He also made a very good profiler. Paul's ability to creep into the minds of unsubs was almost eerie, but it had proved very useful since he joined the team. Paul was very polite. He was proper, courteous, respectful, and always willing to do whatever was asked of him. He was a very capable agent and always completed his tasks as assigned. He was not an attention seeker, which made today all the more curious. He was clearly not comfortable with being the center attraction. However, Jordan felt strongly that Paul was experiencing something personally. She knew that he was not married. She did not think that he was even actually involved with anyone, although she could not say for sure. The only thing she was certain of was that he had been acting odd these last couple of days.

Unbeknownst to Paul, Jordan watched him as he received, opened, and read his letter back in the Minneapolis Control Center. She was very subtle with her observations but she could see that whatever was on that small slip of paper rattled Paul to his core. He was slick about it and he did very well to conceal his discomfort, but Jordan saw it. While it was her job to lead and direct this team, it was also her job to monitor it and she did so with quiet efficiency. She had a fairly strong feel for her team and when something went amiss she could sense it. She just could not put her finger on it as of yet. Hopefully, Paul would manage his way through whatever situation he found himself in; but until that happened, Jordan would have to keep an eye on him. It would be up to Paul to determine how close that eye would be and for how long.

Chapter Eleven

It was a little after 8 p.m. when the B.A.U. touched down in Virginia. As a team, they made their way back to the office to drop off the necessary items and to get things situated for work the next day before saying the requisite goodbyes and going their separate ways. Paul, who managed to get an hour's worth of sleep on the flight back, felt eerily alert and had no desire to call it a night just yet. He headed home to Alexandria, hopped into the shower, tried earnestly to wash his worries down the drain and, upon finishing, managed to feel refreshed for the first time in nearly a week. He was home, which went a long way with regard to finding his comfort zone. By the time he finished dressing it was ten. Despite the fact that he had to be up early the next morning, Paul had no desire to stay in. He needed to get out. He needed to clear his head and think things through. He needed to piece back together the shards of his life and to ascertain exactly what happened to his once peaceful, albeit morbid, existence. And more than anything else, he needed to find out who the hell it was he had unwittingly crossed to bring this nightmare down upon himself.

Paul grabbed his necessities, hopped behind the wheel of his black 2008 BMW 530i and headed for Washington, DC. Although, Paul did not spend much of his time exploring the social scene, when he did go, he preferred to go to DC. For its part, Paul enjoyed the nightlife in DC. It wasn't New York or LA; it lacked the overbearing glitz that sometimes plagued those cities but, on the other hand, it certainly wasn't Tulsa either. Without question, there were some areas around DC that some might consider pretty rough, but Paul always managed to have a good time in the nation's capital and he could use a good time right about now. Paul decided on the Beacon Sky Bar on Rhode Island Avenue NW. It was not exactly a haunt, per se, but it was an establishment where, to Paul's recollection, he enjoyed the atmosphere.

The ride took about twenty minutes. He pulled up the front drive, tossed the keys to the valet and headed in. Despite the hour on a Wednesday evening, the bar had a relatively nice crowd. Paul looked around and liked what he saw. There were approximately forty patrons, most of whom were women. It was a relatively young crowd, late twenties to early thirties. It was a crowd in which he could fit right in without worry that he would become the main attraction. There were a couple of flatscreens tuned to ESPN with the sound turned down, while Nickelback's "You Remind Me" was blaring over the sound system. Paul took a moment to take it all in. It was just busy enough to capture his attention. Waiters and waitresses buzzed to and fro, delivering drinks and food to keep the masses honest. Conversation abounded as friends and acquaintances chatted and chuckled, enjoying each other's company, the ambience, and themselves. The music was loud, but not so much so that it required the patrons to scream to be heard. The symphony of ice jingling in glass gave the environment a festive atmosphere, making the scene pleasant and light. Paul let loose an extended sigh and thought that this was exactly what he needed. He smiled and let his guard down a hair—this was definitely what he needed.

Midway down the bar, which ran along the right side of the room, there were a couple of empty stools that invited Paul to come and have a seat. He made his way to one of the empty seats, dodging a waiter with a tray and a woman who was having such a good time she nearly lost her balance and fell to the floor. He eased himself onto a stool, which happened to be just to the right of a lovely blonde who appeared to be enjoying her drink on her own. She looked up from her drink as Paul got seated and then turned her gaze away from him and to the rest of the room. Paul attracted the bartender's attention and asked for a Heineken. Moments later, the bartender returned with his beer. Paul took a sip and stole a quick glance of the young lady. He surmised that she was probably in her early thirties. She was tall; she looked to be around five feet ten. She was solid, as if she was a lifelong athlete and had been working out for years. She wore a nicely lace-patterned dress that Paul thought was a little thin, given the chilly weather. He figured she would probably do just fine with adequate outerwear. She wore a couple pieces of very fine jewelry: a necklace, bracelet, and earrings set that Paul thought was very classy and elegant. She did not, however, wear a wedding ring. Paul made a mental note.

Just as Paul returned to his beer for another sip, a gentleman approached the young lady to Paul's left. She quickly turned from facing the floor to stare down at the bar, but the approaching gentleman apparently could not or *did not* take the hint.

"Excuse me, miss," he started, managing to be smug and complacent at the same time. "Can I *please* talk to you tonight?" The woman completely ignored the request, the emphasis on "please," and continued to stare down at her drink. Paul rotated slightly to his left and gave the gentleman a long look.

He appeared to be in his early thirties. He was well dressed in professional attire, in a grey suit with dark blue pinstripes. He wore a starched white shirt with French cuffs and dazzling gold links with diamond accents. He had on a bright red, silken tie, accented with blue and yellow dots, that was loosened at the neck allowing the top button of his shirt to be free. The tie alone was probably worth a hundred and fifty bucks.

"C'mon, now. I know you hear me," he continued. It appeared to Paul that he might have already had too much to drink. "Sharon. Your name is Sharon, right? C'mon Sharon, *let me talk to you*?"

The young lady finally looked up from the bar. She turned to the gentleman, just slightly, and calmly explained. "I don't want to talk to you. I really only want to finish my drink. Please, go back over to your friends." The plea was sincere.

The gentleman took an awkward look over his shoulder and back at his friends, four of whom were sitting at a table and giggling incessantly having found his failed attempt to approach this young lady comical. He turned back to her. "Aww, c'mon, don't worry about them," he said as he waved them off. "I just want to talk to you for a little while. You know I've seen you here before. You let me talk to you before, lemme talk to you again."

The lady responded by turning away and saying "Please, just go," trying to bury her head into her drink.

The slightly drunken man, unwilling to accept "no" for an answer, reached out and touched her on the shoulder. She cringed and Paul came to his feet.

"Look, pal," he said, quickly, getting both of their attention. "If the lady doesn't want to talk, she doesn't want to talk. Now, why don't you just go back to your table so we all can enjoy the rest of our evening."

The man took a step back and with more than just a hint of indignation turned his attention to Paul. "Dude, I wasn't even talking to you, I was talking to her," he said as he pointed in her direction.

"I understand that," Paul responded. "But *I* was talking to *you* and she clearly does not want to. So, please—just let her be." Paul managed to stay polite but firm at the same time. He did not want any trouble, and whether he realized it or not, neither did Mr. Silk Tie. Mr. Silk Tie took a few moments to assess the situation. He looked over at the lady one more time, snickered and turned to go back to his table. Paul took that as an opportunity to retake his seat and resume drinking his beer.

"Thank you," she said in a soft, polite voice.

"No problem," Paul said, truly shaking it off.

"You know," she said turning to Paul. "I like coming here. I don't come very often, but I like the atmosphere. It's a good place to unwind and usually, I don't have to worry about guys getting into my face."

Paul nodded. "Yeah, this is a decent place to unwind."

"That guy back there," she motioned over her shoulder. "I made the mistake of having a conversation with him a few months ago, when I first started coming here. It didn't take too long for me to realize that he was an arrogant ass. So now, every once in a while, not all of the time, mind you, but every once in a while, he wants to "resume" our conversation and I am really not interested. He just doesn't get it."

"Yeah, well, to be honest . . ." Paul sighed as he raised the bottle to his lips and took a small sip. "Some guys never do. Some guys think they're entitled. I don't think that there's too much you can do with those guys except leave them alone."

"I couldn't agree with you more," she said truthfully. She extended her hand out to Paul and properly introduced herself. "Hi, I'm Layna."

Paul glanced at the extended hand, accepted it and shook it slightly. "I'm Paul," he offered almost bowing at the same time. He paused for a moment and added cautiously, "You're admirer back there called you 'Sharon.'"

"Uh, yeah. You caught that, hunh?" she started pensively. "That's what I told him my name was. I usually don't come here to meet new friends. So, to most guys that approach me, I'm Sharon. To those I approach, I'm Layna." She smiled bashfully. "I'm me."

Paul considered that thought for a moment. He tilted his head to the side and smiled. "That works for me, Layna," he admitted. "It's a pleasure to make your acquaintance. What are you drinking?"

"This?" she said slightly surprised. "This is just a Shirley Temple." Paul turned to get the bartender's attention. "Another round please? Another Heineken for me and the lady is drinking a Shirley Temple." The bartender acknowledged the order and managed to fill it within moments.

"Soooo, Paul," Layna eased her way into the conversation. "What brings you to this illustrious establishment on a Wednesday night?"

Paul allowed himself to relax just a little bit more. "The Beacon? I'm just letting off a little steam. It's been a tough week on the job so, I figured I'd get my weekend started a little early, even though I have to go into the office in the morning."

"Really? Nothing wrong with getting the weekend started a little early. At least I don't think so." Layna took a sip of her drink. "So, what do you do?"

Paul tilted his head to the side a little bit and gave a small frown. Layna, noticing his reaction, reached out for his left arm and offered, "That is, if you don't mind telling me?"

Paul responded reluctantly, "No." He hesitated. "I guess I don't mind. I'm a special agent with the FBI. I work for the Behavioral Analysis Unit."

"Oh," she responded. Impressed, but not overly so. "So, you're a profiler."

It was Paul's turn to be slightly surprised. "Yes, I'm a profiler. Are you familiar with the B.A.U.?"

"Only from what I've seen on TV," she answered honestly. "Every time I watch something on TV that's got the B.A.U. in it, it's got something to do with profiling."

Impressed, Paul smiled as he finished off his first beer and reached for his second. "The good ol' 'boob tube'. Nothing beats quality television. Well, how about you, Miss Layna? What kind of work do you do?"

"Me," she said, and smiled. "I'm a compliance officer at a department store. "Macy's at the Potamkin Mall? I make sure that all of the store's financial dealings are in accordance with company and federal guidelines."

Again, Paul was impressed. This time he made no effort to hide it. "That's impressive. How long have you been doing that?"

"About six years. I'm a CPA and I worked for an accounting firm right out of college, but I got bored with that after a while. I moved around from job to job for a couple of years until I found this. It's interesting to me and I really like the people I work with. It's not too stressful and I don't have the weight of the world on my shoulders. Not like you do anyway."

Paul chuckled at the notion. She was lovely, bright, and even had some insight. But as for her last statement—she really had no idea.

"I'm sure your job has its own list of challenges that I wouldn't be particularly eager to tackle."

"Well, this is true." Her bashful smile emerged once again. "But once you have all of the right mechanisms in place, it's pretty much smooth sailing after that. That is of course, so long as folks stick to the program, which is sometimes the most difficult part about the job."

Paul paused for a thoughtful moment, adding, "Yeah, sticking to the program can be really difficult sometimes. Sometimes things happen that you really don't expect and you have absolutely no control over."

"That's the truth. So, it happens in your line of work also, hunh?"

"More than I'd care to express."

Paul reached for his beer and was taking another sip when he caught some movement out of the corner of his left eye. Layna had turned to take another sip from her drink when she was all but accosted from behind.

"Hey, Sharon!" Mr. Silk Tie had returned, this time a little more agitated and a little more drunk than before. "I see you can sit here to talk to him, but you can't talk to me? Come on!" He reached for Layna and grabbed her from behind. His intention was to swivel her around on her stool so that she would face him. As he started to make this move, Paul stood quickly and with one fluid movement, stooped a little and, brought his right hand up underneath Mr. Silk Tie's extended right hand and grabbed him by his neck. Holding his neck, he forced the man clear across the bar until they came to a stop against the far wall.

"*Hey!*" the man shouted in protest. Paul pinned him against the wall and spoke with a very calm but firm voice.

"Now I've told you once that the lady was not interested. Now, I'm telling you again. I'm trying really hard to enjoy my night here, pal, but if we have to have a third discussion, it will be time for you to say good night."

The man tried to squirm his way free of Paul's vicelike grip without success. He reached up with both hands to pry Paul's right hand from his neck but the results were feeble. Paul clearly had the superior strength.

"All right, pal, all right!" Mr. Silk Tie spoke weakly but audibly. "I'll leave her alone. I promise." His words were barely above a whisper, but Paul could hear them clear enough. Paul released the man, who subsequently dropped to his knees in a desperate attempt to catch his breath. Paul turned to face his drinking companion, who was now standing by the bar. She quickly made her way over to Paul, grabbed him by the folds of his jacket and whispered hastily.

"Do you want to get out of here?"

Paul turned and looked at Mr. Silk Tie who had been regaining his breath, but kept a wary eye on Paul the entire time. He turned back to face Layna and could see a couple of the waiters making their way over to them, presumably to assess the situation. Paul responded:

"Yeah, let's get out of here. You've got someplace in mind?"

"Are you driving?" she asked hurriedly.

"Yeah, I'm driving. The valet parked it."

"Good then. I have the perfect spot. You get your car. I'll get my coat."

Layna headed to the back of the bar where the coats were kept, and Paul made his way to the valet stand out front after he tossed a fifty onto the bar to cover both tabs and any inconvenience the bar might have suffered from his improvisational intervention. He handed the valet on duty his ticket. The valet picked up a phone and made a call. He spoke only a few numbers and in less than two minutes, Paul's BMW was making its way to him. Layna, having made her exit thirty seconds earlier, sauntered up to Paul's side. She was wearing a full-length leather coat that had genuine fox around the collar and cuffs. It was very elegant and very appropriate, Paul thought. Once the car came to a stop, Layna made her way to the passenger side, pausing only to allow Paul to open and then shut her door as she made herself comfortable inside. Paul handed the driver a five-dollar bill and got behind the wheel.

"Where to?" he asked as he buckled himself in.

"Let's get onto Wisconsin Avenue NW and start heading for the border. There's a place just into Maryland called Friendship Village. Not too much is open there at this hour but I know of a little place where we could go and talk. It's only about fifteen minutes from here—quick, especially, at this hour."

Paul had not planned on doing a lot of travelling on this night, but it was clear that they couldn't really stay here at the Beacon. He threw the car into drive, navigated through the streets of Washington, DC until he found Wisconsin Avenue NW and drove until he left the District and entered Maryland. Once in Friendship Village, he took a couple of direct and accurate directions from Layna until they reached Indique Heights, just across the border in Chevy Chase.

"I hope you like Indian?" Layna queried.

"I do," Paul responded.

"Good." Layna was pleased. "This place is one of the best."

Indique Heights was an upscale restaurant that served Far Eastern Indian cuisine to some repute. It had received several glowing reviews since it opened its doors and catered to a sophisticated crowd both in status and taste. It had a pleasant atmosphere that was conducive to a desire to be discreet without necessarily being covert. Paul was unfamiliar with the restaurant, and he wasn't particularly hungry, but he was very open for the opportunity to have a pleasant conversation.

He pulled into the restaurant's parking lot and found a spot not far from the door. The hour was late so there weren't many customers, but there was time still to get seated and served. Upon entering, a host ushered them to a spot near the rear of the restaurant. The lighting was dim and each table was illuminated by candlelight. The Far Eastern motif was prevalent throughout. There were Indian placards etched in stone that adorned the walls set against traditional Indian drawings of scenery that appeared to be almost sewn into the wallpaper. There were lacy tablecloths that boasted their own Far Eastern designs, intricate and alluring at the same time, exhibiting remarkable detail that was almost inescapable to notice. The sound of Indian music played over the sound system that was pleasant and light and truly heightened the already sensual atmosphere. The restaurant seemed to have an appropriate balance of art, design, ambience, and functionality. *She was right,* Paul thought to himself, *she did have "the perfect spot" in mind.*

In moments, a waitress arrived with two glasses of fresh ice water and slivers of lemon on a dish. Layna and Paul each took some time to peruse the menus in silence. Having decided on the curried chicken and beans with naan, Paul looked up at his companion, who was still completely engrossed in her menu. From his previous observations, Paul concluded that Layna was a lovely woman; however the lighting in the Beacon had not done her justice because now, sitting across from her, he could see how truly beautiful she was. She had very strong features, a strong chin, an almost chiseled jaw line, and again an extremely athletic build. But Paul could see also see a gentleness in her. She was elegant and poised. She was polished and graceful, even with her subconscious movements. She was very effeminate and even posh to a degree. He imagined that she would probably be incredibly tender to the touch, soft and inviting. She had naturally full lips and near perfect teeth that truly glowed when she smiled. Her eyebrows arched ever so slightly, leaving one with the impression that she was perpetually perplexed, and while that look might have looked silly on most people, it looked just fine on her. Her eyes were blue like the morning sky back in Tulsa. They almost sparkled in this light. *Yeah,* Paul thought. *Everything is looking just fine on her tonight.*

On that thought, Layna looked up from her menu and was surprised to see Paul staring at her. Back at the Beacon, she noticed how attractive Paul was when he walked through the door. Although she spoke honestly when she told Paul that she did not go to the Beacon in search of new friends, when Paul first walked through the door she had three immediate wishes: one, that Paul had come alone; two, that he was not there to meet someone, especially someone special; and three, that he would somehow, someway, manage to make his way over to the empty seat just next to her. She didn't expect that a conversation would necessarily ensue, or that it would lead to them ducking out together. In all honesty, she really just wanted to get a closer look. All the rest of this was simply a bonus.

She began to smile bashfully again. "Everything okay, Paul?"

Paul jerked back to reality with the question. It was the second time he heard those words come from a woman's lips today.

"Yeah, I'm okay," he said softly. "It's just the light in here." He feigned a brief look around, leaned forward and whispered. "You know you're quite beautiful?"

Slightly embarrassed, Layna instinctively raised her right hand and began to play in her hair. "Well, I'm glad you think so," she responded, looking down at her menu because she was too embarrassed to return his gaze.

Paul, with his glare never wavering continued, "I do think so. You are very impressive, Layna. I'm happy to have this opportunity to sit and share a meal with you—get to know you a little bit."

This time Layna managed to return his gaze. She smiled and reached out with her hands to touch his. "You know what, Paul. I'm glad too. I wasn't even going to go out this evening. I usually don't on a Wednesday. But for some reason, I just didn't feeling like being home, alone, again." She paused for a moment, gathered her hands and looked down at her menu again, once more trying to hide her bashfulness. "This is nice," she said.

Upon the waitress's return, the two placed their orders and took a moment to simply enjoy each other's company. Without words they were able to communicate to each other the relief each of them felt to be away from the previous, tense situation. Paul, however, was a little out of his element. He did not "date" often, and was a bit uncomfortable. Astute, Layna was able to sense her companion's unease.

"This is all a bit strange, huh?" she asked, sounding a bit uncomfortable herself. "You know if you want to just go . . ."

"No," Paul interrupted. "You were right. This is nice. It's not anything that I've ever done before, but it's nice."

Paul paused for a moment. "So, I'm gonna just take a wild leap here, but why is it that you're single? You're clearly a very lovely woman. You have a good job . . . " He looked around the restaurant, "And good taste. I'm sure that you could probably have your pick when it comes to men."

Layna smiled at the assumption. "I suppose I could do all right, if I was so inclined. But I really don't have time for the petty games. A lot of the guys I seem to meet have a game about them. It's not that I want to get married and have kids within the first month, but if someone is serious about being with me, then they need to foresee some kind of future. Don't get me wrong, I've had my fun. I guess you could say that I've done my fair share of dirt along the way. But after a while, it's just time to grow up. I guess that's where I am right now, and none of my male friends are there with me."

She sighed wistfully and sat back into her chair. "I would rather be by myself than with someone who wants to be with me for only the moment. I don't like being by myself, but it is the better option."

Paul nodded. "I understand," he said. "I guess I'm kinda the same way."

"Now, don't get me wrong," Layna continued. "I'm not trying to marry every guy I meet, and I understand, and even appreciate, the ability to just be able to go out and hang with friends. But as for the personal side of things, I need to feel that it's going to be leading somewhere."

Paul nodded again and sat quietly for a moment.

"I hope I haven't scared you off," Layna offered. "None of this refers to you . . . I mean we just met and you really got me out of a jam back there. This is just my way to say thank you and hopefully, a chance to get to know you a little bit."

Paul smiled. "No, I'm not scared. It takes a lot to scare me." *Not as much as it used to,* he thought to himself. "I'm good. I'm happy to be here."

Paul reached forward with both of his hands, which Layna promptly and tenderly took. He looked down at her hands. He observed the elegance in them. They were long and slender and there was a creamy white texture to her skin tone. Her nails were perfectly manicured and like the rest of her, they seemed to be just perfect. He looked up and saw that she was watching him observe her. Their eyes met yet again and seemed to convey more than their words would say.

The waitress returned with their order. Her motions broke the couple's gaze. Paul looked over at the order and without conferring with Layna asked that everything be packed up to go. Layna, neither surprised nor offended, did not object. The waitress, completely surprised, took one look at the couple and completely understood. She returned to the kitchen with the food. Moments later she returned to find Paul and Layna standing with their coats already on and ready to go. She handed Paul the bill, who promptly paid in cash, tipping the waitress nearly thirty percent.

"Where to?" Paul turned to Layna.

"I know someplace close."

Paul picked up the bags. "Lead the way."

Chapter Twelve

Layna directed Paul to a Marriott Hotel that was nearby in Chevy Chase. They booked a room and upon entering Paul sat all of the food down on the nearest secure surface while Layna relieved herself of her coat by tossing it at the bed—but she missed, so the expensive, leather, full-length coat with fox at the collar and on the cuffs lazily fell to the floor. Almost immediately, the two found themselves locked in a powerful embrace. He kissed her so hard that she nearly retreated from his advance until she found herself backed into a wall. With his right hand, Paul brushed her hair out of their faces and reached down to grab her left leg. His large hands nearly engulfed her thigh as he pulled it near him. She sighed softly and the two continued to passionately kiss, tongues touching in the process. Paul lowered her leg and reached up to take off his jacket. Layna was eager to assist him, but did not stop there as she quickly moved to unbutton his shirt, relieve him of his undershirt, then turning her attention to his pants. Once his pants were unzipped and discarded, Layna removed her dress in one smooth movement. It was done properly and even politely, but completely without haste.

The two embraced again, then slowly but deliberately made their way to the bed. Paul sat at the foot of the bed. Layna stood in front of him and acquiesced as his strong arms pulled her close. Paul reached up behind her and, with a certain dexterity, managed to unhook the clasps of her bra to free her ample breasts. Layna arched her back to allow him full access to his newfound bounty. Paul tenderly began to kiss her about her right breast and slowly made his way through her cleavage to her left. Layna wrapped her arms around Paul's head to draw him closer to her bosom while at the same time Paul massaged her back and gently used his fingers to ease her panties down her legs and onto the floor. Standing, he quickly removed his own underpants. He grabbed Layna underneath her arms twisted and heaved her unto the bed. Surprised by the move, she was taken aback slightly but was impressed at his strength. She giggled as she bounced on the bed. Paul climbed on top of her. He kissed her again and, instinctively, Layna threw her arms around him as they embraced yet again.

She ran her fingers through his hair and tried to remember the last time she was so utterly excited by someone, anyone. She could not. She had absolutely no idea where they would go from here, but for the moment, she really did not care and as Paul gently eased himself into her, as she could feel his strength and his size throbbing inside of her, she promised not to let herself get carried away. She promised to take this one day at a time, one moment at a time. But more than anything else, she promised to enjoy this moment for what it was—a passionate, spontaneous moment. Much to her enjoyment, it was a passionate, spontaneous moment that lasted well into the night.

Afterwards, as Layna slumbered silently, exhausted from the lovemaking that relieved her of her inhibitions and her strength, Paul eased his way out of the bed and into the bathroom to take a steaming hot shower. He had hoped to find a diversion tonight. He had no idea his diversion was to include the company of an incredibly lovely woman.

He got the water started, and as soon as the steam crept over the top of the shower curtain he eased himself into the tub and underneath the spray. The water felt good against his skin, but to his chagrin, he could feel his worries and trepidations creep back into his psyche. He was amazed at the physical effects that this enigmatic fear seemed to create. He grabbed the complimentary bar of soap and lathered himself completely. Again he tried to wash away his despair, somehow corresponding a clean body to a clean conscious. As before, he was unsuccessful. No manner of diversion, even an incredible one such as Layna, would free him from this nightmare. This was something that he had to face head-on, and there was only one way to do that.

Paul stepped out of the shower, dried himself off and re-entered the main room. He walked over to the bed and looked down at her thoughtfully as she slept. He wasn't one for one-night stands. He really wasn't one for relationships either. Over the years, Paul had managed to occupy his time with other things. In reality, relationships often conflicted with those "other things." They complicated things.

He, once again, marveled at how beautiful she was. He did not know much about her, but somehow in a strange and interesting way, he felt a connection with her. It was something that was different than anything he had felt for anyone before. He wasn't quite sure where to place it, but he felt an underlying need to protect her.

He gently eased back into the bed beside her. She moved a little bit, moaning softly as she did. He comfortably placed his left arm around her waist. She subconsciously backed into him, allowing him easier access as they snuggled together. He thought for moment once again—*this was nice.* After spending some time of simply enjoying the moment, Paul drifted off to sleep.

***

As was his custom, Paul awakened at the break of dawn. He took a moment to look at his companion, who was still sleeping soundly. He watched her breasts rise and fall beneath the covers as she took the long, lingering breaths that normally accompany deep sleep. He thought about last night and felt a pinch of remorse as he recounted all of the events. He could have handled himself better at the Beacon. He could have handled himself better with Layna. Paul thrived on his

Midwestern values and was not accustomed to such a speedy encounter.

Layna stirred just a bit. Reluctantly, Paul gave her a nudge to assist her in her journey to consciousness. She responded well.

"Hey," Paul whispered softly.

"Hey," she whispered back.

"It's a little before six. I gotta get you home and then swing by my place so I can get ready for work."

Layna bounced up almost immediately, shook her head a bit, to clear the cobwebs. Paul admired how her breasts reacted to her sudden movements; he could not hide his satisfaction.

"That's right," she said, still a little groggy. "I've got to get ready for work, too."

Paul and Layna both got dressed rather quickly. Paul was amazed at Layna's speed. It had always been his experience that the fairer sex was always a bit lengthy when it came to personal appearance. The two of them managed to get dressed, check out, and head back to the District in less than twenty minutes. Paul was impressed and pleased. Layna lived in Georgetown: she had a very nice three-story brownstone. It looked to be very old, yet very well cared for. Paul liked the neighborhood. He thought that perhaps here, Layna could avoid many of the seedier elements that she might encounter in some of the other sections of the city.

"This is me," she said as he pulled up to the door.

"Nice," he nodded.

"Yeah, I was lucky to get this. The previous owner's husband died and she wanted to move back to Montana to be with her family. If we had more time, I'd invite you in."

Paul turned from gazing at the house to be greeted by her incredible smile. "Maybe some other time."

"Yeah?" she asked in questioning tone. It almost had a hint of longing attached.

"Yeah," Paul said with conviction.

Layna smiled again. She reached for the center console of the car and grabbed Paul's cell phone. She activated the phone, made a mental note of his number and then, very adeptly, entered her name and number. She leaned forward, gave him a gentle kiss and darted out of the car, up the front steps and into the house. Paul touched his lips gently with the fingers of his right hand, smiled, threw the car into gear and headed home. There was work to do.

Chapter Thirteen

Thursday morning, Paul walked into the B.A.U. headquarters to a chorus of cheers and congratulations. Word of his stunning, one-man rescue and apprehension had made its rounds via the grapevine even all the way back home. Paul found himself harried on his way to his desk after shaking a hand here and receiving a pat on the back there. It was nothing over the top, mind you; nothing like the reception he received back in Minneapolis—but the circumstances here were different. Back in Minneapolis, everything had just happened. It happened all so fast—almost too fast—and for many of the folks there, it happened firsthand. Here, everything was second-, third- or even *fourth*-hand so it was a quite bit more subdued. Besides, many of his colleagues were the low-profile type anyway. This was all part of the job, and everyone knew it. Sure, they were more than ready to congratulate one on a job well done, but it *was* part of the job after all.

Finally free of his admiring fans, Paul set to work on his case summary for his closing electronic communication. He organized his notes and got to work. Paul always endeavored to make his reports as thorough and concise as possible. This often meant spending a great deal of time on the details, but that was never a problem. The details were essential to every faction of his career, his life, even his extracurricular activities. If this meant spending a little more time to make sure everything was included and accurate, then he would spend the extra time, even if it required staying late. All of this was a non-issue for Paul. Today would be no different.

Midway through completing his report, Paul began to suspect that he was being observed. He marveled at how funny that feeling was and how it probably had no basis in reality—yet, it was uncanny how accurate that particular feeling could actually be. He slyly looked around the office to his right. Everyone he could see appeared to be working studiously. He slowly looked around to the left and found more of the same. As he brought his gaze back around to resume his own work, he caught a glimpse of Connie Jordan who was sitting in her office, staring at him, without being bashful about it—at all. Once she recognized that Paul noticed she was staring, she motioned for him to come into her office.

Paul made a couple more notations, made his way over to Connie's office, stuck his head in and asked, "You need to see me, Connie?"

Connie, still seated, motioned towards a chair. "Yeah, Paul. Come on in. I'd like to talk with you for a minute."

Paul entered the office, closed the door and sat in the seat that Connie offered. He took a moment to look around the office. He could not recollect the last time he was actually in this office. He only knew that it was some time ago.

Connie Jordan's office was very modern in its décor. Newfangled, as Paul's grandfather always said. Everything was modular. The bookcases to the rear consisted of tempered glass shelving held in place by a modular skeleton. To Paul's right was an oversized painting of something that Paul couldn't quite recognize. It appeared to be a faux Picasso, but Paul couldn't be sure. He simply noted that the painting consisted of a lot a pale colors and geometric shapes. To his left there was a water environment attached to the wall that operated like a waterfall behind a pane of glass. He supposed that the sound and motion of the piece was intended to have a soothing effect, but that was lost on Paul. He didn't particularly care for those types of items. Just in front of Paul, Connie sat behind a large—*too large for her needs,* Paul thought—tempered-glass desk, set securely in a tempered steel frame. To Paul it looked like an oversized computer desk but it was a small matter, as it was not his desk or his office.

"What's up?" he asked.

"Well, let me start by congratulating you again on the Konetchy case. What you did yesterday was tremendous. I really don't think that that scenario could have ended any better than it did."

Paul tried to shake it off. "Drake didn't really want any trouble. I think when he learned who he had—he realized that he might have bitten off a little more than he could chew. I honestly don't think that he really wanted to start any real trouble."

"Maybe not," Connie agreed. "But that doesn't mitigate your actions. You did one helluva job back there. Don't forget that."

"Well, thanks."

"Listen, Paul," Connie said as she leaned forward a little bit, folding her hands in a forward posture across her desk and speaking in almost a hushed tone. "You know, it's not just my job to lead this team, it's also my job to make sure that all of the working parts are operating at peak level."

Paul shrugged as if to say, *"Okay."*

"Now, over the last couple of days," she continued, "I've noticed a few different behaviors on your part that seem to be a bit out of character for you. At times, you've seemed distracted, almost as if you were in a different place as opposed to the here-and-now. At other times, you seem . . . " Connie hesitated, not quite sure how to put it. "You seem as if you're ready to explode on anything or anyone. I'm not quite sure if that's the best way to put it, but there's definitely something there."

Paul sat back in his seat, his glance never wavering. He had hoped that he had hidden his emotions from observation, but Connie was good. She was well respected and well regarded, both with very good reason.

"Well . . . " Paul tried to minimize his reaction. "I really don't know what to say."

"I know I asked you this yesterday, but is everything okay, Paul?"

"Yes, I'm fine." Paul tried to be as reassuring as possible. "I really am. I can't imagine what it was that you're seeing. I'm really okay."

"I hate to probe, Paul, but is everything okay with the home life? Are you having any issues there?"

Paul was a bit put off by the question. He had never discussed his personal life with any of his colleagues and never would—even if he had one to discuss. Connie noticed his reaction.

"I realize that you're a very private person. You have every right to be. And it's not that I'm interested in knowing your business, because I'm really not. I just need to make sure that everything is okay with you. When we're out there in the field, we count on each other tremendously, which means that we all must be on our "A" game. That can't happen if we have distractions that are preventing us from working at our best."

Paul understood. She was right of course, but there really wasn't anything that he could say.

"Listen, Paul. I'm always available if you need to talk. But if you don't want to talk to me, we have a host of resources here at the Bureau that you can take advantage of that can help in practically every area of need. If you need to talk to someone, please do not hesitate to let me know. We'll set you up with the right people, and perhaps they could give you the help that you need."

They wouldn't be able to help me, Paul thought. *Trust me on this.*

"Really, Connie, I'm fine. The Konetchy case had me a little highstrung, everything happened so fast. But I'm cool. This weekend, I'm gonna wind down and come Monday I should be good to go."

Connie looked at Paul for a moment. He was an exemplary employee. There really wasn't any reason to disbelieve his assertions. But something wasn't quite right. She couldn't put her finger on it, but she needed to keep an eye on him. Hopefully, whatever the issue was would pass and everything would return to normal.

"Okay, that's great." She sat back in her seat and spoke with a newfound cheeriness in her voice. "I just wanted to let you know that I'm here for you. If there's anything I can do . . . "

"I got it, Connie. Really, I do."

"Good enough."

Paul stood. Connie smiled. He made his way out of her office and back to his desk. He sat down and took a moment to think. He reached into his pants pocket and pulled free an old Swiss Army knife. It was his father's many years ago and it was given to Paul on his thirteenth birthday. It was one of the few items from his childhood that he still had, that he still cherished. He had it with him at all times and it was always kept it in his front right pocket. The knife always seemed to make it into his hands whenever he needed to think deeply about something—anything. It was one of his few idiosyncrasies and it occurred on the subconscious level. Once in hand, Paul would flip it, turn it, twirl it. He would open and close all of the different little attachments without realizing what he was doing. He would normally be so deep in thought that all of these actions, which his hands apparently would carry out on their own, would occur without any forethought whatsoever. Whatever magic the knife held, Paul hoped to draw from it now.

I need to be more careful, he thought to himself. If Connie was truly going to be eyeing him like a hawk he needed to be extra careful about everything. The last thing he needed to do was to draw attention to himself. There was much too much at stake for this to happen now.

Paul looked around his desk. He needed to finish his report but his in-bin caught his attention. He had some mail. After being away for nearly a week that was to be expected. Using the knife, Paul sorted his way through the mail. The first few items held little interest, a couple of industry circulars, followed by a couple of inter-office memos and an invitation to a birthday party for the wife of one of his coworkers. It was the final item that truly caught his attention, an overnight envelope with no return address. Paul froze at the sight of the envelope. He was now wary of everything that came addressed to him anonymously. He took a moment to look at it. He didn't want to touch it, let alone open it. He looked around; everyone seemed to be minding themselves. He glanced over at Connie, and she was in her office talking to Terry. He steeled himself, reached for the package, and opened it.

Inside of the envelope was one full-length piece of paper. The letter consisted of one sentence, which was typed and centered right in the middle of the page. It read:

You should have left her well enough alone. Now, you will pay.

Paul simply stared at the words. He could feel the blood rush from his face, yet again. He had become intimately familiar with the feeling. He could feel the pressure increase within his bladder as he now, all of a sudden, had an excruciating desire to relieve himself. This nightmare was causing his bodily functions to go haywire. It was causing a clash of emotions that he could neither control nor abate. Paul needed to get to the bottom of this situation. He needed to eliminate his tormentor, but he needed to do a little tormenting of his own first. He could feel the blood rush back into his face. It was accompanied by a wave of anger and frustration. He looked away from the letter and caught Connie looking directly at him. "Damn it!" he whispered under his breath. He did not know how long she had been looking, but he immediately worked to regain his composure. With a few frenetic movements, he cleared his mail out of the way. He eased the letter into an empty, standard-sized, manila envelope and returned his attention to his work. It took a few moments, but after getting his mind back into the groove of his work, he was able to regain his normal demeanor. He managed to focus on his report and occasionally stole glances toward Connie's office to see if she was still looking. The first couple of looks, he could see that she was. However, after about fifteen minutes, she had a couple of other agents in her office, so her attention was completely diverted. He took the letter and slipped it underneath some of the other items on his desk, turned back to his report and did not stop until it was completed.

Chapter Fourteen

As soon as Paul completed his report, he called the Bureau's forensics lab. He asked to speak with David Iannetta, the lab's supervisor and someone whom Paul had built a very good working relationship with over the years. He waited anxiously for David to pick up the line.

"Forensics lab, Iannetta speaking."

Paul was relieved to hear his voice. "Hey, Dave, it's Paul Andersen from the B.A.U."

"Oh hey, Paul. What's going on? We heard about Minneapolis. Good job, my man."

"Thanks, man. Just another day in the corps. You know how that goes."

"Um, no, not really. But I'll take your word for it. What's up?"

"Yeah, listen. I need you to do a little favor for me."

"What kind of favor?"

"Nothing too big. I have a letter that I'd like completely analyzed. It's a longshot, but if we can find any evidence on it, even a shred, then I can use it."

"I don't see how that's a favor, Paul. I mean that's what we do down here."

"Yeah, I know, but I kinda need you to do this for *me*. This isn't anything official, at least not yet. I would appreciate it if you could keep this between us."

David paused for a moment. "I don't see any problems with that. It's just a letter, right?"

"Right. One sheet of paper with one sentence on it."

"Yeah, okay. Just stop through and I'll take care of it for you."

"Thanks, Dave. I really appreciate it. I'll see you in a few minutes."

"Good enough. See you then."

Both gentlemen replaced their respective receivers. Paul collected a few things, including the manila envelope, stopped by the men's room for a long overdue visit, and headed to the lab. On the way, Paul wished that he had kept the slip of paper he received in Minneapolis. There might have been something to tie both pieces of evidence together but, as he admitted to David, he figured that finding any evidence on this note was a longshot. But, he had to get started somewhere, and folks did make mistakes.

It took Paul just under ten minutes to reach the lab. He walked in and looked around. There were a few technicians at work in the expansive, expensive lab. This place was always abuzz. He didn't know what half the items were, but everything was state of the art and if there were any evidence to be found on this letter, David and the utilization of this equipment would find it.

"Paul!" David emerged from his office, which was to the far left of the lab.

"Hey, Dave."

David Iannetta was a tall man at six-feet-one, was strongly built and had a very approachable demeanor. He was roughly forty or forty-five years old but always seemed younger when one engaged him in conversation. His hair was almost completely gray, save a few streaks of black here and there, but he wore the silver mane well. He wore a white lab coat, the customary attire as everyone in the lab was adorned with one, which apparently protected an expensive suit, if the pant legs were any indication. David also sported a pair of eyeglasses that were rounded to complete circles and seemed almost too small for his face. In totality, David looked like a forty-five-year-old version of

Harry Potter, who at some point in his life decided to shed his cape and wand for a white lab coat and a pair of tweezers.

David motioned Paul over. He spoke a few words to one of his lab techs and by the time Paul reached him, had concluded that conversation. Both men shook hands, David stepped back to allow Paul access into his office and closed the door for privacy.

"So whatcha got?" David asked as he walked around to his seat, which was situated behind a clutter-filled desk.

Paul reached out his hand and presented Dave with the manila envelope. "The envelope is mine," he offered. "The overnight envelope I received it in is back at my desk, but the letter inside is what I'm interested in."

David moved a few things around on his desk and sat the envelope down into the clearing. He quickly grabbed a pair of latex gloves from a desk drawer to his right and then reached into the breast pocket of his lab coat to pull free his trusty set of tweezers.

Carefully, he examined the envelope, then, utilizing the tweezers, he began to pull the letter from its casing. Once free of the envelope, David turned it over a couple of times. "Now, you've touched this right?"

"Unfortunately, yes. You should find my prints on that, but anything else is what we're looking for."

David turned it over again and this time read it out loud: *"You should have left her well enough alone. Now, you will pay."* He paused for a moment. "What do you suppose that means?"

"I have a few suspicions, which is why I'd like to get it analyzed." Paul looked down at the letter then back at David. "So, do you think you could help me on this?"

"Yeaaahhh." David subconsciously drew out his response while he squinted through his spectacles. "I don't think it would be too much of a problem. Give me a couple of hours. We've got a few things going on right now, but I'll make sure this gets done for you. I have your number. I'll give you a call."

Paul closed his eyes and made a small sigh. He quickly came to his feet, his gratitude was apparent. "Thanks, Dave, I really appreciate this. I'll be waiting for your call."

"No problem."

Paul left the office with David still giving an ocular examination of the letter. On his way back to the B.A.U., his cell phone rang. At first glance, he didn't recognize the number. He stopped in his tracks, depressed the talk button and hesitantly lifted the phone to his ear.

"Hello," he said, listening intently for the voice on the other end.

"Hey, Paul, it's Layna. Busy?"

Letting loose a long sigh, he was very relieved to hear her voice on the other end of the line. He just couldn't be too sure of anything right now.

"Hello, Layna. Um, I'm working but I'm not extremely busy at the moment. What's going on?"

"Not too much. I just wanted to tell you that I really had a good time last night."

"I did too. It was, uh, special."

"Yeah," Layna agreed apparently ignoring his hesitant response. "It really was."

Both paused for a moment; neither one quite knew what to say next.

"Well, you know," Layna finally broke the uncomfortable silence, "I was thinking that since it was almost the weekend, kinda— it being Thursday and all, and if you weren't busy, that maybe we could get together tonight?" She asked the question as if she feared the answer.

Paul remained silent a bit longer. He was uncomfortable with the idea. He was still uncomfortable with last night.

"Oh, um, tonight, um . . ."

"I know," Layna admitted. "You weren't really expecting to see me again so soon."

"Um, no. It's not that. Uhh . . ." Paul was truly at a loss for words. He really did not want to get into anything right now.

"Well, let's do this." Layna had a little more confidence in her voice. "You have my number. Why not just call me and . . .?"

Paul interrupted. "No, Layna. I would like to see you. You just caught me off guard a little bit."

"Good," she sounded more relaxed, then suddenly. "I don't mean 'good' I caught you off guard. I mean 'good', that you would like to see me." She did not succeed in hiding her embarrassment.

Paul could not help but smile. "It's all right, Layna. I know what you mean. Listen, I'm right in the middle of something right now. How about I give you a call back?"

"Sure, I understand. You're out there keeping us safe from all the creeps in the world. Just give me a call." Layna tried her best to hide her disappointment.

"Yeah, I'll give you a call."

"Talk to you then."

"Okay. Bye."

Paul hung up his phone and thought for a moment. He could not help but think that all of this was happening a little too fast and entirely at the wrong time. On the one hand, he really did not know Layna and he wasn't all that sure that he wanted to. But, on the other hand, he could not deny that there was "something" between them worth exploring. Nothing about her, thus far, had seemed frivolous or loose. Last night, they both simply seized the moment. It didn't

162

happen often, but it happened. It happened to folks from time to time, and they were no different than anyone else in that regard.

"Let's just see what happens," he said aloud and to himself. He slid the phone into his pocket and headed back to the office.

Back at his desk, Paul sat down and got to work on his desktop. He jotted down the lot number of the overnight package, intent on finding out exactly where it was purchased. After conducting some preliminary research he was able to ascertain that the package was mailed in town, yesterday, from a local courier. He picked up the phone and dialed the courier's office. He verified that the package originated from that location and that the person to whom he spoke with was on duty yesterday. With that information, Paul quickly hung up the phone, took a brief look around, and then slyly made his way out of the office and to his car.

Twenty minutes later, Paul was standing at the counter of a Ship & Go talking to a clerk named "Marie" with regard to the package that was processed at the location the day before.

"Hi, Marie, listen—I received this package yesterday. I was told that it came from this location. Can you verify this for me?"

Marie took the envelope and using a scan gun, scanned the barcode and then turned her attention to the monitor just adjacent to the workstation.

"Yup," she said in a rather nonchalant tone. "This was processed here. What else do you need?"

"Where you the person on duty, yesterday?"

Marie looked at the time stamp on the screen and turned back to Paul. "Yes."

"Is there any way that you could tell me anything about the person that might have brought this in here yesterday?" She gave him a blank stare.

"I know, it's a stretch . . ." Paul reached for and showed his credentials. "But, I could really use any help that you could give."

Marie read the credentials. In her mind, she figured as much. She looked at the envelope again and nothing significant jumped out about it.

"Sorry, mister."

"Okay, okay." Paul shrugged off that line of questioning. "What can you tell me about this envelope?"

"This?" She took the envelope and looked at it. "See this here." She showed Paul a few red markings at the top of the envelope and then a red shaded area near the bottom.

"Yeah," Paul responded expectantly.

"This means that this is a pre-paid envelope. Folks can come in here, or into any store, and buy these in bulk. Then, they can mail them from any store at any time."

"Well, can you tell me where this one was purchased from?" Marie looked at it again. "It's kinda old. We don't use these envelopes anymore. A lot of our packages have been updated. They have a different kind of layout on them now." Paul continued to look at her.

"This looks like it's at least three years old."

"Three years?"

"Yeah, that's what I mean. It's kinda old. But people can still use them though."

"Okay." Paul tried his best to not sound impatient. "But can you tell me where it came from?"

The woman looked at her monitor again. She typed a few things into her keypad and did a minor bit of scrolling. "This was bought as a part of a batch in August, three years ago in St. Petersburg, Florida."

"What?" Paul could not hide his disbelief. "Are you sure?"

"That's what the computer says, mister."

Paul stared blankly at the clerk for a few moments. Other patrons in the store began to grow restless as they too had mailing and packaging concerns that needed to be addressed.

Tentatively, Marie handed Paul his envelope back. He took it, and as if he was in a daze, he turned and walked directly out of the store and got into his car.

There he sat. Thinking. Remembering. August—three years ago—St. Petersburg, Florida. Her name was Adriana Montejo. She'd been the state beauty pageant winner. She was very beautiful, so much so that Paul didn't really want to taint her. But he did. Her case was still unsolved.

"But, there can't be a connection," Paul reasoned aloud. "There just can't!"

Unsure of what to do, or where to go next, Paul threw his car into gear and headed back for the office. Along the way he received a call on his cell, which he had patched through his car's hands-free system.

"Paul Anderson," he answered.

"Hey, Paul, it's Dave."

"Hey, Dave. That was quick. What have you got for me?"

"Well, I've only done some preliminary tests so far, but there's nothing on the letter. Outside of your fingerprints, there's absolutely nothing here."

Paul was not disappointed. He did not expect that anything would be found.

"Hey, I figured as much. Thanks, Dave. I'll swing by a little later and pick it up."

"There're a couple more things I'd like to try. But I wouldn't hold my breath if I were you."

"I hear you, my friend. Thanks."

Paul disconnected the call and continued the drive back to the office. Nothing learned, but nothing lost. Now, he had to figure out the St. Petersburg angle, if there truly was one.

Back at the office, Paul sat at his desk, knife in hand, and tried to recall everything about St. Petersburg. He had been there for a conference about crime scene analysis. He didn't find anything particularly stimulating about the conference except for when he encountered Adriana Montejo.

Adriana had been a stunningly, beautiful young lady. She was tall at five feet nine. She'd had very dark features, which were enhanced by her brilliant black hair. She was poised. She was graceful. She was just the kind of young lady that one would want to represent one's home state in any kind of venue. She was very well spoken. She was clearly educated and to Paul's recollection of his own, private research, she had been training all her life for that one achievement. Unfortunately for Adriana, Paul had known for months that she would be his next victim, and while there were scores and scores of people still looking for the lovely Adriana, they would never find her. *Well,* Paul thought, *they would never find all of her.* Her body parts were spread along the eastern seaboard from Florida all the way up to and including Virginia.

Paul continued to think intently about the circumstances of that particular "venture". He continued to fiddle with his knife as he tried to recall every little detail with regard to Adriana. She was single. She had a younger brother and a single mother. Her father died in the Gulf War. She attended school in Gainesville and was finishing up her degree in English lit. She was well liked and, by all accounts, fairly grounded. Not stuck up and full of herself because of her looks or accomplishments. In fact, if Paul could recall correctly, the family was rather poor. They only got by on the monthly stipend that the government gave them because of the father's death. There was

166

nothing significant that stood out at all to Paul, except for the fact that her death coincided with the purchase of an envelope that was sent to him today that referenced another one of his victims.

"This shit is going to drive me crazy," he murmured. He rubbed his face with his hands and peeked between his fingers to take a look around the office. He was ready to leave the office for good. He needed to wind down. He reached into his pocket and grabbed his cell. He looked at it for a moment, pondered the consequences of what he was about to do, scrolled through the contacts, and did it anyway.

"Hello?" She picked up after only one ring. "Paul?"

"Hey, Layna, it's me. Do you still want to get together tonight?"

"Sure."

"What did you have in mind?"

"Well, I was just thinking that maybe you could swing by my place and I could fix dinner and we could just—I don't know, just talk and get to know each other a little bit. Nothing fancy, *nothing deep.* Just two adults enjoying each other's company."

Paul smiled into the phone. "You know. That's exactly what I need."

"Good. What time can I expect you?"

"Well, I've got another hour or so before I can knock off here. Give me enough time to run home, grab a shower, and change. Let's say seven-thirty."

"Seven-thirty sounds good to me. See you then?"

"See you then."

Paul was still smiling when he disconnected the call. There was something so real about Layna—it was refreshing. He looked at his desk. There were still a few things that he could attend to that would pass the time. He gave those items his full attention and before he knew it, he was out of the door and on his way home. He grabbed a quick shower, changed clothes, and headed out. He made a quick run to the local spirits store and picked up a bottle of red and a bottle of white. Unsure of what Layna might be serving, he wanted to be prepared. To his own surprise, he was actually excited at the thought of seeing her.

Again, he smiled.

Chapter Fifteen

At exactly 7:30, Paul was standing at the threshold of Layna's three-story brownstone. He was still quite impressed with the home. He had already pressed the doorbell and was simply awaiting her response. Moments later the door swung wide and Paul had to gather himself at the sight of her. She answered the door dressed in a full-length, white satin dress that accentuated her curves perfectly. She had her hair down—more or less to be comfortable at home—but it was perfect for the dress. He almost couldn't take his eyes off her, and as his gaze returned to her smiling face and their eyes met, Paul knew that coming to see her tonight was definitely the right decision.

"Are those for me?"

Her question broke the silence and his haze. "Um, yeah. I didn't know what you were fixing so I got both to be covered."

"Good man," she said and smiled. "Come on in."

She took a step back and moved to the side to allow Paul access. Paul walked in and was greeted by a series of sensations. The first "hello" was the atmosphere of the home. It was moderately lit by a variety of candles and softly burning wall sconces that seemed just perfect for the mood and the home. The home essentially invited one to make one's self comfortable without the utterance of words. The atmosphere was sensual without being seductive, sexy without being vulgar. It was just—nice, and it seemed to fit Layna perfectly.

The next sensation filled Paul's olfactory system with the most exquisite aroma. "What is that I'm smelling?" he was compelled to ask.

"Oh that," she said with a sly grin as she closed the door behind him. "*That* is dinner: poached salmon with dill sauce, spinach, and wild rice. I've also have a nice loaf of challah baking in the oven."

169

"It smells incredible." Paul had never been more honest.

Layna smiled. "Wait 'til you taste it." She, too, had the propensity to be quite straightforward.

Paul continued to look around as he entered the home. The next sensation he encountered, if it could be called a sensation, involved the sense of *being* he experienced while in Layna's lovely home. Layna's brownstone had a very traditional layout. There were original, but newly refinished, hardwood floors throughout. The walls were adorned with the type of wallpaper that boasted conservative patterns and were textured with an almost woven, cloth-like feel. There were nine-foot ceilings hoisted upon the shoulders of exquisitely designed and meticulously crafted crown moldings that he assumed also ran throughout. To Paul, it appeared that this was one of those brownstones, which had probably been built nearly 100 years ago, but had been completely and painstakingly restored in an effort to recapture its once brilliant standing with regard to residential magnificence. By any and all standards, Paul mused, the restoration was a success.

Within the foyer there was a grand set of stairs that ran along the wall on the left that headed all the way up to the third floor. Just ahead was a hallway that led to the back of the house where the kitchen was situated and from where all of the mouthwatering aromas originated. Off to the right, a few steps in from the front door, there was an archway that led to a formal sitting room. Paul stepped into the room and was impressed by the authenticity of everything he saw. To his right, there was a picture window that was flanked by two smaller, openable windows that faced the street. There was a traditional window treatment that adorned the windows—a bar stretched across the top with drapes imaginatively wrapped around it and releasing down. At the base of the window was a radiator that ran nearly the entirely length of the wall and was encased in a cherry-wood, handmade cover that also exhibited a great deal of detail in its design and construction. Atop the radiator were a series of aloe plants of different sizes and in different pots, each unique enough to embolden its host plant with its own special character. A few feet away from the radiator sat two Elizabethan-style chairs that faced away from the window and into the room. They were separated by a cherry coffee table that supported a small Tiffany-style lamp and a few magazines.

Just to the left of the front windows and against the far wall, there were built-in bookshelves that appeared to be original to the home. From his vantage point, Paul could see that the shelves were clothed with books and collections that ranged from the classics to contemporary fare. Layna apparently had eclectic tastes with regard to what she liked to read. In the center of that far wall and directly across from the archway was a grand fireplace. It was nearly five feet tall from hearth to mantel and almost seven feet wide in length. The mantel itself held a variety of photos, trinkets, and novelty items, while a fire danced gracefully in the firebox, spilling its heat well into the room and out into the foyer. Off to the left of the fireplace, along that same wall, was her entertainment center. There were open shelves that displayed her collection of CDs and DVDs, along with a few other media items. In the center of the console, behind a set of closed doors, rested a 42-foot plasma television that she rarely watched on her own but welcomed the opportunity to share with the right person. Across from the unit, just to Paul's left was a modest leather sectional that looked both inviting and expensive.

There was no left wall to the room as the opening, accentuated handsomely by columns at both sides, spilled into a Victorian decorated dining room that appeared to be furnished more for show rather than practical use. It, too, was dimly lit but Paul suspected by the settings that they would actually be dining elsewhere.

Layna tapped Paul on the shoulder. "Follow me," she said with a smile. He was happy to oblige.

They left the sitting room, entered the foyer, and followed the central hallway to the back of the house and into the kitchen. The kitchen was expansive and completely modernized. It encompassed the entire rear of the house. Unlike the classic or antique-like feels of the foyer, sitting room, and dining room, the kitchen had all of the latest appliances: a Sub Zero refrigerator/freezer combo, a six-burner Viking stove with a matching double wall oven, a double sink, and a wine chiller. There were granite countertops, cherry wood cabinetry, and porcelain tiled flooring; it was like stepping into a renovation designed by HGTV just upon completion.

"This is impressive." Paul simply stood at the threshold.

"You likey, huh?"

"Yes," Paul said and grinned. "I likey a lot."

Off to the right of the room was a small nook that held a round, slate-tiled table and two chairs. On the table were two place settings and a lovely, three-tiered candelabra that was already lit. Layna motioned toward the table and Paul obediently made himself comfortable.

"Ahh," he sighed as he took a seat. He looked around the marvelous kitchen once again and was truly awed. Paul had never considered himself particularly domestic, but in all his travels he had never seen a kitchen quite like this one.

"I don't know what I'm gonna do about you," he said as he watched her walk over to the double oven, slip on an oven glove, and open the lower door.

"And what do you mean by that?" she asked without looking back.

"You keep impressing me. That could get you into a lot of trouble."

"Really?" She smiled as she withdrew the challah from the oven—the aroma was intoxicating. "And what kind of trouble could that be?"

Paul smiled and shook his head. *She really is too much*, he thought.

Everything was ready to be served. Chatting aimlessly, the two worked together, getting the table set and the food plated in a matter of minutes. Because they were having fish, they silently settled on the bottle of white. Paul uncorked the bottle, let it breathe for a few moments, and poured. They took their respective seats and sat in silence for just a moment. They each took stock of this special time that they were sharing together and gave their appreciation for the opportunity as they smiled and began to eat.

For the majority of the meal they ate in silence. For Paul's part, he was completely taken with Layna's culinary skill. He conceded to himself that the meal was not particularly difficult to make, but the combination of tastes were exquisite to his palate and he truly could not recall if he had ever enjoyed a meal so much. It was an experience that he truly was not accustomed to. As for Layna, she was just happy to cook again. Though she prepared food daily in order to provide her sustenance, it was not the same as actually *cooking.* Cooking for someone else was always different. It always required more care, more forethought. It was something that she enjoyed doing; but she found herself doing it less and less as her taste in men became more selective. She silently hoped that this would not be the last time she cooked for Paul.

They finished the meal and playfully cleaned the kitchen together. During the process, they would poke and prod all in good fun. They were very relaxed in each other's company and that fact was not lost on either of them. Having finished the bottle of white, they grabbed the bottle of red and made themselves comfortable on the sofa in the sitting room. Layna turned on her stereo system and light jazz spewed forth from a modest set of Klipsch speakers, adding just a little more depth to the already near-perfect ambience. It was nice. Paul refilled their glasses and they casually sipped, seated close together, bodies touching. They sipped and again, enjoyed the moment.

That single moment became twenty minutes of listening, swaying, sipping, and touching. Paul had even managed to steal a few kisses as they continued to enjoy the evening. Then suddenly, and as far as Paul could tell, without warning, the mood changed. Layna changed. The playfulness and cheerfulness changed to brooding and sorrow. Paul was at a loss.

He reached out, grabbed her by the chin, gently turned her face towards his and asked, "What's wrong, Layna?"

She turned away from him, pulling free from his hand. A tear that she really did not want him to see trickled down her cheek. He repeated his actions and his question.

"What's wrong, Layna? Talk to me."

Her gaze had been downward in his hand. He lifted her chin and they made eye contact.

"I'm sorry." Her apology was genuine. "I'm really sorry. I really didn't want you to see this."

"What's wrong?" He was insistent. "I still don't know what's going on."

"Well," she started slowly, hesitantly. He wiped the tear from her cheek and looked at her thoughtfully. "I just . . ." She was still unsure of herself, not truly willing to talk, but feeling obligated.

"I really like you, Paul. I really do." Paul's look was unwavering. "I know, I know," she continued, sounding embarrassed and ashamed. "It's only been a couple of days. There's so much that we don't know about each other. It's just that—it's just that I feel so comfortable with you. Connected, somehow."

"I know what you mean, Layna. I'd be lying if I said I didn't feel it too."

"So, you do feel there's something here?" She sounded encouraged.

"I do. At least the start of something."

"Well, that's good." She wiped another tear from her eye. "That's very good." She sounded a slightly bit more composed. "Then, I really need to share something with you." Paul brushed her hair from his face. Their eyes met again. He remained silent.

"Last night was a little more than just a night out for me." Paul had a quizzical look on his face. He wasn't quite following. Layna sank back into the sofa. She took a sip of wine, gathered herself, and continued.

"Four years ago, my best friend at the time was picking her daughter up from daycare. She had already had her son in the car. On the way home, while she was stopped at a stoplight, a guy approached her car with a gun. He ordered Melissa out of the car, but she didn't want to leave her kids in the back. I guess she resisted—I really don't know exactly what happened—but this guy—this guy *shoots* Melissa. He dumps her body into the street and takes her car. He takes the car with the kids in the back!"

Layna paused for a moment to wipe away fresh tears. "It was one of those Lexus SUVs— you know what I'm talking about?"

Paul nodded.

"Anyway, he takes the car and drives off, leaving Melissa in the street. He sees a patrol car and starts to run." She paused again. "Before you know it, he runs a light. He slams into the side of another vehicle, some kind of delivery van or something, and the guy and Melissa's two kids die."

"My God." Paul was barely able to utter his words.

"It didn't make any sense. All she wanted were her kids. I'm sure she would have been willing to let him have the truck. We've talked about things like that. But the kicker was . . ." Her frustration began to come through. "The kicker was that the cops weren't even chasing the guy. They hadn't even gotten the call yet. They just happened to be passing by."

She buried her face into his chest. She was sobbing softly and desperately trying to compose herself. In moments, she sat back again. She looked at Paul. She had his undivided attention. He maintained his thoughtful visage.

"The worst part was that Melissa didn't die right away. She died almost two hours later. *After* she learned that her kids were killed." She paused again. "That was four years ago." Her voice was still a little weak. "Four years ago, yesterday." Paul recognized the significance and understood.

"So, when you saw me. When we met. That's what I was dealing with. That's why I had my head buried in my drink. That's why I really didn't want to be bothered with that asshole. That's why I really didn't want to spend the night alone. I just needed to be with somebody and honestly . . . when I saw you . . . after you came to my rescue when that nut got into my face. I really wanted that somebody to be you."

Paul was unsure how to react. He was unsure of what to feel. Layna continued.

"I'm really happy you called me back today. I'm glad you came over. I'm glad we've had this time together. Paul, I really want to get to know you, but I thought you should know what happened with us last night wasn't just a fling for me. It actually meant something and it still does. You were there for me, in more ways that you realize."

Paul looked at Layna and without knowing what else to do, he kissed her. He kissed her tenderly. He kissed her lovingly. More than anything, he kissed her in a manner that was reassuring to her. It let her know that everything was okay and that yes, there was something special between them.

After the kiss, Layna stood and offered Paul her hand. She then slowly led Paul upstairs to her bedroom. Upon entering the room, Layna turned to Paul and slipped out of her dress. She then helped relieve Paul of his shirt, his pants, everything. She led him to the bed. They laid together. They held each other. They kissed each other. They comforted each other throughout the night.

More than she would ever know, Layna comforted Paul in a manner he had not previously known. Considering all that he was dealing with, Layna had a calming effect on him, which was exactly what he needed. She was the right person at the right time. Paul *knew* it. He could feel it.

They spent the night making love—not only with their bodies but also with their spirits. They fell asleep in each other's arms and for Paul—it was the best night's sleep of his life.

Chapter Sixteen

It was 8 a.m. Monday morning and every member of the B.A.U. had been called into the conference room for a briefing on their next assignment. Paul, on time and ready, felt refreshed and rejuvenated. While the previous Friday was uneventful during the workday, he spent the entire weekend with Layna save for a few irrelevant hours apart. It allowed him to regain some of his perspective. Of course, he was well aware that he had work to do. He had a killer to find, some shit to settle. But, having recharged his batteries, he felt better equipped to take on his challenges. He felt on top of his game.

In the conference room, the other team members assembled. Paul found a seat to his liking near the rear of the room and looked earnestly as he noticed that the board at the front of the room was covered. He also took note of Connie who was standing and conversing softly with a couple of men he did not recognize. It was unusual to see strangers here at the B.A.U. Usually these types of meetings took place on location, not here at HQ. Paul refused to take too much stock in it and reached in his pocket for his trusty knife. Sometimes, these initial meetings were a little intense, so Paul endeavored to get his thinking cap a little warmed up before the party began.

"Good morning, team," Connie said, turning to face the room. She stood at one end of a long conference table that had eight chairs at either side and a single seat at either end.

"Good morning, Connie." An uncoordinated chorus returned her greeting.

"As you can see, we have a couple of visitors with us here today." Connie turned toward the two men. "The gentleman to my far right is Captain Richard Lee, and this gentleman right here next to me is Special Agent Thomas Chen. Captain Lee is from the Kansas City, Kansas, Detectives Division and Agent Chen is from our Kansas City, Missouri, branch. I've been in contact with Agent Chen over the past couple of weeks, and now it appears that our services have been retained to grant him some assistance. There have been a string of murders in the Midwest that these men believe are linked. During the course of their investigation they've found significant evidence that suggests that a serial killer is at large and has been for quite some time." Connie turned to Agent Chen. "Agent . . ."

"Thank you, Agent Jordan. Good morning, everyone."

Thomas Chen was sharply dressed and well polished. He stood approximately five feet nine and had a very solid, stocky build. He looked to weigh nearly 220 pounds, all of which appeared to be muscle, even through his well-tailored suit. He stood very erect and talked in short controlled bursts, clearly the mark left by superior military training. Agent Carter quickly recognized the traits. He smiled.

"As Agent Jordan said, I'm Thomas Chen from the Kansas City branch. Over the past few weeks we've been coordinating with a few of the local law enforcement agencies across the Midwest. We've reviewed a few cold cases and have compared them with more recent killings. As a result, we believe that we have uncovered the trail of a serial killer. We were still trying to connect the dots when we received word of another murder last night." Chen paused briefly and then continued. "Two days ago, I was contacted by Captain Lee with regard to a murder that occurred in his jurisdiction—the murder of a young lady. Initially, we saw nothing to connect her to the others, but upon closer inspection, we were able to ascertain that she was another victim. Another one among many."

Agent Torres raised his hand and was acknowledged. "When you say others, what are we talking about? How many others are there?"

Chen turned to Connie and nodded. She walked over to the board and was quickly joined by Captain Lee. Together they uncovered the board, and revealed the pictures of seven slain women strewn across the wall. Under each picture was the name of each woman and a series of pertinent notes that pertained to their individual murders. Off to the right of the pictures was a running list of everything that linked these deaths together.

As Paul began to scan the board, look at the pictures, and read the names of the victims, a familiar sickening feeling began to take hold of his body. His knife slipped out of his hands and as he attempted to catch it, he managed to cut his left hand in the process.

"Damn it!" His exclamation broke the room's concentration and immediately attracted the attention of Connie Jordan.

"Excuse me." Holding up his wounded left hand, he hurried out of the room and headed directly for the men's room. He burst into the restroom and immediately began to run hot water over his wound. He squeezed his hand to curb the bleeding; the wound was long but not particularly deep. He grabbed a few paper towels and applied as much pressure as he could. While he applied the pressure, he looked into the mirror that hung above the sink.

"Jesus," he whispered. His skin looked bleached. He had begun sweating profusely and hadn't even realized it. He grabbed more towels and hurriedly wiped his brow. He looked like he had seen a ghost then realized that for all intents and purposes, he had. His mind's eye recalled the pictures that were hanging just down the hall in the conference room and he shuddered. Of those seven victims pinned to that wall, three belonged to him. Three were murders *he* committed and now the team he worked for—*the team he worked with*—would be investigating his own work. His incredible, terrible nightmare had just gotten worse.

Terry entered the restroom. "Paul? Are you all right?"

Taken by surprise by Terry's entrance, Paul was momentarily speechless. However, he recovered quickly.

"Oh, hey." He turned his attention back to his hand. "I dropped my old knife and cut myself trying to catch it."

"How bad is it?"

"Not too bad. It looks a hell of a lot worse than it actually is."

"Well, I went and grabbed the first aid kit. I thought you might need it."

"Thanks."

Terry opened the first aid kit and reached for the hydrogen peroxide. Together they properly cleaned the wound. Terry applied a healthy amount of Neosporin before carefully and effectively bandaging it.

"Thanks, man."

"No problem. You've got to be careful with that thing. Those Swiss Army knives are deadly."

Both men smiled and walked back toward the conference room. Terry quickly returned the first aid kit to the break room and rejoined the bigger group shortly after Paul.

Paul apologized for the interruption and returned to his seat. Everyone at the table had a look of concern that slowly turned to relief when they were sure that Paul was all right. Connie, on the other hand, was not so forgiving. She turned back to Chen and sharply said, "Please continue, Agent."

Chen turned to Captain Lee, who now had a stack of manila envelopes that he began to distribute around the room.

"What we're handing out is a composite of everything we have here on the board. You'll see that each of these women was killed in a distinctly different manner and that they have no obvious connection with each other. There's nothing overt to link them. They all looked different. They had different occupations and came from different walks of life. Of their similarities, they all were relatively young, ranging from the early twenties to early thirties. They were also fairly productive in society—good jobs, respectable occupations. They were all different but similar at the same time, if that makes any sense. Anyway, from what we've learned, there's absolutely nothing that actually linked these women together. At least while they were alive."

"Okay," Terry offered. "I'll bite. What does link them together?"

"Well, on the board and in your packet, these women are ordered in a specific manner. You see, from left to right, at each of the subsequent murder scenes we found an item that belonged to the previous victim. Here . . ." He walked over to the board. "Our first victim is Vanessa Hayes. She died of rat poisoning in Jackson, Mississippi, five years ago. Of course her murder is still unsolved and it had been cold until we realized that a small, framed picture of her daughter was found with this victim, Myla Prentiss, at her home in Memphis, Tennessee, a year and a half later around Christmas. Here, in Appleton, Wisconsin, . . ." Chen pointed to a photo on the board." We found a pair of prescription eyeglasses that had the DNA of Prentiss's sister, who lived with her at the time, with the body of Susan White at the site where White was found beaten and strangled. And, according to her friends and family, Ms. White had perfect eyesight and had no need of eyeglasses. It just goes on down the line. Katana Lopez, killed in Chicago, was wearing a bracelet that belonged to Susan White. Eunice Flowers died from an allergic reaction to bee stings, if you can believe that. She didn't register with us at all at first. She was visiting her sister in Little Rock and wasn't there but for a few days and we had no cause to believe that her death was anything more than an accident, an allergic reaction. That was until we learned that the baby teeth sealed in a vial among the items found in her purse belonged to Katana Lopez's daughter."

"Damn," Terry said, shaking his head.

Chen continued down the line. "Paige Traxler was suffocated. She died of carbon monoxide poisoning. It was initially thought to be a suicide until we learned that the earrings she was wearing belonged to Eunice Flowers. And finally, our most recent victim. Sabrina Burnett, twenty-two, just graduated from college. She had her own apartment, not far from her parents' home, by design, mind you—they wanted to keep an eye on her. She was killed with a single stab wound at her apartment. No signs of forced entry. She was found half dressed but not bruised. We're not sure if she was sexually assaulted. The lab results aren't in. Just a note—none of the other victims were sexually assaulted."

"What did you find?" Terry pressed the issue.

"Here we found a birthday card that was addressed to Paige, from her mother, but displayed among the items found on Sabrina's nightstand in her bedroom."

The team was quiet. This was far more involved than anything they had previously worked on. This not only seemed like a killer of opportunity, but one of cunning and forethought. This unsub seemed to be well organized and extremely clever. The weight of the task ahead left the room quiet.

Paul, however, was quiet for yet another reason. While he had absolutely no knowledge of Vanessa Hayes, Myla Prentiss, Eunice Flowers and of course, Sabrina Burnett, he was very knowledgeable with regard to Susan White, Katana Lopez, and Paige Traxler. He knew a great deal about each woman's life, but he was even more knowledgeable about the circumstances of their deaths. He could not fathom how they could've been linked, not only to each other, but to these other women who he had absolutely no connection with.

As Agent Chen continued to talk, providing the elements behind his theories, Paul became consumed with the ramifications of what he was hearing. It began to dawn on him that there was a possibility that he could be linked to all of these murders. That at some point, his team could turn its focus his way and unless he could clear all of this up before that happened, there would be no escape.

He listened as each death was described in greater detail. He listened as his fellow agents hypothesized, with fairly decent accuracy, as to how the killings might have occurred. Paul's mouth had become so dry that he could barely draw a breath. He started to think of ways to tamper with the evidence, ways to clear any possibility of suspicion that might come his way. He began to feel desperate about his situation, but quickly caught himself. Desperation was the last thing he needed. Desperation led to mistakes. He was sure he had made no mistakes during those killings. He was being set up and he knew it. There was no other explanation. Paul knew who killed those other women. It was him. *He killed those women and now he's pinning them all on me. I've got to catch this bastard. I've got to bring him to his knees and make him pay for all of this.*

Paul snapped back to the present. He had to regain his emotions, his control. He glanced at Connie. She was intently listening to Agent Chen. Hopefully, she didn't observe him as he drifted away.

Captain Lee took the floor to briefly explain his stake in the case. He was tall and thin with only the memory of hair left on his head. He was very soft-spoken, yet managed to maintain an air of respect. He explained that in his nearly forty years on the force, he had never encountered anything quite like this and he was intent on catching whoever this monster was, even if it was the very last thing he did as an officer.

The team completely understood the captain's sentiments. The trail of items with each subsequent kill was intriguing, but it also showed a great deal of planning and arrogance. Connie took the floor again.

"As I mentioned earlier, I have been in contact with Agent Chen for the past few weeks. He's kept me abreast his latest developments. Of course, we were tied down with the Konetchy kidnapping last week, but we're on tap for this one, for sure.

"There are a few things I'd like to point out before the agent continues. Clearly, we, and when I say we I mean all of law enforcement, are being taunted by this guy. The only reason to place an item from one victim onto the scene of another is to show that there's a link. And since we can find no other link, that link *must* be the killer. He had to know that we'd discover these items sooner or later. He wants to spar. He wants to play. There really is no other explanation for this behavior."

At this point, Emiliano Torres chimed in. "True. Killers often take souvenirs for private, personal reasons. These things are for their own personal collections, used to relive the murders, recapture the euphoria. Usually, it's compulsive and instinctive. From what you've told us so far, these items were not only chosen carefully, but they were carefully placed in the subsequent scenes. All of this shows not only malice of forethought, but an intent to snub his nose at us. We've got to catch this guy. This is *not* a game."

Dr. Hermanski leaned forward. "Do you have anything that could help us with our profile?"

Agent Chen resumed. "We have almost no evidence against this guy. Like I said earlier, the only links between these women are the items our unsub has left at each of the crime scenes. We need you guys to piece together the profile."

At this point, Paul decided to join the conversation. "Well, based on the little information that we have so far, tentatively I would we think the standard parameters would apply: white male, thirty-five to fifty, fairly decent shape, nondescript—wouldn't stand out in a crowd, dysfunctional upbringing, but smart, careful, complete attention to detail, meticulous. Of course, this really doesn't get us any closer to catching the guy, but I think if we could agree . . ." He looked around the room and found his colleagues nodding, "Then that's as good a starting point that we could have right now."

"Yeah, I think you're right, Paul," Connie said stepping forward. "That's probably where we'll start. Captain Lee has preserved the crime scene of our latest victim, Sabrina Burnett. Correct?"

"Um, yes. That is correct." The captain was caught slightly off guard.

"Good. You each have your packets. I want you to take some time to review all of the materials. Grab your things, because we'll be heading out to Kansas City in two hours. We'd leave sooner but our plane has been delayed. Agent Chen, is there anything else you'd like to cover at this time?" The agent shook his head.

"Very good. Team, you have two hours. I expect to see you on the tarmac then. Gentlemen," she said turning to her visitors, "I'll need a few minutes, and then I'll be right with you."
Jordan turned to face Paul.

"Yeah, Connie?" He knew it was coming.

"My office, please."

She was curt. Paul thought that following his wonderful weekend, his week would start off pretty well. The reality was that it couldn't start off any worse. He walked solemnly into Connie's office and took a seat.

"Paul, I'm gonna make this short and sweet. I don't know that the hell is going on with you, but you have got to get it together. If you cannot manage to do that, I will relieve you of your duties."

"I'm really sorry about that, Connie. I dropped my knife and . . ."

"I don't want to hear it. No more outbursts, no more staring off into space, no more talking to yourself as if you're on another planet. Got it?"

"Got it."

"Get your head into the game! Now go and get ready."

Paul stood and looked at Connie for a moment, then left the office. He began to realize that it wasn't so much that he had cut himself or disrupted the meeting, but that he embarrassed her. Of course, that was never his intention, but he had done so just the same. On the heels of their talk last week, this did not bode well at all.

Paul grabbed his things and headed home to retrieve his travel kit. On the way, he decided to make a quick detour. He headed into DC to stop by and catch a quick moment with Layna. She had planned to take the day off—just because. It didn't take him long to reach her home. The traffic was unusually light for it being not too long after rush hour ended. He parked his car right out front and had a certain bounce in his gait as he took the steps leading to her front door. He rang the bell and awaited her response. He peered through the prism-like glass of her front door and thought he saw movement. He waited for the door to swing wide, but it didn't happen. He looked into the glass again and the movement he thought he saw was no longer there. He felt a small tinge in the pit of his stomach. He reached for his cell phone and dialed her number but the only response he received was that auto reply that reported: "All circuits are busy." Next, he dialed her home number and received her voicemail greeting.

"Hey, this is Layna," even the recorded version of her voice had a soothing effect. "I'm not available right now, so please leave a message. Thanks!"

"Hey, Layna it's me. Um, Paul. I'm just letting you know that we got a new assignment this morning, so I'll be heading out of town for a while. Give me a call when you can. Um. Actually, it might be better if I gave you a call a little later. I'll talk to you." He disconnected the call.

Paul looked in through the glass again. Again, he saw no further movement. He caught the glimpse of a car passing by, a reflection from the street. He thought perhaps that that's what he caught the first time. Disappointed, he turned from her door, got back into his car, and continued home.

He wasted little time once he made it home. Paul discarded the dressing on his left hand and replaced it with a fresh bandage. He grabbed his travel kit, which he stored in the bottom of his bedroom closet. The kit consisted of a medium-sized suitcase and a smaller toiletry bag, containing a week's worth of clothing and all of the personal items he would need. He, along with his colleagues, kept a travel kit prepped and ready to go for situations such as these. It was something that was easy to grab, when they needed to be out in a moment's notice.

For a moment Paul paused and thought again about what he had seen—or did not see—at Layna's house. He was sure he had seen movement but was aware that he couldn't actually be sure. The only thing that he felt he could be sure of was that his adversary was wily and that Paul could not put anything past him. He grabbed his cell again and attempted to reach Layna again. Still no answer. He was worried, but there wasn't anything that he could do about it. He had to bury his worry as deep as possible because he was sure that once he was back with the team, he would be under Connie's watchful eye.

Apprehension had been getting the best of him; he shook his head and attempted to clear his thoughts. He gathered all that he needed, packed his car, and headed for the airport where the team's plane would be ready and waiting. He met up with the rest of the B.A.U. just before Connie and her two guests arrived. They all boarded the plane and moments after take-off, Agent Chen and Captain Lee began to resume their debriefing. They discussed, in a little more detail, the scene in Kansas. Chen wanted to stress all of the differences between the scenes as opposed to the similarities. He believed that the distinctness of each scene was actually a clue in itself. It was as if everything was different by design. That thought struck a chord with Paul. Throughout his ventures, he made a point that with each of his killings each of his scenes was different— distinctly different. It was as if the variation itself was his calling card. He truly did not think that there could be any way that his victims could be linked. All of this, he truly believed was beyond the realm of probability.

Each member of the team turned attention to the dossiers. Paul had glanced lightly over the material earlier but intended to take a good look at it now. Unfortunately, he found his concentration lacking. He could not focus. His mind drifted from Minneapolis, to his anonymous letters, to Layna, to his victims in this case, to what he thought he saw at Layna's house, to Connie's concerns, back to Layna, to his current situation, and back to Layna again. At the very least, he could not afford to let anything happen to Layna. He put the package down. He stared out of the window and drifted. He knew that, without a doubt he was on the clock; for if he did not catch this killer, and catch him soon, sooner or later, the eyes of his team would turn to him, and that would be the end of everything.

Yes, he thought quietly to himself. *I'm on the clock now.*

And that clock was ticking.

189

Chapter Seventeen

Kansas City, Kansas

When the team finally landed, each member was intimately acquainted with all the information provided them in their packages. Even Paul found the time and the energy to prepare himself for the task ahead. Upon landing, the team was immediately ushered to waiting vehicles, which took them to the Detectives Division of the KCK Police Force. The Detectives Division was in a modest building centralized in downtown Kansas City. Although the city was often overshadowed by its Missouri counterpart, KCK offered a great deal with regard to its own identity. Formed in 1868, the city held historic significance especially with regard to the American Civil War. It boasted significant historical architecture among its skyline and despite its little sister status, managed to maintain its own identity in the annals of American relevance. The Detectives Division Headquarters was a little dated and not abundant with space, but it was practical and it was not overcrowded with unnecessary items. It was more than adequate to serve its purpose.

"All right, everyone. I'm sure we've made all of the necessary introductions by now. Most of you in this room know me. I'm Special Agent Thomas Chen from the KC Branch office. I have worked side by side with many of you in one manner or form over the years.

"Three nights ago, a young lady in your jurisdiction, Sabrina Burnett, was brutally murdered in her condo. She died of a single stab wound to the base of her skull. We believe her death is the latest in a series of killings that go back at least five years, possibly longer. The crime scene investigators found a birthday card on her nightstand that belonged to another victim who was killed nearly a year ago in Nebraska. That's the background. Given the complexity of this case, I have requested and been allowed to designate this case with a codeword designation. As it stands, the code name is "Mephisto." The case number is 62D-KC-3748267.

"Agents," he said, turning to them. "The officer there will be handing you a note with all the pertinent information, including the proper file number."

One of the detectives proceeded to hand each of the agents a small slip of paper with the information.

Chen turned back to the floor. "As you can see, we've managed to secure the services of the Behavioral Analysis Unit. We hope that their input would create a profile of this character and give us a leg up on how to catch him. Agent Jordan?" Chen surrendered the floor.

"Good morning, everyone." Jordan stepped forward. "My team and I have a lot of catching up to do, so if you don't mind I'd like us to get right to it. There are a couple of things I'd like to stress that I think are important. Since there are strong indicators that these murders are linked, Agent Chen will continue to run point on this investigation. As it stands, my team and I are here in a support capacity only. Don't get me wrong, we will conduct our investigations, and we will need your complete cooperation to do so, but our goal is to create the profile. Any questions?" There were none.

"Agent Chen, if you don't mind we'd like to dive right in. Where is the body now?"

Captain Lee answered. "It's down in our medical examiner's office."

"Captain, if you don't mind, I'd like Dr. Hermanski to go down and examine the body if she could."

"I don't see that being a problem. I'll have an officer take her over."

"Thanks. Jacob . . ." she said turning to him. "I'd like you to stay with Agent Chen. Agent, if you don't mind, I'd like Jacob to have a closer look at what you have."

"That's fine by me. I always appreciate a second set of eyes."

"Good. Thanks. I'd like the rest of us to take a look at the crime scene."

The captain chimed in, "We'll get you over there pronto. Tommie?" He turned to Agent Chen, who simply nodded.

"Okay, let's head out." Captain Lee was ready to go.

Jordan turned to Leisa. "Leisa," she spoke in a bit of a hushed tone. "See if you can find any and all of the media coverage that might have covered any of these killings. When Agent Chen and Jacob are all set, maybe you and Chen could get together on that. I'm not sure what you'd find but I want to know everything. We need to make the most complete profile possible and we need to get on top of this fast. If word leaked out about this, it could turn things into a complete mess."

"I understand. I'll let you know if I find anything."

"Thanks." Jordan turned back to the remaining members of her team. Their faces were a little grim. Each one of them knew the seriousness of this situation. They had a beast on their hands.

"Captain?" she said in an apprehensive voice. "Please lead the way."

***

Sabrina Burnett's condo was left in exactly the same manner in which the officers found it, save the removal of her body. On the evening of her murder, Sabrina was to spend some time with one of her girlfriends, Lacey Schepner. When she did not show up at the appointed place, at the appointed time, Lacey became worried. She called Sabrina's cell phone but only reached her voicemail. After an hour, and no word, Lacey went to Sabrina's place, used her spare key, and entered the unit to find her best friend dead in the middle of the living room floor.

Now, three days later, Captain Lee cut the police barrier tape and granted access to the accompanying members of the B.A.U. As was her custom, Jordan reached into her purse to pull free her digital recorder as she and her team prepared to analyze the crime scene. She took a quick look into her bag, found the small slip of paper she was looking for, and began recording.

She began by stating the date, the time, and the location. She gave a brief description of the day's weather and made a note to check the weather conditions on the night of the murder. She identified all of her present team members and included the names of the accompanying officers. She gave the name of the case and the corresponding case number. She designated Terry the custodian of evidence and with the assistance of her colleagues began to meticulously describe the scene.

Sabrina Burnett lived in a very nice one-bedroom condo near the center of the city, yet was only a five-minute drive from her parents. Her place was on the fourth floor of a six-floor building, a renovated warehouse that housed traditional condos, as well as some respectable loft space. There was no main lobby—hence no doorman, which meant a potentially helpful, added layer of security did not exist.

Upon entering Sabrina's unit there was a closet immediately to the right. A few steps in, and to the left, was a galley kitchen with an open hutch that spilled into an expansive dining area–living room combo. The dining area was just beyond, and adjacent to, the kitchen. It consisted of a small, circular, glass table with four chairs in a matching set. Atop the table was a vase of plastic flowers and display settings for two. It was small but practical and more than likely rarely used. The rest of the room was the living space. There was a large leather sectional that faced an impressive fireplace which supported a forty-eight-inch plasma television on its mantle. Off to the left, along that wall, but beyond the dining area, there were four windows that ran from floor to ceiling and provided a breathtaking view of downtown Kansas City. There was wall-to-wall, plush carpeting throughout that was light beige in color and in pristine condition. There were a few other chairs accompanied by side tables and lamps strategically placed throughout. There were carefully chosen prints of places she had visited during her young life, as she was well traveled. Jordan noted that all of the items therein were of a high quality. She moved deeper into the unit.

Just to the right of the fireplace was a walkway that led to the back of the unit where both the bedroom and the unit's only bathroom were located. The walkway from the living room to the bedroom was approximately twenty feet long. Midway down the hall and on the left was the bathroom. Jordan peeked into the bathroom and immediately noticed that it was much larger than she suspected. Immediately to the left was a large vanity with an impressive mirror looming over top. The vanity had a large basin, double the normal size Jordan thought, which was flanked by antique-styled faucets. There were various personal and grooming items situated neatly atop the dark grey granite counter. From the items displayed Jordan believed that Ms. Burnett spared no expense when it came to personal hygiene.

Beyond the vanity was the toilet and beyond the toilet was a triangular-shaped, jetted garden tub. It was large enough to seat three healthy-sized bodies with perhaps a little room left to spare. On the opposite side of the bathroom, across from the toilet and sink was a well-sized standalone shower. The shower was nicely tiled in mosaic fashion both on the wall and on the floor. It was enclosed with a dense glass door that was as clear as an autumn day in Georgia. Much like the rest of the unit, the room was immaculate. Everything sparkled. Everything was in its place. Jordan shook her head slightly, left the bathroom, and headed to the bedroom.

"She appeared to have so much promise," Jordan softly whispered to herself.

While the bedroom was nicely furnished and decent in size, in Jordan's mind, it was not as impressive as the bathroom. Upon entering, the queen-sized bed jutted from the wall on the right. It faced an eight-drawer dresser on which stood a thirty-two-inch flat screen television and a few more personal items. There were more floor to ceiling windows on the far wall and a large, though not quite walk-in, closet to the left of the dresser. Jordan made note of the two nightstands that flanked the bed. She identified every item on top of the nightstands, including the birthday card which did not belong.

She walked back into the living room and rejoined Captain Lee.

"Have your guys itemized everything here?" she asked plainly.

"Absolutely," he replied. "We didn't want to miss a thing."

She nodded. "Good. Do you know if anything's missing?"

"No. Not yet. We need to run our list past someone who really knew Sabrina and had a strong grasp of what she owned."

Jordan nodded again. "Have you talked to her parents?"

"Yes, we had a preliminary discussion with them. It wasn't anything too deep. We were giving the notification at the same time so, they were still dealing with the shock of it all."

"Yeah, we're gonna need to talk to them too. We're gonna need to try and understand Sabrina as much as possible. We have to try and find out why she was targeted—what made her so special."

"Well, you can be my guest, Agent. Just let me know when and we'll make sure to get you over there. It's not far."

"Good."

Jordan turned back and looked into the room. Paul, Terry, and Emiliano were going over the space with a fine-toothed comb. Jordan thought that was where Emiliano was at his best. She hoped that he would be able to find something here that perhaps had been overlooked. Something significant that could give them a clue.

Paul, who had been crouching down over the area where the body was found, stood and shook his head. Jordan caught sight of that action and pondered it. Paul looked around, caught Connie looking, and walked over to her.

"What's up, Paul? I saw you shaking your head."

"We're not going to find anything, Connie. And if we do, I wouldn't trust it."

"What do you mean?"

"This guy is slick. If all of the information is correct, he doesn't make mistakes. Everything he does is for a reason—it has a purpose. It's gonna be difficult to get a read on him."

This was the first time Jordan had ever heard Paul sound discouraged with regard to tracking a killer. It usually took him a little while, but he was always confident that he could get a lead on an unsub. This time was different, but given the circumstances, she understood why.

"Keep at it," she encouraged him. "We need to get this guy. I'm sure you'll come up with something."

Emiliano re-entered the living room after having briefly examined both the bathroom and the bedroom. He too was shaking his head.

"This place is clean," he announced. "I can't find a thing. I'll need some more time obviously, but I can tell you right now that I doubt very seriously that we'll find anything here."

It was now Jordan's turn to shake her head. "We should be able to find something. There's no blood. She was stabbed—there should be blood. That is, if she was killed here. If she wasn't, we need to find out where."

Terry Carter joined the party and approached Jordan. She turned to him and asked solemnly, "What do you think?"

Terry answered in a very practical tone, "I'm thinking we got bubkus. We're working with a real smart one here. That means he's real dangerous. We're gonna have to bring it this time around, folks."

Emiliano looked around the scene once more. The lack of blood was a big clue, an important clue. They needed to determine whether or not this was the crime scene. He looked at the furniture. Everything seemed to be in place. There was no indication that anything had been moved. He walked over to one of the chairs and looked very closely at its legs. He overturned the chair to get a closer look. With his naked eye he believed he saw small flecks of green on the bottom of the leg. He moved to another chair, overturned it, and believed he saw more of the same.

"The murder scene was here. Right here, in this living room." He was sure of it.

His colleagues gathered around. "How can you tell?" Terry asked. "What have you got?"

"Look." They did. "If you look closely, you'll see small flecks of green on the feet of these chairs. It's on that other one over there. Ten will get you twenty that it's on a few others too. We'll have to take these back and get them analyzed but I'm certain that these flecks are plastic. Our guy used a tarp. When he came, he laid a tarp down and used the furniture to anchor it. He wanted to keep this scene as clean as possible. He didn't stop to consider the soles of this furniture."

"Bag 'em up." Jordan was satisfied that at least they had something.

Paul chimed in. "If this guy used a tarp then his planning might be a little more developed than we realized. He had to have known what the layout here would have been. He would have been here before with or without Sabrina's knowledge. He comes completely prepared."

Jordan took a moment to consider the thought. The more they learned about this guy, the worse it got—and the more important it became to get him off the street.

She turned to Emiliano. "Keep working the scene. Give me a call if you find anything else."

"No problem. You leaving?"

"We're leaving," Jordan motioned toward Paul and Terry. "We're gonna have a talk with Sabrina's parents. See what we can dig up there."

She turned to Captain Lee. "Captain, we'd like to talk to the parents."

"Sure. Like I said they're nearby. We'll be there in ten minutes."

Captain Lee gave a few orders to a couple of his officers; he wanted to make sure that whatever Agent Torres needed, he got. He also wanted to remind them that this was a secure scene and that no one was to be admitted without his prior approval. Afterward he led Jordan and her team out of the building and back into their vehicles as they took the seven-minute drive to the grieving Burnett household.

Chapter Eighteen

At the medical examiner's office Dr. Eva Hermanski prepared to do a review of the previously conducted autopsy. She had already read the report and though she had no intention of conducting a complete and independent autopsy of her own, she did want to get a close look at the body with the hopes of finding anything that might bring them closer to their killer.

At the ME's office she met with the coroner, Dr. Stephen Gastfield, and his assistant, Arnold Baxter. Although, both men seemed a little hesitant at first, neither man could resist Dr. Hermanski's charm and, ultimately, gave her full access to the facilities. They led her to the main lab where Sabrina Burnett's body lay waiting.

"This is Burnett's body over here." Dr. Gastfield pointed to a slab in the middle of the room. He was an older gentleman. Dr. Hermanski couldn't put a number on his age, but by the way he moved she believed that he probably should have retired years ago. He stood at a hunched five feet seven inches. He was probably closer to five feet nine erect, but it appeared that years of leaning over bodies had taken a toll on his posture.

"Have her parents been in to identify the body?" She spoke softly but with confidence.

"Yes," he answered swiftly. "We actually were here for that. It was one of the more disheartening scenes that I have seen in a long time. The mother completely broke down, and it took everything the father had to keep them both from collapsing. Right, Arnold?"

Arnold Baxter was a much younger man. He looked fresh out of high school although Dr. Hermanski was aware that he had to have had at least some medical training for the job. He was a smallish man, five feet six,, maybe 140 pounds soaking wet. He was very timid, the mousy type. Dr. Hermanski surmised that he probably spent most of his work day chasing behind Dr. Gastfield, agreeing with everything the good doctor had to say.

"Yes, sir, you're absolutely right."

Dr. Hermanski could not help but smile.

"Well, let's see what we have here."

Dr. Gastfield uncovered Sabrina Burnett's body and Dr. Hermanski took a close look. She scanned the body from the crown of Sabrina's head to the soles of her feet. She carefully looked underneath each fingernail and each toenail. She looked between the fingers and between the toes. She took a significant amount of time scanning Sabrina's scalp. After painstakingly examining the body in its totality, she turned her attention to the murder wound.

At the base of Sabrina's skull, there was a singular stab wound that penetrated clear through into her mouth. The wound was small and circular. The weapon would have been sharp and long. Very similar to an ice pick, Dr. Hermanski thought. The entry area appeared a little wider than one would expect from an ice pick. The length was about right, but she questioned the diameter.

"Any idea what could have caused this wound?" she asked without looking up.

"Not really. Not yet." Dr. Gastfield was sincere in his response. "At first glance, you'd think ice pick."

"Yes," Dr. Hermanski agreed. "But . . ."

"But, the diameter is all wrong."

"That's what I was thinking."

"We really don't know what it was as of yet, but we have a weapons division here. That unit does a very good job identifying murder weapons that have caused strange wounds. It might take them a little time but they'll find it, whatever it is."

Dr. Hermanski looked up at Dr. Gastfield and nodded at his last comment. She returned her gaze to the wound. She grabbed her digital camera from her purse, took a few photos, and returned the camera to her purse. She stood erect and was relieved to ease the pressure from her back. She gave Sabrina the onceover once more and shook her head. Sabrina had been a beautiful young lady: great shape and good skin. Her teeth looked well cared for. She apparently put forth a great deal of effort with regard to her appearance. She had her own place, a good job—which was very hard to come by straight out of college. From all appearances, she had a bright future ahead of her. Until, of course, this monster decided to take her future away from her. Dr. Hermanski really couldn't understand the madness behind it all.

"Have you run her blood?" she asked again without looking up.

"We've done a preliminary blood screening. No alcohol or drugs to speak of. We have a private company that does our full workups for us. That usually takes a few days. We haven't gotten the complete results back as of yet."

Dr. Hermanski nodded. She understood the growing trend of outsourcing to private companies, functions that traditionally belonged to the government; federal, state, local or otherwise. She turned back to her hosts. "Are any of her personal items here?"

"Um, yeah." Dr. Gastfield was both surprised and relieved at the question. "Actually, her purse is here. Not exactly sure why, but we have it. We've logged everything in it in. You can take it if you wanna sign for it."

Dr. Hermanski tilted her head at the suggestion. "Sure, I'll take it." She concluded that it wasn't serving any purpose here. Perhaps the team could examine it closer and find something.

Arnold Baxter retrieved the purse along with an inventory list. Carefully, Dr. Hermanski matched the items in the purse with the items on the list. Satisfied that everything was a complete match, she signed the list and asked for a copy. Dr. Gastfield was all too eager to oblige.

Dr. Hermanski gathered the items. She thanked the two gentlemen for their assistance and made her way out of the medical examiner's office. She walked slowly to the patrol car that had been waiting to take her back to the Detectives Division. She reached the patrol car and slid into the passenger seat beside the waiting officer.

"Anything good?" He asked.

"Not really," she answered. "Maybe."

She looked down at the purse, which was secured in a clear plastic bag. The officer glanced at the purse, shrugged and headed back to the Division.

Chapter Nineteen

The somber atmosphere in the Burnett family home was so thick it could have been shaved with shears. Connie Jordan sat in a single chair opposite a sofa that seated Andrew and Patricia Burnett, Sabrina's parents. Also seated in the modest living room were Tina Burnett, Sabrina's seventeen-year-old sister and Andrew, Jr. (Andy), her thirteen-year-old brother. Patricia was completely distraught, the preceding two days did absolutely nothing to ebb her grief. Jordan saw immediately that a competent interview with her would not be possible, at least not at this time. She hoped to extract pertinent information from Mr. Burnett, but he seemed preoccupied with consoling his wife. Little Andy was staring off into space; he was clearly somewhere else. Tina was the most helpful. She was the most alert. She was the most lucid. Jordan suspected that in this household, that was probably the normal case.

Jordan tried to press the parents without pressing the issue.

"Mr. and Mrs. Burnett, we really do hate to have to ask you these questions at this time, but any information that you could give us can help."

"I'm sorry, Agent," the father responded weakly. "As you can see, this is still very difficult for us. It's just too much at one time." He paused for a moment. "But please, ask your question again?"

"I understand how difficult this is for you. I really do. Unfortunately, we see cases like these all too often. It takes a toll on the victim's family and loved ones. It's okay to grieve for Sabrina."

Jordan paused for a moment, then asked her question again. "Had Sabrina given you any indication that she was having trouble with anyone?"

MINE!

Mr. Burnett shook his head and looked down at his wife who had her head buried into his chest. He pulled back so he could see her face and she too only shook her head. Jordan looked over at Tina and she offered a blank stare.

"Well, what can you tell me about Sabrina? What kind of young lady was she? Did Sabrina have many friends?"

"Breen . . ." Tina injected.

"Excuse me?" Jordan was taken a little off balance.

"We called her "Breen." Everybody called her Breen, and she was my best friend." Tina had effectively caught Jordan's attention.

"Tell me more."

"I could talk to Breen about anything. And she could talk to me about anything. We talked about school, friends, boys, everything. She was always there for me." Tina worked hard to fight back tears. "She would do anything for me. She never hurt anybody. I don't know why anybody would want to do something like this."

"It doesn't make any sense to us either, Tina." Jordan was sincere with her consolation. "It really doesn't, but we're gonna do our best to find out who did this to your sister, okay?"

Tina simply nodded her head.

"What can you tell me about Breen's friends? Did she have a boyfriend?"

Tina shook her head. "No. No, boyfriend. She was too busy for anything serious. She dated. She had friends, but nothing serious."

"Who were her closest friends?'

Tina let loose a long sigh. "Well, you know about Lacey. She was the one who found—Breen."

"That's Lacey Schepner?" Jordan confirmed.

"Yeah," Tina shook her head. "I think so. I'm not really sure what her last name is. There's Brooke Balcena, um, Trish, uh, Trishelle Looney, I think."

204

After finishing a note, Jordan asked, "What about who she was dating?"

Tina switched gears effortlessly. "She saw this guy Brian a few times. I don't know his last name. He works at her job. She said he was nice, but it wasn't anything serious. She saw another guy named Mark Lansford or something like that. She thought he was cool too but she didn't like him as much as Brian. I don't know where she met Mark."

"Sabri–" Jordan started and then corrected herself. "Breen was a salesperson right?"

"Yeah. She was a marketing major in college. She came out and got a job selling for a big medicine company. "Fi– something.""

"Phizer, maybe?"

"Yeah, that's it."

"Had she met anyone new, do you know?"

Tina remained silent, but Jordan could see on her face that she had something to say; something that she probably didn't want to share in front of her parents. Jordan took the clue. She turned to Terry who was standing nearby. "Terry, could you sit here with the Burnetts for a moment?" Then back at Tina. "Tina, could you show me Breen's room?"

"Um. Sure." Tina was nervous, but she completely understood. She headed to the stairs and took each one tentatively. Jordan was close behind. Moments later they were both in Sabrina's old room, sitting on her old bed, talking softly and frankly.

"What can you tell me, Tina?" Jordan was reassuring in her tone.

"Well, there was this one guy that kinda freaked Breen out. A few weeks ago, she was either going to work or coming home, I can't remember, anyway some guy came up to her and asked her for directions. I forget where he wanted to go. In fact, I don't think she ever told me, but she gave him the directions. He thanked her and went about his business, but it made her feel, I don't know. Kinda eeww like."

"Why was that, do you know?"

"Nooo. I don't think Breen really knew. But she did say that she thought she had seen him someplace before. She just wasn't sure when or where."

"Did she ever describe the guy to you? Give you any idea of what he looked like?

"Actually, yeah. She said that he was older. Like early forties or something. He was tall. He was kinda muscular. And he was smoking one of them brown cigarettes—or maybe a thin cigar."

"Really?" Jordan was a little surprised at the details. "She told you all of that?"

"Yeah, because she wanted me to stay away from this guy if I saw him. You know she didn't live that far, so if this guy was in the neighborhood, she wanted me to be careful."

Jordan nodded. She appreciated the "big sister" love.

Tina continued without taking a breath. "She was always like that. She always looked out for me. She looked out for all of us. Now, I don't have her to talk to. Now, I can't see here anymore. I don't know what I'm gonna do."

Tina broke down and into Jordan's arms. Unbeknownst to the agent, this was the first time that Tina actually let her emotions run free. For the past couple of days, she had been keeping it together for the benefit of her family. She had been cooking the meals, answering the phone calls, assisting the police as best she could, maintaining contact with extended family members and friends, and even keeping the house in order. Patricia Burnett was awash with grief and totally withdrawn. Andrew, her father, had been preoccupied with keeping her mother from going off the deep end. Andy was just there. He was walking around like he was on another planet. He had had a very special relationship with Breen. She'd often played sports with Andy and had given him a lot of one-on-one attention. It was almost as if Breen were his big brother as well as his big sister.

So, it was up to Tina to keep it together. It was a role that came naturally for her, but it often came at the expense of something else. Thus far, she had been unable to properly grieve for her big sister, her best friend, her confidante. Thus far, she really didn't have a moment of her own to just be herself. Here, now. With Agent Jordan she could actually express how she felt about her sister and in doing so, it all poured out.

Connie recognized the indicators. She had seen it before—all too often as far as she was concerned. She placed her arms around Tina and let her cry. After a few moments, Terry poked his head into the room. He caught Jordan's attention, but she shook him off. He understood. She was willing to give Tina all the time she needed. This cry was the healthiest thing she could do right now.

It didn't take long for Tina to gather herself. Once she regained her composure she was embarrassed and apologetic.

"I am so sorry. I really didn't mean to do that. I don't know what happened. I just started crying and I couldn't help it."

"It's okay." Jordan was patient and tender at the same time. "It's okay. You needed to cry. Trust me. I know."

Jordan gave her a few more moments. "Are you ready to go back down?"

Tina nodded and let loose a sigh of relief. "Yes. I'm ready. I feel better. Thank you so much."

"It's not a problem. Here . . ." Jordan reached into her jacket pocket. "Here's my card. It's got my cell number on it. If you want to talk, you can call me anytime. Day or night, okay?"

Tina nodded.

"My name is Connie. Just call me, okay?"

"Okay."

The two headed back downstairs. Jordan caught Terry's eye and met him at the entry of the living room.

"I just spoke with Eva. She has Sabrina's purse back at the station. She thought that we might want to examine its contents."

"Did she find anything at the ME's office?"

"Nothing of any significance." Terry then whispered softly, "They just haven't identified the murder weapon yet. It wasn't a garden variety instrument."

"Hmm." Jordan processed the information. "Okay." She walked into the living room.

"Mr. and Mrs. Burnett, we'd like any information that you might have on Sabrina's—I'm sorry—Breen's friends and acquaintances—names, addresses, phone numbers, things of that sort."

"I don't know what we have, but whatever it is we'll give it to you," Mr. Burnett responded openly.

"Tina," she said turning to the young lady. "If you can get us any of that information, I would appreciate it."

"I have Lacey's cell phone number. She can give you all of the others. They all know each other. I'm sure she'd have them."

"Good." Jordan turned to Terry who caught the cue and retrieved the information from Tina.

"Mr. and Mrs. Burnett, I want you to know . . ." She paused and gave Tina an understanding look. "I want you all to know that we will do everything we possibly can to catch Sabrina's killer. You have my word on that."

"Thank you, Agent." Mr. Burnett replied. "We're sure that you'll do your best."

Jordan turned to Tina and smiled. Tina did her best to muster a small, but genuine, smile. Jordan winked and turned to her colleagues.

"Let's head back. Eva has done her examination and she has Sabrina's purse. Don't know what we'll find, but I want to have a look at what's there and maybe determine what's not. We also need to talk to all of her close friends. We need to find out if Sabrina shared anything recently that might have given them any cause for concern."

"Well, I've got Lacey's cell number," Terry offered. "If this Lacey was truly her best friend, she should be able to give us a good deal of useful information."

"I would agree. She should be the first person we talk to."

Jordan looked around. "Listen, we're done here. Let's head back. We need to keep the momentum rolling on this until we have a profile that's sharp enough to catch this guy."

Jordan took a deep breath, and she and her team headed for the door.

Chapter Twenty

Back at the Detectives Division the team reassembled in the conference room. The contents of Sabrina's purse were spread across the conference table spaced in such a manner as to allow each item to be viewed independently. Dr. Hermanski, who had already crosschecked all of the items against the copy of her signed transmittal was now checking the list aloud so as to receive a confirmation of the items from her colleagues. She simply went down the list.

"Eyeliner, tan lipstick, brown lipstick, small bottle of hand sanitizer, small bottle of lotion, travel toothbrush and toothpaste, wallet; three twenties, one ten, two fives, three ones, three credit cards, coin purse with eight dollars and seven cents, three pens, one pencil, ID wallet with driver's license, Pfizer ID card, Bally's membership card, Social Security card, voter's registration card, small baggie of peppermint candy, small notepad with various work-related notes scribbled on a few of the pages, one set of car keys." Dr. Hermanski paused for a moment. "I'm sorry, two sets of car keys." She corrected herself. "One set of gold earrings, one small gold bracelet, a small package of tissues, three receipts.

"That's everything." She lifted her head from her list. She looked at her colleagues and each was intently focused on the items on the table.

"It's all here, Eva." Jordan confirmed. "Thanks."

"What do we have, guys?" Jordan asked openly.

"Not too much," Emiliano offered.

"Well," Jacob started slowly. "I don't know about this." He pointed at two of the items on the table. "Did she have two cars? I mean, those sets of keys don't belong to the same car."

Everyone was silent for a moment. There was a bit of uneasiness.

"Wait a minute, wait a minute," Paul broke the silence. "That wouldn't make any sense. I mean he already left us his souvenir, right? That was the birthday card. He hasn't left two items at a scene before, has he?"

He turned to Agent Chen who also was in the room. "Not to my knowledge. If he did that here, it would be a first."

With that bit of information the tension in the room eased a bit for everyone, except Paul. While his assertion with regard to the multiple clues might have been a valid one, he recognized one of the items on the table. He actually recognized the change purse. That change purse belonged to Lorri Massey; she kept it in a dish on her mantle in her living room. It was her godmother's. Lorri never knew her birth parents. They were killed in an auto accident when she was very young. She was adopted by her godmother at an early age, and the purse was a gift when she turned fourteen. Lorri cherished that purse. Paul actually liked Lorri, at least from what he had learned about her, but he killed her just the same. He drowned her in her bathtub. He was able to make it look like an accident.

With all the time and energy he spent in choosing and surveilling his victims, Paul came to know them intimately well. He knew their likes, their dislikes, their habits, their possessions. While he didn't personally know Lorri, he knew her well just the same. He did his homework. Lorri never kept money in that purse. She kept it in a dish, on display atop her mantle. He killed her in August of 2007. Eight dollars and seven cents.

Man, he thought. *How long has this guy been on my ass?*

Internally, a storm of panic started to brew at his core. The scope of his adversary's aggression toward him had started to take place and it appeared that he, himself, had been a mark for quite some time.

Paul looked again at the change purse on the table. His mind started to race. He started to calculate the different scenarios by which he could retrieve—or *lose*—that change purse. He stopped himself almost as soon as he started.

Don't be an ass, he thought to himself. *There's no way you'll be able to get rid of that purse. Everyone here has seen it. What are you gonna do? Tamper with evidence now? What the hell is wrong with you? Get it together!*

He looked at the other items on the table so as to not focus on the purse too much. He felt as if he was shaking with frustration and angst but believed that he was hiding his emotions well.

He turned to Agent Chen. "Is there anything else that you can tell us about these killings, or the victims?"

"Nothing more than what I've already told you. They were all killed in different ways and in different locations."

"Well, that's an interesting point." Paul stopped him. "They were all killed in the Midwest as if there were a range or a radius, if you will. So our unsub is probably centrally located in the Midwestern states."

Chen agreed.

"All of them were relatively young ladies, really just getting started in their new lives and new careers," Chen continued.

"It was as if he was preventing them all from becoming," Jacob offered.

"Becoming what?" Agent Chen asked.

"Becoming anything," Jacob answered frankly. "All of these young ladies were just getting their feet wet with regard to the rest of their lives. They were becoming beautiful flowers but this guy plucked them before they got the chance. He's keeping them from "becoming.""

"These women call to him," Paul took the conversation. "There was something about each of these women that made them his targets. Even with Eunice Flowers, the woman who was killed visiting her sister in Little Rock. I bet that she lived somewhere in the Midwest and that she was probably a target long before she was killed."

Chen checked his information. "Flowers was from Michigan. In fact, the entire Flowers family is from Michigan—the sister she was visiting was the displaced one."

"That's what I mean," Paul continued. "Our unsub learned she would be visiting her sister and decided to kill her there. Just as he learned that she would have a fatal allergic reaction to bee stings. Our guy studies his victims. He learns about them. He also has access to them. He learns their habits, where they work, how they live. He has access to their homes and their personal items. He doesn't take these items by chance, he takes them by choice. He's good—and he's dangerous. We've got to stop this guy." Paul's assertion nearly became a plea. He had to watch himself.

"So," Terry jumped in. "Our preliminary profile still holds. Only now we know that he's able to get detailed information on his targets. He studies them as Paul says. There has to be something about him, maybe his occupation, that allows him to learn so much about these women."

"He also needs to be able to get around," Emiliano took the floor. "He's killing these women in different places at different times. Whatever he's doing he has to be able to travel, though his travelling seems to be restricted to the Midwestern states."

"He's also very effective in his killing technique," Dr. Hermanski entered the fray. "He has tailor-made each of these women's deaths. I looked at the wound on Sabrina's body, it was perfectly placed. He used the perfect weapon, whatever it was, to get the desired effect." She shook her head and shivered as a chill ran through her body.

"The thing that gets me is his planning." Emiliano started to pace a little as he talked. "He knew how he wanted to kill Sabrina, and he came completely prepared. There isn't a drop of blood anywhere in her condo, and yet there had to be a lot of blood with the way he killed her."

"And there were no signs of struggle."

"I'm sorry, Paul. Could you say that again?" Emiliano did not quite hear.

"Oh, I was just saying that there were no signs of struggle. Was she drugged?"

"According to the coroner, the toxicology results haven't come back yet. They outsource those exams," Dr. Hermanski answered the query.

"We need those results." Jordan, who had been quiet, listening, took the floor. "The crime scene was immaculate. Sabrina was a healthy girl. For someone who was as guarded and alert as she appears to have been, she would've put up one hell of a fight—if she could. There's something else in play here. There has to be."

Her team was in complete agreement.

"We need to get Sabrina's friends in here," Jordan continued. "We need to track down all of these items. We need to make sure all of these things belonged to her. Jacob, I'm a little curious about the two sets of keys as well. Although, that would seem a little sloppy given the way our guy has handled everything else.

"Terry," she turned to him. "Give that Lacey Schepner a call. Let's see if we can get her in here. Maybe she can identify all of these items and maybe tell us if anything is missing. I also want her to give us all of the information she has on the rest of Sabrina's friends."

"Actually," Agent Chen offered. "We have all of Lacey's contact information from the initial interview. You're welcome to it if you need it."

"Thank you, Agent." Jordan responded. "Please share that with Terry." She looked at Terry and nodded. Terry and Agent Chen gathered to exchange information.

Jordan took the opportunity to share the information with her colleagues that she was able to glean from Tina Burnett. She relayed the story and included the brief description of the stranger. This might be their first actual lead, and Jordan wanted to make sure that this stranger was explored with each of Sabrina's friends when they were interviewed.

Paul acknowledged the lead, but could not prevent himself from focusing again on the change purse. He knew that if any of Sabrina's friends really knew her, they would know that that purse was not hers. That would lead the team to learn who the actual owner was. They would then conclude that the accidental death of Lorri Massey was actually a murder. There are entirely too many arrows that were starting to point into Paul's direction. Things were becoming entirely too much out of his control. He had to stop this, but it was becoming increasingly too complicated for him to find ways how. He needed a breath of fresh air. He started to walk out of the conference room.

"Paul?"

He turned toward the sound of his name and saw Connie standing there. The ashen look had begun to reclaim his face. "I'm okay. I'll be right back. Gonna step outside for a minute."

Paul didn't wait to see her reaction; he simply turned and left the room. He made his way out of the building and on to the street. It was a little chilly as expected for this time of year. Spring was upon them, but the accompanying warmth had not arrived. Paul found the street and started pacing back and forth. For what it was worth, he wanted to recap all of the things he had encountered over the past week or so. He just couldn't fathom how things could have collapsed so quickly and so completely. He attempted to talk himself through it. He had to figure out how someone had gotten to know him so well without him ever having had a clue. He paced and he talked. He worked to gather himself and to get his mind straight.

As he walked, talked, and tried to wrap his mind around things, Paul was completely unaware that he was being observed. As he was making his way out of the building, Connie Jordan was making her way over to a window that covered the entrance into the building. She found one in Captain Lee's office. She looked on as Paul paced back and forth and talked to himself. It was another bizarre behavior. This time, however, Jordan thought things were a little different. Jordan began to suspect that Paul was somehow involved in this case. She didn't know how, or in what capacity. In fact, she didn't have any true basis for her belief. But there was *something*. First at the debriefing in Quantico, and now—something was definitely amiss. Maybe Paul was scared of this guy. From the looks of things, he was starting to scare the willies out of Jordan. But she believed it was more than that. There was a connection. She was sure of it, and she was going to find it.

Chapter Twenty-One

Within the hour, Terry Carter managed to contact Lacey Schepner and retrieve the contact information for Brian Hansen, Mark Lansford, Brooke Balcena, and Trishelle Looney. He was able to contact each of them. All agreed to come in for an interview. Captain Lee dispatched officers to bring them in. Once inside, they were each placed in a different interview room. Terry interviewed Brian Hansen. Emiliano interviewed Mark Lansford. Jacob sat with Brooke Balcena, and Dr. Hermanski spoke with Trishelle Looney. Jordan and Paul interviewed Lacey Schepner—by design. Jordan wanted Paul to take the lead. She wanted to see where his head was. Ms. Schepner was more than accommodating.

"Good afternoon, Ms. Schepner." Paul spoke in a frank, but not unforgiving, tone.

"Good afternoon." Lacey Schepner was still dealing with the death of her best friend.

"I'm Special Agent Andersen. She's Supervisory Special Agent Jordan. We're both with the FBI. The gentleman standing in the corner is Captain Lee of the KCK Detectives Division."

She gave a small wave to the Captain. "Yes, I've met the Captain before. On the day I—on the day I found her."

Paul paused for a moment. "Yes, I understand. We know that finding Sabrina like that must have been a really big shock for you. We're sorry for your loss—and I want you to know that we will do whatever it takes to find and catch her killer."

"I hope so." Her voice was weak and cracking. "Because Breen really didn't deserve to die like that. She never did anything bad to nobody. *Nobody!*" She began to sob weakly. Jordan left the room and returned with a box of tissues. She handed the box to Paul who then handed a few to Lacey.

"Thanks," she said, and immediately began to dry her tears.

"Lacey, was Breen in any kind of trouble? Was she having any problems with anyone?"

"No, no. Nothing. She had a good life. She had a good job. She had a nice place. She had guys that were interested in her. Good guys. No creeps. She was doing fine."

"No problems at work?"

"No, no problems at work. Ask Brian, they worked together. He can tell you. She was doing well on her job. She was making good money. Her clients liked her."

"Okay." Paul paused for a thoughtful moment. He took the opportunity to read Lacey's facial expression. He didn't see anything that indicated she was trying to deceive him, trying to hide something from him.

"What can you tell me about the stranger who asked for directions?"

"Oh—that guy! I forgot all about him."

"What can you tell me about him?"

"He was some creep that stopped Breen in the street to ask for directions. It was kinda weird because where he wanted to go was only, like, two blocks away. Breen said he started to go in the direction she gave him, but then turned off the street to go somewhere else."

"Really?"

"Really. I mean if you're not gonna bother to follow the directions that somebody gives you, why ask for them in the first place?"

"Do you know if she ever saw him again?"

"Actually, I do think she saw him again. That's what made him stand out. The first time was creepy enough, but when she saw him again, that's when she got a little concerned."

"When did she see him again?"

"It was a couple of weeks later. I think she was with Brooke, shopping or something. Ask Brooke, she'll tell you."

"We'll ask her, thanks. What about you? Have you seen this guy?"

"No, I haven't. But I'm sure Brooke has."

"Okay, okay. From what we've learned so far, you were Sabrina's best friend."

"We were both best friends."

"What I'd like you to do, if you don't mind . . ." He turned toward Captain Lee who simply nodded his head. "An officer is going to take you into another room and have you look at some items on a table. These are items that we found in Sabrina's purse. If you would, take a look at these items and let us know if there's anything there that doesn't belong to Sabrina."

Lacey had a puzzled look on her face.

"I know. It's a strange request." Paul tried to reassure her. "We just want to make sure that everything there belonged to Sabrina. It's pretty routine."

"Okay." Lacey shrugged at the request.

"Also," Paul added, "let us know if there's anything missing. Like, if you know of something that she carried with her everywhere that's not on the table, please let us know that too."

"Sure, whatever you need." Sabrina looked at Paul, then at Jordan, finally at Captain Lee. "Is that it?"

Paul turned to Jordan who nodded. "Yes, that's it for now. We'll get in contact with you if we need anything else." Lacey and Paul rose together. "Thank you so much for your help." Paul extended a hand and Lacey took it. Captain Lee opened the door and showed her to a detective who escorted her to the conference room to identify Sabrina's items.

"Good work, Paul." Jordan was genuine in her praise.

"We really didn't get anything."

"No, we got something. There's the possibility that she saw this guy more than once. There's also the possibility that someone else saw this guy, too. It's something."

"Well, I have to say this. If that's truly the case, it was done by design. This guy is too good to make these kinds of mistakes."

"I'm inclined to agree. Let's check on the others."

As they left the office and headed back into the main office, Jordan mentally acknowledged that Paul did a good job with his interview. However, she still could not dismiss the feeling that he was somehow involved.

Paul, on the other hand, could not escape the feeling that he was being framed. He was sure that the change purse would be indentified; Lorri Massey's death would eventually be revisited. He knew that he needed to apply complete due diligence if he was going to catch this adversary before things became too dire.

***

After forty minutes, the entire investigative team was situated in the main office of the Detectives Division. The hour was getting late and the team wanted to go over what they learned before they broke for dinner.

Agent Chen was the first to take the floor. "As you may know, with the exception of a few excursions, I've been working with Agent Nance-Roberge trying to gather any and all media-related information with regard to each of these deaths. Of course, the information is a little uneven—there was some coverage that was a little more complete than others. Unfortunately, there was nothing to indicate that these deaths were related. Most of them flew beneath the radar and rated only a passing mention on a few of the newscasts. But the good thing is we believe that we have all of the coverage, so it's available for review if you need it." Agent Chen relinquished the floor, moved over to the side of the room, and found a seat.

Connie Jordan headed to the front of the room. "We might have found a couple of interesting clues. In our interview with Lacey Schepner, we learned that Sabrina spoke of this mysterious stranger and that she might have seen him more than once. In Jacob's interview with Brooke Balcena, we learned that she might have actually seen this stranger, as well. Apparently, Sabrina and Brooke went window-shopping once and Sabrina caught this stranger's reflection in a store window. She turned to point him out to Brooke, who claims she saw his profile as he turned away. Brooke was able to confirm that the description Sabrina gave Tina on this guy was fairly accurate. So, it's possible that we've got a viable person of interest on this, if we could actually find this guy.

"Now, I must say this." Jordan spoke in a cautionary tone. "Paul made an interesting comment at the end of our interview with Lacey. If this guy was seen by Sabrina—twice—and Brooke as well—he let himself be seen. This guy hasn't made any mistakes thus far, so it's naïve to think that he would allow himself to be seen if he really didn't want to be. He allowed these girls to see him for a reason. We have to figure out why."

She turned to Captain Lee. "How did the item identification go?"

"Well, we'll start with the car keys, because I know that they were items of interest. Both sets actually did belong to Sabrina. One set belonged to her Mazda, and the other set was a spare set for her parents' car. She had a second set of keys to their car, their house, and even to a storage unit that they have rented for years. So, that explains the keys.

"Now, neither Lacey nor Brooke recognized the change purse."

Paul could feel the temperature rise in the room; accordingly, the sweat began to bead on his forehead.

"In fact," the Captain continued, "both ladies told us that Sabrina hated to carry change. Whenever she had change she would dump it in the ashtray of her car or convert them to bills as soon as possible. As far as they were concerned, that change purse was not hers."

"That's odd," Jacob said. "So, in this particular case there are possibly two souvenirs at the one scene. There has to be a reason for that."

"Well," the Captain turned to Jacob, "we don't know if the purse actually belongs to another victim as of yet. We have to check it out. But if it does, it does mean that something was definitely different about Sabrina Burnett's murder."

Jordan was quick with her orders. "Either way, let's get that bagged back up immediately and sent to Quantico for analysis."

"We're ahead of you on that." Captain Lee turned to Agent Jordan. "It's bagged and Tommie Chen has it all ready to go back east."

Jordan looked at Agent Chen and smiled.

"What about anything missing?" Jordan turned back to the Captain. "Was there anything missing from her purse?"

"Actually, there was." The captain's response brought the room to attention. "According to Brian Hansen, who by the way, as far as we can tell, was the last one to see Sabrina alive, he had given Sabrina a friendship ring that she placed in her purse on the day she was killed. Now, this ring wasn't anywhere in her condo. It wasn't in any of her jewelry boxes—it wasn't on her dresser or in her nightstand. It was nowhere to be found. Hansen said he had given her the ring, she tried it on, it fit, and she liked it. She placed it in her purse because she was about to shower and dress before going out to meet Lacey. As far as he was concerned, it should've still been in her purse, and it's not."

The team took a moment to let that sink in. Jordan stepped up.

"Let's get Hansen back in here. Let's find out where he bought the ring and if there's any way we could get a picture of it. If we truly can't find this ring, than I have no doubt that our unsub has taken it. We need to find this ring."

There was a certain tension in Jordan's tone. This unsub was clearly toying with them and she did not like it one bit. She was being mocked. They all were being mocked. They needed to turn the tables on this guy, and they needed to do so fast. She looked sharply at Paul. He knew something. She was sure of it. He seemed to be fully participating in the investigation but she could not suppress her suspicions.

"All right, everybody, it's late. Let's break for the evening. You all have your hotel assignments. I believe the good Captain here has made some transportation available to us."

The Captain nodded. "I've been able to arrange a few vehicles for you."

"Good. Thank you, Captain." She turned back to her team. "You should all have directions to the hotel. The evening is yours. We'll meet here tomorrow at eight-thirty, our usual starting time."

"Connie, do you want to grab some dinner?" Terry asked expectantly.

"No, Terry, you go ahead without me. I have a few things that I want to wrap up before I leave out tonight. You guys go grab something. I'll catch up with you all at the hotel."

On that note, Jordan turned to Captain Lee. "Captain, if you don't mind, may I have use of your office for a few minutes?"

"By all means, young lady." The captain was a complete gentleman.

Jordan left the main office and headed for Captain Lee's office. On her way out, she saw that Paul was already gone. He apparently had received a set of keys for a vehicle and wasted no time heading out. Jordan shook her head and continued on her way. She entered the captain's office and closed the door behind her. She reached for her cell phone and dialed a familiar number. It rang four times before a gentleman on the other end answered the line.

"FBI, Simmons speaking."

"Mickey?"

"Speaking."

"Hey, Mickey, it's Connie Jordan."

Michael "Mickey" Simmons was an administrative officer with the FBI. His responsibilities included tracking and monitoring work assignments. He kept a running record of the B.A.U. team members with regard to where they're assigned and when. This included all trainings, conferences, competencies exams, and so on.

"Hey, Connie. What's up?" His voiced perked up a bit.
"Mickey, I need you to do me a favor."

Jordan, reading from a list of notes she had previously prepared, proceeded to give Mickey Simmons a series of dates and locations. Mickey jotted them down.

"I need you to cross reference those dates with Paul Andersen's assignments schedule."

Mickey was quiet for a moment. "Paul?" He sounded completely confused. "Paul Andersen? *Your* Paul Andersen?"

"Yes, *my* Paul Andersen. Will you do that for me?"

"Well," he was still quite hesitant. "Sure. I can do that for you, but are you sure?"

"Yes, I'm sure." Her tone confirmed it. "Get back to me when you can. Oh, and Mickey . . . "

"Yeah?"

"Please don't let anybody know about it."

"Not a problem. I should be able to get back to you by tomorrow afternoon." Mickey was still in disbelief.

"Thanks. Talk to you then." She disconnected the call.

She held the phone close to her chest and closed her eyes. She could feel her heart pounding heavily in her chest. She had hoped that she was wrong. She needed to be wrong, but there were just too many peculiarities to ignore what was obvious. She opened her eyes and slowly walked back to the main office. She slowly gathered her things; Captain Lee had a vehicle waiting for her. She didn't have much of an appetite but knew she needed to grab something. She decided that she would order room service once she made it to the hotel. All she really wanted to do was to take a long, hot shower. She suddenly felt dirty and she needed the shower to sluice that feeling away. She longed for that shower and, as far as she was concerned, she couldn't take it soon enough.

Chapter Twenty-Two

Paul Andersen made one stop to grab some fast food on his way to the hotel. He needed some time alone, away from everyone else while he tried to put all of these things into perspective. He and his team were piecing together a profile. The unsub was thirty-five to forty-five years old. He was a white male, nondescript; he would probably blend well into a crowd. He was very detail oriented, meticulous, in fact. He spent a great deal of time learning about his targets. He knew them well. He was a proficient killer and unbeknownst to everyone else, he apparently had been stalking Paul for years. He knew Paul well enough to know Paul would return to retrieve that pendant back in Minneapolis.

Paul continued eating, almost as an afterthought. While his hands, mouth, teeth, and tongue went through the motions, Paul's mind rested solely on the events of the day. It appeared that Sabrina Burnett got a look at the guy. It also appeared that Brooke Balcena might have seen him too. Paul made a mental note. Though it was unlikely, the police department might want to grant Brooke some protection. There was no telling what this guy had in store.

It was clear to Paul that this unsub had known all about his murder of Lorri Massey; the stolen change purse was proof of that. It was only a matter of time before his colleagues knew of that murder as well. Her "accidental" death was bound to be re-examined. Paul believed that this killer was centrally located in the Midwest. He had the ability to travel, probably throughout the country, and he had the ability to learn all about his targets.

Just like me, Paul thought. *This guy operates just like me. It's just that . . .* He paused, dreading the impending thought. *It's just that he's a hell of a lot better at it than I am.*

At that thought, he put down his food. That thought had been sneaking around in the shadows of his mind almost since the beginning. It had stayed hidden, lurking from corner to corner, from shadow to shadow; but now along with the realization, the thought had moved from the shadows to the light and its countenance was hideous and grotesque.

Paul wished that there was a way he could have intercepted the change purse, but he had to remind himself that that issue was dead. It was bagged. It was gone. Sooner or later it would get traced back to Lorri Massey. Sooner or later, he was sure, it would be traced back to him. *He* would make sure of that.

And Connie—Paul knew Connie was watching. He knew that if she were to catch on to something she would not let it go. She was the last person he needed on his ass. She was relentless. What he needed to do was to bring this unsub to the surface—bring *him* to light. If he could do that, then Connie would have no choice but to focus all of her attention on him and possibly leave Paul alone. That was the hope anyway.

There were just so many things to consider. So much that seemed to be just going wrong and not nearly enough solutions to all of the problems. He was helpless. He was on an island with nowhere to turn for help. He had to handle all of this on his own. His despair was numbing.

Paul stood up and walked to the center of the room. It was a typical hotel room: a queen-sized bed adorned with a tan, beige and brown comforter set. The room consisted of two side chairs over by a big picture window, separated by a small side table. Against the wall across from the bed was a set of drawers that supported a modest, twenty-four-inch, flat-screen television. Also along that wall was a small desk with chair that granted the occupant free Internet access if he or she so desired. Just off the entry into the room were a respectable sized bathroom to the right and a practical sized closet to the left. On the nightstand beside the bed were a phone and a clock radio that displayed the time two minutes too fast according to Paul's watch. Wanting to break the silence, he headed for the radio to find a local station that he could tolerate, even if it was just for a little while.

Just as he reached the nightstand, he was startled by the ringing of his cell phone, coming from his jacket which was hanging from the back of the chair by the desk. He turned to look at his jacket. He had a peculiar look on his face, it was as if he had never seen that jacket or heard that sound before. He slowly walked over to the desk.

The phone had rung a fourth time before he finally reached into his jacket, retrieved it and answered it.

"Hello?"

"Hey, Paul." It was Layna. "Is this a bad time?"

"Layna!" He was surprised and relieved at the same time. "What's going on? Are you okay?"

"I'm fine. I'm fine. I'm sorry I got your message late. You're on a new assignment, huh?"

"Yeah, I tried to call you to tell you about it, but I couldn't get through. I was starting to get a little worried."

"Oh, I'm sorry. You didn't need to worry. This morning, right after you left, I went to go see my girlfriend. She lives in the sticks just across the line in Maryland. The reception out there isn't very good so it's hard to get cell phone calls."

"Well, just as long as you're okay."

"I'm fine, really. Well, you know I wanted to take the day off, so I figured I'd spend it with my friend Michele and her family. She has a couple of young children, so she doesn't get out much. I just spent the time hanging out with her, talking, laughing, chatting, giggling. You know—silly girl stuff."

Paul could not help but muster a small smile. "Let me guess. You spent some time talking about me?"

"Who? Moi? Nooooo. Believe it or not, I have other things to talk about than *you,* Mr. Andersen." Layna giggled softly. "Actually— I spent the entire day talking about you." She giggled again. "It was a very good day."

"Well, I'm glad to hear it."

"How about you? How was your day? How's the new case coming?"

"It's coming. My day was productive. I work with a great group of people. We made some headway today, I think."

"Well, that's good. Isn't it?"

"Yeah, it's good. But I gotta tell you . . ."

"Tell me what?" Layna spoke in a very bashful tone.

"The best part of my day so far—is talking to you."

"Awww. Really?"

Paul could just imagine the look on her face. "Really."

"So you miss me, hunh?"

Paul was almost embarrassed to admit it. "Yeah, I miss you."

They both were silent for a moment, but unlike, in a previous conversation, this was not an awkward or uncomfortable silence. Paul used the moment to reflect upon how important Layna had suddenly become to him. She actually *meant* something, which was a completely new experience for him. He found comfort in her tone. He found comfort in her touch. He was slowly and quite uncontrollably becoming reliant on her companionship and, to her credit, she was handling it well. With all of the madness that he was presently dealing with, to have an anchor that was as sincere and as real as Layna was, at this time in his life, immeasurable. He knew that no matter what, he had to protect this woman and not allow his madness to creep over into her reality.

Layna took the moment to simply enjoy it. She had had a wonderful day with her girlfriend, talking, almost exclusively, about Paul. Yes, it was early and, yes, there was still so much to learn about each other—but the potential was incredible. She had never really dealt with anyone before who had demonstrated so much potential. It was refreshing. It was enlightening. She simply hoped, beyond all hopes, that it was real. Time would be the real test. Would he be there tomorrow, next week, a month from now? She really did not know. But, she did know that for right now, she was going to simply enjoy the moment and she prayed that this moment would simply go on forever.

Paul broke the silence. "So, what did your girlfriend have to say about me?"

"Not too much." Layna smiled into the phone. "She wants to meet you though."

"Is that so?" Paul was not surprised.

"Yep. Since she is my dear friend, Michele has to approve of anyone that I want to date."

"Really?"

"Yeah. My track record with men hasn't been all that great as of late, so she figured that if I was really thinking about getting serious with someone, she would scope him out first, just to make sure that I wasn't hitching my wagon to a pony that wasn't going in my direction."

Paul chuckled. "She sounds like a very good friend."

"The best. She was there for me when I lost Melissa. She knew how close Melissa and I were. I don't know how I would've made it through without her."

"Did she know Melissa?"

"They'd met on a couple of occasions. They weren't best friends or anything like that but when we all got together, we knew how to have a really good time."

"Hmm. That's cool. I'm still really sorry to hear about the loss of your friend."

"It's all right. With each passing year, I'm getting stronger and stronger . . ." Layna took a moment.

"Anyway," the cheerfulness and vibrancy returned to her voice, "I didn't know you had a key to my house, Paul."

"What?" He sounded genuinely surprised.

"You heard me, young man. I didn't know you had a key made to my house. I guess you snuck it over the weekend."

"Layna, I don't know what you're talking about."

"Yeaaahhh, okaaayy. You knew I was going to find it."

"Find what?" Paul began to become agitated.

"C'mon, Paul, stop kidding. Your little gift."

"What little gift? Layna! Please, tell me what you're talking about!"

"Okay, okay. When I got home this evening, I got my mail, poured myself a glass of wine and was about to have a seat in the living room where I could enjoy it, when I decided to change my clothes. I came upstairs to the bedroom and on the middle of the bed I found the cutest little friendship ring with a note attached to it saying:

"You are mine."

"Now, I thought it was a little presumptuous, mind you. I mean, you know I like you
but . . ."

"Layna!" Paul tried to interrupt. There was clearly panic in his voice.

"Well, I guess you could've left it on the bed when you left this morning and I guess I could've missed it but . . ." She was simply rambling on.

"Layna! Listen to me!" Paul was beside himself.

"What? What's wrong?" A tinge of fear crept into her voice.

"You have to get out of there. You need to go, right now."

"Why? What are you talking about?"

"Listen to me. I can't go into a lot of detail right now, but you need to leave the house immediately. You need to leave and don't come back until it's okay."

"Paul. You're scaring me. What's wrong?" Her fear was slowly becoming fright.

"Layna, right now, I'm working on a very serious case. We're trying to catch someone who is extremely dangerous, and I believe that that person was in *your* house. Now, you need to get out of your house right now and don't come back until I say it's clear. Go back to your girlfriend's house. Don't take anything, just get out. Now!"

"*My* house! Why would he come here?"

"Layna!"

"Okay, I'll go! What should I do about this ring?"

"Get rid of it. Get rid of the ring, and get rid of the note. Just get the hell out of there now, Layna."

"I will." She was clearly flustered.

"Goodbye. Go—no, wait!" Paul nearly disconnected the call. "Listen, while you're at your friend's house I'll need you to think. I need you to think back and recall if you've talked to any strangers lately, anybody that might have approached you with something simple like directions to someplace or anything like that. He would've been an older gentleman in his early to mid-forties. He would've been tall, in decent shape—he might have smelled of cigars or rich tobacco. If you remember seeing or talking to anybody like that, you give me a call from your girlfriend's, okay? Now go, get out now. I'll talk to you later."

Paul disconnected his line. It was then he realized that he was trembling. He was now sure that he *had* seen someone in Layna's home. He was also now sure that this guy had the complete upper hand at every turn and that now, even the peripheral people in Paul's life were in danger.

Paul was filled with rage and nervous energy. He knew that sleep was out of the question. He could only hope that Layna would make it out of the house and over to Michele's without a problem. He would be anxiously awaiting her call. In the meantime, he had to do *something*. He tossed his food into the wastebasket, grabbed his coat and laptop and headed back downtown to the Detectives Division.

Chapter Twenty-Three

When Paul returned to the Detectives Division he found the building nearly deserted. There was no third shift to speak of. Most of the detectives here worked on-call throughout the night. It was a consequence of budget cutbacks that KCK and most other cities throughout the US had had to endure.

He found a relatively empty space at one of the desks. He pulled out his laptop and immediately got to work. He logged into his FBI-issued laptop and began an extensive search. He presumed that Agent Chen was a very competent agent, and considered that this search had probably already been conducted, but Paul wanted to expand upon what had already been done. He wanted to use the present murder pattern, expand the search beyond the Midwest, and go back more than five years.

For the next few hours he searched open case after open case. He searched cold cases and even those that were lukewarm. From coast to coast, and as far back as twenty years, he wanted to find out just how busy his adversary had been—considering he could tie those cases together.

The impetus for Paul's search surrounded murders that might have indicated missing items that have yet to turn up. Paul conceded that it was a stretch. Serial killers took souvenirs; it simply went with the job. He expected that some of these cases would indicate missing items. What Paul wanted to focus on were the types of items that were missing. This killer was very particular. He was cunning, and he was creative. He didn't take panties or locks of hair or shoes or pictures. He took eyeglasses, baby's teeth, friendship rings, birthday cards— items that weren't usually high on the serial killer list of souvenirs.

Paul believed that he could tie murders to this killer by the profile of the victim and the type of items that were missing.

So, he searched extensively to find something, anything that might indicate the mark of this killer; and in time he would. In one case, seven years before, a young woman was murdered in Alabama. She bled to death in her home. She was missing a Christmas ornament, a family heirloom that was never found. In another case, twelve years ago, an even younger woman was killed in Wyoming. Barely out of high school, she'd been her high school valedictorian and the lapel pin she received to commemorate the honor was missing. Her family said she always kept it in her jewelry box and it was gone. In a third case, thirteen years ago, another relatively young lady was killed in Nebraska. She asphyxiated on her own vomit. Initially thought to have been a victim of a cocktail of drugs and alcohol, it was later learned that she was murdered and the deadly substances were introduced into her system by virtue of an injection at the base of her spine, in a place that she could not reach. She'd faithfully kept a diary that had gone missing immediately afterward. There was some speculation that perhaps a jealous ex-boyfriend might have taken it, but there seemed to be nothing that really substantiated that belief. Paul believed that he knew better. He believed that he knew who took that diary.

As Paul continued his search, he found nine cases that he thought belonged to this killer. There was nothing to indicate whether or not there were items at these murder scenes that actually did not belong. It probably would not have occurred to anyone to conduct that kind of search. But Paul felt certain that if he had the opportunity to dig deeper, perhaps examine the inventory lists of each of these crime scenes, that he would be able to find something out of place. He was sure of it.

Paul was inclined to share everything he found with the team, but he knew that he needed more. Many of these cases go back much further than they anticipated. There was simply too much speculation at this point to simply dredge up all of this, with regard to the families and all of the investigators that might have been involved at the time.

Paul leaned back into the chair. He stared at the fifteen-inch screen as if he expected it to talk to him. He was a little unsure of how to proceed. He thought for a moment, closed his eyes. He decided to look at the oldest of the killings. His assumption was elementary. He figured that the earlier the killings, the newer his unsub was at it. He would be less experienced, just finding himself as a killer. Being less experienced, and just getting his feet wet, the unsub might have made some mistakes that, with Paul's experience and skill, could uncover—and perhaps those mistakes could give him a lead with regard to his adversary's identity.

Paul leaned back into his chair when his cell phone rang. He didn't recognize the incoming call's number but he did recognize the area code as coming from Maryland.

He quickly answered the call. "Hello, Paul Andersen."

"Hey, Paul. It's me," Layna said. "I'm at Michele's."

"Good. Did you have any problems getting there?"

"No. No problems. I mean, I'm scared as hell. I really don't know what's going on."

"I know you don't, Layna. I know you don't. Everything is a little crazy right now. But if what I believe is right—if the guy we're looking for was at your house tonight? Getting you out of there was the first thing we needed to do."

"But why, Paul? Why would he come here? Why would he be in my home?"

"Because, this guy is toying with us. He's mocking us, Layna. I don't know what else to say. We're just now understanding how sick this guy really is and he seems to know a lot about us."

"Paul, I'm scared."

"I know. I know. Honestly, I'm a little scared, too. But stay put for now. At least there you'll be away from DC and with people you can trust."

"Yeah, I guess I should be fine here."

"Hey, I'm assuming the number that showed up on my phone is Michele's land line."

"Oh, yeah, it is. That's where you can call me, if you need to."

"Good. Listen, I gotta go. I'm going to do everything I possibly can to catch this guy. You just stay put. I wouldn't even go to work if I were you. Take the week off if you can. In the meantime, I'll keep checking up on you just to make sure you're okay."

"All right. I've got plenty of personal time and there isn't too much going on at the office. I should be able to take the week. Just— call me, Paul. Call me, and please come home as soon as you can."

"I will do my best, darling. You have my word on that."

They both sat silently on the phone a moment before saying their goodbyes. One of the now mounting burdens upon Paul's shoulders had been lifted. Layna was able to make it safely out of the house and to her girlfriend's. He was unsure of just how long this guy's reach extended, and he could only hope that it did not extend as far as the sticks in Maryland.

Paul went back to work, hoping to find mistakes, error of judgments, anything that could lead him to the identity of this killer. As earnestly as he searched throughout the night, he would find none. As the night turned to day, Paul only accomplished in turning his desperation into frustration.

Chapter Twenty-Four

Paul was still working diligently through a magnificent sunrise when KCK personnel started to file into the building. He was so focused on trying to identify the mistakes that he was sure were there, he did not notice that Agent Connie Jordan had arrived. Jordan looked at Paul as he worked at his laptop. He was reading, scrolling, typing, and taking notes and by the looks of his notepad, Jordan surmised that he had been doing all of the above for quite some time.

"Anything good?" she asked, taking him by complete surprise. So much so that when he looked up he nearly pulled a muscle in his neck.

"Oh, Connie. It's you." The butterflies in his stomach collided.

"Yes, it's me. Good morning."

"Good morning. I'm sorry. I had no idea you had come in. What time is it?" Paul looked at his watch. It was seven o'clock.

"Are those the same clothes from yesterday, Paul?"

"Hunh?" Paul looked down at his own attire. Changing clothes had completely slipped his mind. "Uhh, yeah. I didn't get any sleep last night."

"So, I see. Have you been here the entire time?"

"No. Not really. I went to the hotel, grabbed something to eat and was planning to call it a night until I got this little brainstorm. I decided to come in to see how far it could fly."

"And does it?"

Paul had a puzzled look on his face.

"Fly, Paul. Does your brainstorm fly at all?"

"Oh, um, it has wings but not flying just yet. There are a few more things I'd like to check out first. If I come up with something, I will definitely let everyone know about it. It's just a hunch right now, nothing solid."

"All right," Jordan said, pretending to shrug it off. "If it develops into anything, please don't hesitate to share."

"Sure thing."

Jordan turned and walked away. Paul slowly turned his attention back to his notes. Jordan suspected that Paul might be on to something. She was certainly sure that he knew more about this case than he was letting on. Just how much, or in what capacity, she couldn't be sure.

Over the next hour, the daytime members of the Detectives Division and the other members of the B.A.U. began to file in. They exchanged their morning pleasantries but quickly settled down to get to business. Agent Chen was the first to address the room.

"Good morning, everyone." He maintained his military posture. "I have some news that might get us off on the right foot this morning. After we conducted our interviews yesterday, I asked Captain Lee to forward the description of our mysterious stranger to the jurisdictions of some of these other murders, just on the odd chance that we get a hit. It appears that we have. Two of them."

The news added a little energy to the room.

"The Captain has informed me that he has received messages from both Jackson, Mississippi, and Memphis, Tennessee. It appears that friends of Vanessa Hayes, Jackson, and Myla Prentiss, Memphis, have come forward with a description of a mysterious stranger. We don't have any of the particulars as to the nature of these sightings but both claim that the victims had been approached by a stranger that apparently irked them enough to warrant mentioning. There's no mention of any descriptions, so we can't be sure if this is our guy.

"Do you know if any of the vics saw this guy multiple times?" Emiliano called out.

"Not to my knowledge," Chen admitted. "But this is a new line of inquiry. It hasn't been fully explored yet."

"What we need to do," Jordan suggested, "is get a couple of teams down there to these locations. We need to interview these folks. We need to get as much detail from them as possible. Thanks, Tommie."

Jordan turned to the floor. "We need to get to Memphis and to Jackson. We're gonna also need to keep working this case from here. This is the hub."

"Tommie, if you don't mind," she said turning back to him, "I'm gonna send Emiliano to Memphis, and Jacob and Eva to Jackson."

"Fine by me."

"I want our guys to ask some questions. We know what we're looking for better than the authorities there."

Jordan turned to Leisa Nance-Roberge. "Leisa, please work out the logistics with the Captain here and HQ. We might need to get some assistance from the KC branch—work with Tommie if it comes to that. I'd like them to get moving on this as soon as possible."

"No problem," Leisa replied before calling the appropriate agents over to a less populated area of the main room to discuss possibilities.

On her way over to talk with Leisa, Dr. Hermanski asked openly, "Has there been any word with regard to the murder weapon?"

Captain Lee fielded the question. "No, nothing as of yet, although . . ."

"Yes . . .?"

"I received an email from the Weapons Division of the M.E. office last night. I think they've already exhausted their list of weapons, but one of the guys in that office thinks that it might have been a horseshoe spike."

"Pardon?"

"You know, horseshoes are, like, nailed into the hooves of the horses. They use these longs spikes to secure the shoe onto the hoof. It's just a guess right now. They don't really have one of those spikes to actually compare to the wound, but one of those kids down there grew up on the farm and that was his guess. They're gonna look further into it and get back to me."

"Well, if that's the case," Terry said, joining the conversation, "then we're gonna need to get that tox report back."

"I was just about to say that," Dr. Hermanski agreed.

"Yeah," Terry continued, "in order for this guy to use something like a horseshoe spike for a murder weapon, Sabrina Burnett would either have had to be willing, which I doubt, or incapacitated, which I strongly suspect."

"That murder wound at the base of her skull was clean and precise." Dr. Hermanski spoke reservedly. "It appeared to me that whatever the weapon was, it was used in one single, powerful thrust. She would have to have been still for that to have happened. She might have even been unconscious. But I'd like to be sure. Without there being any other trauma on her body, I have to suspect that there was another agent involved to keep her from fighting back."

"Well, I'll get on the horn to see what I can do about expediting that report. You know we outsource those reports?"

"Yes, we know."

"Oh. Well, um, er, yes. I'll see what I can do to get those results back to us pronto." The Captain gave the room a quick nod and headed back to his office and directly to his phone.

Jordan looked over into Paul's direction. She had hoped that he would have something to offer to the group, but he remained silent. She was intent on finding out what his angle on this thing was. She had hoped that she would have an idea before the end of the day.

"If, I may . . .?" Jacob had something to offer.

"By all means, Jacob," Jordan acquiesced. "Please do."

"I think the key to really finding this guy, or at the very least, creating a more accurate profile is by trying to find out how he is learning so much about these women. I mean, look at it this way. There are a lot of occupations that could lead a person to travel extensively, especially within a specific region. A truck driver, a salesperson, a field service tech—any one of those jobs, and probably a couple dozen more, would allow our guy to get around the region and commit these murders. But our guy takes it a step further. He learns about these women. He knows their habits, what they like, what they're allergic to. These are rather intimate details that wouldn't be available to a truck driver or a salesperson. Whatever this guy does for a living, gathering information on people is a part of it."

"Like someone in law enforcement?" Terry concluded.
Jordan stiffened at the suggestion. It was a conclusion that she had been flirting with but had hoped she could avoid. Everything Jacob had to say made sense but she wasn't quite ready to go all the way there just yet.

"Yeah, I guess. I mean something like that," Jacob said. "The different levels of law enforcement have varying levels of access to information, so it's definitely something that we'd need to think through. But I think if we can find out how he's learning so much, we'll have a better chance of nailing down this profile."

Paul remained motionless as the conversation took place. He wanted to remain as stoic as possible as to not allow Connie Jordan to add any more fuel to her now burgeoning fire. Paul knew that sooner or later, the team would be looking at him. That was the plan. Paul realized that that was the plan all along. He needed to throw Connie's suspicions elsewhere. Finding this guy was the only way to do that.

"Jacob," Jordan said, sounding her usual, confident self. "I think you make some valid points. We're gonna have to consider this thing from all angles. How he's learning about these girls is just as important as anything else."

Just as Jordan finished her statement, her cell phone rang in her jacket pocket. She reached for the phone, looked at the incoming number and offered a surprised reaction as she did not expect to receive this call until little later in the afternoon. She excused herself, walked out into the hallway and answered the call.

"Hey, Mickey, it's Connie. Whaddaya got?"

"Connie, I gotta admit that your request sat so uncomfortably with me last night that I decided to run these checks as soon as I got into the office this morning."

"Yeah, I'm really sorry to put you on the spot like that."

"Paul's a good guy, Connie." His voice was almost pleading.

"I know he is, Mickey. Trust me, I do. Now, tell me. What do you have?"

Mickey proceeded to inform Jordan that of the seven dates and corresponding locations, Paul was in the vicinity at the appointed time three times. Of the other locations, Paul was nearby but not at the specified times. He was in those areas either months before or months after.

"Thanks, Mickey, I'll talk to you later." Jordan disconnected the call. She took a moment to think. Paul was on hand for three of these murders. She didn't want to believe. She couldn't. There had to be some other explanation, but it was like she felt before. She did not want to be in a position where she was ignoring the obvious.

She felt compelled to share her suspicions. She needed to get a second opinion on this. She needed to bounce her thoughts off someone else. She needed to know if she had something tangible or whether she was simply off base.

She turned to go back into the main office. She caught sight of Terry and thought that maybe she should confide in him. She had done so in the past; there was no reason why she shouldn't do so now. It was just that everything was so circumstantial.

She walked back into the room. She glanced over at Paul and saw that he was engaged in a conversation with one of the detectives. Leisa, Jacob, Emiliano, and Eva appeared to be finished with their conversation. Jordan had hoped that all the appropriate arrangements had been made. She wanted her folks to talk to those potential witnesses as soon as possible. Terry was having a discussion with Agent Chen. He looked up as she entered the room. The two of them made eye contact, and Jordan tilted her head to the right ever so slightly. Terry, caught the nod, took the hint, said a few last words to Chen, and started to make his way over to her. In just that instant, Jordan decided to share what she suspected. In just that moment, the entire dynamic of her very efficient team was about to change.

Terry reached Jordan's side. They shared a few hushed words and walked out into the hall. Jordan led Terry up the hall until they were able to find an empty office. They entered the office, closed the door, and Jordan talked while Terry listened.

Chapter Twenty-Five

By the end of the day, a few more elements had been established. Emiliano Torres flew to Jackson, Mississippi, and spoke with a few of the friends of Vanessa Hayes; three to be exact. In each of the conversations, he was able to glean the same general description; white man, forty to forty-five years old, six-one to six-two, clean-shaven, well built. None of Vanessa's friends had seen the gentleman but he came up in a conversation after Vanessa reported seeing the man three times. She was uncomfortable with the encounters, so to be sensible, she mentioned it to a couple of her friends. One of her friends, DuJuan Davis had even offered to confront the guy, but Vanessa argued against it. Since it had later become clear that Vanessa was probably murdered, Mr. Davis had become increasingly distraught with the passage of time. This was more than evident when Emiliano talked to him. Mr. Davis was convinced that had he confronted the guy that perhaps Vanessa would still be alive. Emiliano did what he could to dissuade the notion but he was not sure that he was successful. In reality, had Mr. Davis truly confronted this man, he might have become a victim as well; one that might not have been tied to this stranger at all, given the possible circumstances of the death.

Jacob and Dr. Hermanski had similar results in Memphis. They were able to speak with Myla's friends and family and found that she too had mentioned the stranger but she did so only in passing. Myla had seen the gentleman on a couple of occasions but thought he was attractive. She had a penchant for slightly older gentleman and this particular man caught her eye. She had intended on approaching him around the time she was murdered. Her friends made no connection between the gentleman and her death. They simply believed that under no circumstances did she commit suicide; she did not intentionally jump off the A.W. Willis Ave. Bridge. Of this, they were certain and accordingly, Ms. Prentiss's family and friends would not rest until her killer was brought to justice. Jacob and Dr. Hermanski were both very impressed with the dedication this group exhibited. They both could feel the passion and the determination from everyone that they spoke to. They believed sincerely that, at some point, their efforts might actually assist in possibly apprehending their unsub.

In both locations, the agents mobilized the local authorities in an attempt to ascertain whether or not their unsub was still in the area. While everyone concerned believed that it was extremely unlikely, they did not want to leave any stone unturned. This "person" had to lay his head somewhere. There was someplace that he actually called home. It might be in one of these locations, it might not. However, it was extremely important to explore the possibility. As long as everyone kept pressing, sooner or later, someone was going to know this guy and then, the real investigation could begin.

Upon receiving all of this information, Jordan processed everything very carefully. The alleged unsub had been sighted in multiple locations—that could not be a coincidence. She also considered that this particular unsub had been seen by design. He was too good, too cool for it to have been otherwise. She also admitted to herself that these descriptions that the team had been receiving did not fit Paul at all. Sure he was tall, fit, and carried himself in a gentleman-like manner, but every description they received spoke of a man who was older than Paul. They were very consistent on that point. Therefore, they were definitely looking for someone else, but she could not shake the feeling that Paul was somehow involved. Considering he had opportunity on at least three of the murders, she had no intention of shaking that particular feeling loose.

With the way things stood presently, Jordan did not expect her disembarked comrades to return for a couple of days. This was clearly a multi-jurisdictional investigation and coordination was going to be paramount if this operation was going to be effective. For his part, Agent Chen had organized everything extremely well. All of the contacts were in place and the communication network he had established proved to be working quite efficiently. When her agents landed in their assigned locations, the local authorities were waiting and the prospective witnesses had already been corralled. There was nothing like efficiency as the backbone of an investigation.

Meanwhile, Captain Lee created a temporary workspace for Jordan. She was using an office that was normally assigned to a duty sergeant. It wasn't much to speak of; it was small with a single metallic desk that had probably been in use for the past forty years. There were two wooden chairs that faced the desk, each looked to have been repainted, reupholstered and reincarnated many times over before they landed in this room. They were pieces of paper taped to various places on the walls. Some were copies of pictures; others appeared to be old assignments going as far back as six years. There were a couple of calendars posted and a few other things that Jordan took very little interest in. The bottom-line however was that the office served its purpose. It gave Jordan the privacy she needed, when she needed space, quiet, time to think.

Of course, the case was taking its toll. There was a monster loose in the heart of America and at least seven jurisdictions were working together to bring him down. But, Jordan feared that she had a monster of her own right underneath her nose. She shared her fears with Terry Carter, her right hand man, her second in charge, her confidante, her friend. Terry listened intently; he didn't have much to offer. He did, however, assure Jordan that he, too, would keep an eye on Paul and take note of any strange behavior that he might observe.

He admitted that Paul's whereabouts, on at least three of the deaths, were intriguing but he wanted to caution Jordan against reading too much into things. Paul was a good kid, but he was interesting; strange in fact. His odd behavior could be the result of any number of things, but Terry conceded that he could see why she would be concerned. So, with that, he promised to keep a second set of eyes on Paul and together maybe they could get to the bottom of things.

Paul Andersen was in the main office working on his laptop, determined to link some of these other cases to their present investigation. He had uncovered some definite similarities but as far as he was concerned none of it was strong enough to bring to Jordan—at least not yet. In the middle of a thought regarding the possibility that their unsub was in fact a member of the law enforcement community, Paul's cell phone rang. He looked at the number and this time he recognized it as being from Layna's friend Michele's residence. He answered the line.

"Hey, Layna." He spoke in a hushed tone.

"Hey, Paul. You got a minute?"

He could hear the worry in her voice. "Yeah, I have a few minutes. What's wrong?"

"Paul, I'm just really scared. I really don't know what to do. The more I thought about some creep coming into my house, the more all of this scares me." The fear was evident in her tone. "Why, Paul? Why would this man want to come into my house? What have I done?"

"It's not you, Layna. It's me."

"You? How is it you?"

"This guy . . ." Paul was really unsure of how to proceed. "This guy has been playing with us. Sending messages, leaving notes, that kind of thing."

"But how does he know about me, Paul?"

"I don't know, Layna. I guess he's been tracking me. All I can tell you is that we're doing everything we possibly can to catch this guy."

"But, Paul," Layna sounded at the point of exasperation. "How are you gonna find him out there in Kansas, if he's here in DC?"

Paul pondered for a moment. That very question had been bouncing around in his head for a few hours. He also believed that the unsub was presently back east. He had hoped that if he could find something perhaps he could persuade Jordan that she needed to send the team back home. But as far as Jordan was concerned, Sabrina Burnett was the latest victim; this location was the freshest. He would need something concrete to pull the team away from this location and back to Virginia.

"This guy gets around, Layna." It was the best explanation he could provide. "He travels a lot. Even though I wanted you to leave your house, it's quite possible that he has moved on to his next location."

Layna accepted the explanation but it did very little to ease her anxiety. "I don't know, Paul. I'm scared. I think he's still here. I went shopping with Michele a little earlier. While we were out I checked the messages on my cell phone. One of my neighbors called me. He complained that a lot of noise was coming from my house. He said he tried knocking on my door but that I didn't answer. He thought I was being rude, that I was ignoring him."

Panic crept into the edges of her voice. "Paul, I wasn't even there. Please, Paul. Look, I don't want to be a pain in the ass. I really don't. But I need you to come back. I'm scared and I really don't know what to do."

Paul could hear the sincerity of her plea. She was genuinely and legitimately scared. In fact, if she knew how truly dangerous this guy was, she would be absolutely frightened. Paul needed to get back.

This guy was back east and if he planned on doing something, *anything* to Layna, Paul wanted to be there to set things straight.

"Layna, please just stay put. I'll see what I can do about getting back home. But, I need you to stay with Michele. Just stay there until I can figure something out. Okay?"

"Okay. I mean, I really am trying to keep it together."

"I know you are. I know that you weren't expecting any of this. Quite honestly, neither was I. I really don't know what to say about all of this. All I can tell you is that I'm with you. I will find away to make things as safe as possible for you. Okay?"

"Promise?" she said through the tears.

"Promise."

Paul disconnected the line and leaned back onto the chair. He had to find a way to get back home; get back to Layna. He needed to find out what this guy was doing in her home. He thought for a moment. There was no way he was going to be able to convince the team to go back. He arrived upon an idea. He could only hope that it would be enough to make it past Jordan.

He rose from the chair and walked cautiously to the office that Jordan was now occupying. He looked in and she was busy writing. He knocked on the door and poked his head in.

"Connie, can I talk to you for a minute?"

Jordan looked up from her notes and squinted her eyes just a bit. The office had no window so it was devoid of natural light. Occasionally, purely artificial light did a number on her eyes.

"Yeah, Paul. Come on in. What's up?" She put the pen on the desk and leaned back into the relatively uncomfortable chair.

Paul slipped into the office and down into one of the even more uncomfortable chairs facing the desk. "I was thinking . . ." he started slowly, his voice nearly wavering. "about some of the things we talked about before."

"Yes," Jordan was very intent on hearing everything that Paul had to say.

"Well, I'm having some personal issues back home."

She waited.

"I have this . . . uh . . . friend. And, um, things started off pretty well, but now things have gotten . . . a little, uh, complicated."

"Okaayy."

"I know we're not supposed to let our personal lives interfere with our professional lives, and you know that this has never been an issue with me before."

"This is true," Jordan conceded. "I've never had any kinds of issues with you before, Paul—on any level."

"Well, I really need to straighten some things out, clear my head a little bit. You know I've hardly taken any personal time since I joined the Bureau, let alone the B.A.U."

"Yes, I'm aware that you have a great deal of time on the books."

"I know this is really bad timing. I know that we're in the middle of something very heavy right now, but I'm just . . ." He bowed his head a little, placed both hands along the side of his face and began to rub his temples with his fingers. "I'm just out of it right now. Every time I think I have something, it just doesn't seem to fit. I need a little time. Not much, a few days maybe. Just enough time to recharge my batteries a little bit."

Jordan looked at Paul thoughtfully. There was no escaping the timing of this request. There was no escaping that something was definitely amiss where Paul was concerned. He wanted to get out of Kansas for a reason. She wanted to know why.

"Paul, I told you before that I thought something was a little off. You need to take some time for yourself. Of course, we need you on this case, but it's like I said before, you're really no good to me if you're not working on all cylinders. Go ahead. Take a few days. Take the rest of the weekend. At the rate we're going, we're gonna still be out here come next week. You can come back to us then, fresh and ready to go."

Paul was surprised at how understanding Jordan appeared to be. She had implied previously, that he might need a break. Maybe she was pleased to see that he was finally taking her up on her suggestion.

"Now, I don't know if I can authorize a flight back home for personal reasons . . ."

"No, that's okay," Paul rushed his response. "I can catch a commercial flight. That's not a problem. I should be able to find something that's headed my way."

"All right. You're sure that this is what you want to do?"

"Actually, no. I'm not. But I am sure, that this is something that I need to do."

"Well, that's good enough for me. Talk to Leisa on your way out. Maybe she can help you with the arrangements. One way or another I hope to see you first thing next Monday, okay?"

"Yes, ma'am." Paul paused for a moment. "Thank you, Connie. I know that this was inconvenient for you. But thank you very much."

"No problem, Paul. Now, get out of here, before I change my mind. I'll see you next week."

Paul rose from the chair. He truly was grateful for Jordan's compassion. He gave her a weak smile and then left the office. He went back to the desk and gathered his things. Jordan had risen from her seat and slowly followed Paul into the main office area. She watched as he collected his belongings and then made his way over to Leisa Nance-Roberge.

Jordan caught the eye of Terry, who had been huddled with Agent Chen and Captain Lee. She tilted her head in Paul's direction and Terry subtlely glanced toward Paul. Terry was not sure of exactly what was transpiring but he was sure that Jordan would bring him up to speed later.

With the assistance of Leisa, Paul was able to make arrangements to be on the next flight to DC. On his way back to the hotel to get his things, he made a call to Layna. He informed her that his plane would be leaving in about an hour and that he wanted her to meet him at the airport. He really wanted to see Layna, not simply so she could feel a little more secure that he was back home, but for his own gratification. He needed to make sure that she was okay—that she was safe. He couldn't get home quickly enough.

Back at the office, Jordan told Terry about Paul's request. Terry was surprised that Paul would make such a request in the middle of such an intense investigation. He started to feel that Jordan was onto something, that this particular request was a little too convenient. Jordan wanted to expand her search into Paul's activities. She had already managed to learn that of the seven cases they were presently investigating, Paul was in the area for three of them. Now, she wanted to know more. Now, she wanted to dig deeper. With Paul actually away, she could dig with a little more freedom and without the fear of alerting him to her suspicions.

"Terry," she began, "this is what I'd like you to do."

On the heels of the information that Jordan had shared with regard to Paul, she wanted Terry to get a list of all of the assignments Paul had been on since he had joined the Bureau. Once Terry was able to determine when and where Paul had been in his six-plus years of service, she wanted him to cross reference that information with any unsolved murders that might have occurred during those times. He was to look for any cases that might bear the same markings as the cases they were looking into in this investigation.

"Now, wait a minute," Terry objected lightly. "We do have a description of our possible unsub, and accordingly to the people we've talked to, this guy doesn't look anything like Paul."

"I know, I know. I recognize that there's a discrepancy there. But look into it anyway. I need to know."

Jordan stared at Terry for a moment, and then said, "Look, I want to be wrong. Hell, I need to be wrong." She shook her head and looked away. She stared at the copy of a picture of a 1957 Chevrolet that was taped to the wall across the room. "It's just that I don't think that I'm wrong."

Terry followed Jordan's gaze to the car. "Okay. I'll look into it. I know about you and your intuition. I'll grant that over the years it's proven to be real accurate. But I guess there's a first time for everything."

Jordan chuckled. She turned back to face Terry. "What do you mean?"

"Well, for the first time that I can remember, I am actually hoping that you're wrong."

Terry dipped his head a little, turned and left the room. He would call and speak to Mickey about getting the rest of the dates. Since Paul had not spent his entire time with the B.A.U., Mickey would probably need a couple of days to create a complete list starting from day one. Afterwards, Terry would need to log onto the FBI database and make the appropriate calls in order to track down all of the open cases that occurred during those specific dates. This assignment was going to take a while, but Terry suspected that it needed to be done. Connie's nose for things like these was uncanny. Though, he wanted her to be wrong, he was inclined to believe that she was right. She almost always was.

Connie stood in the middle of the small office for a little while before making it back to her seat. She sat down and looked at the last note she had written. While she had Terry working on Paul's assignments since he had joined the Bureau, Connie decided that she wanted to go back a little further. She had Human Resources fax her Paul's personnel file. She was in the process of creating a list of all of the places that the HR office could provide with regard to his pre-Bureau life. This included his collegiate life, high school, prior work experience, and so on. The application process to the FBI was extensive and Jordan was using that information to track Paul's whereabouts as best she could. She would then take those locations and dates and do exactly what Terry would be doing: cross reference them against open cases or any cases that were similar to what they were dealing with now. Most serial killers started young. And when they started and got their feet wet, so to speak, they often made mistakes. Connie Jordan was going on a mistake hunt.

Chapter Twenty-Six

It was late afternoon when Paul's flight landed in Virginia at the National Airport. Since he only had a carry-on bag, he was able to eschew the laborious ritual of going to baggage claim and wading through the passengers as everyone sought to grope for their own luggage like hungry tigers during a feeding frenzy. He made his way over to the pick-up area and initially did not see Layna. He had never seen her car, so he was unsure of what vehicle he should be looking for. He heard a series of car horns, each one grabbing his attention, as he wanted to make sure that he didn't miss seeing her in the sea of waiting autos.

He ducked and weaved between his fellow travelers trying to make himself as visible as possible when he heard a familiar voice come from just behind.

"Looking for me, soldier?"

He spun, looked, smiled and said, "Absolutely."

Layna thrust herself at Paul who instinctively engulfed her in his arms. They held each other tightly, so much so that Paul could actually feel Layna's tension ease in the midst of the embrace.

"It's okay," he whispered in her ear. "Everything will be okay."

He held her by the shoulders and pushed her away to look at her face. As he suspected, she was crying. He used the back of his right hand to wipe her tears away.

"Button up, sweetie. I'm home now. Why don't we get out of here?"

"Yeah, sure. I'm parked right over here. Actually," she sounded almost naughty now. "We should probably hurry before I get a ticket."

S. E. Robinson

Paul smiled and both trotted through the crowd to Layna's mint-green 2008 Volvo S40. Having tossed his bag into the back seat, he entered the passenger side of the vehicle and secured the seatbelt. He then turned to Layna with a smirk on his face.

"Nice car," he said.

"It's okay." Layna was being modest. "It gets me around."

"I'm sure, I'm sure."

"Where to?"

"Well actually, I need to go home first to take care of a couple of things. Then, if you don't mind, I want to get your keys. I want to go by your house and see what's going on there. If this guy has been there, and especially if he's made a mess, I'd like to know why."

"Sure."

Layna took her keys out of the ignition. She removed the house keys from her ring and handed them to Paul. "Here are the keys. This is the top lock." She pointed to one key. "And this one's for the door handle," she said, pointing to the other.

Paul made the appropriate mental notes. "Okay thanks. I live in Alexandria which really isn't that far."

"I tell you what." Layna replaced the ignition key and started the car. She got out of the car and trotted around to the passenger side. "You drive. You know the way."

Paul acknowledged the logic in the reasoning, got out of the car and made himself comfortable behind the wheel. Within moments they were on their way.

Twenty-five minutes later, they pulled into the parking lot of his condo complex. He turned to Layna.

"Listen, I want you to go straight back to Michele's."

"Can't I come up?" she asked, mildly disappointed.

He shook his head slowly. "Under normal circumstances, it wouldn't be a problem. Trust me." He tried to be as reassuring as possible. "But right now, I don't want to risk it. I want you safe, and right now, I think Michele's is the safest place you can be."

Although she would have liked to spend at least a little time in Paul's home, Layna did not argue.

"Okay. I understand."

"Just go. Stay with Michele." Paul got out of the car, reached into the back to retrieve his bag, and through the driver's side door said, "Give me a call when you get there. Let me know that you're all right."

"I will. I promise." Layna slid across the center console from the passenger seat and into the driver's. She readjusted all of the accessories and looked at Paul. She was unable to hide the sadness in her eyes. She closed the door and blew Paul a kiss from the window. Paul looked at her thoughtfully and placed a hand against the window. Layna matched the action with her own. Paul turned from the car and headed in. He listened intently as Layna pulled out of the spot, turned her car around, and headed back to Michele's. He wanted to turn and watch her leave but he didn't dare. He needed her away—with no reason to linger any longer than she should.

Paul hastily made his way into his unit. He dropped off his bag and headed straight for his bathroom. He took a quick shower and prepared to get dressed, when he looked around. He had the sneaking feeling that something was different. He couldn't put his finger on it but something seemed amiss. He looked around his condo as he got dressed. He tried to uncover anything that might either be misplaced or missing. He couldn't find anything. Not wanting to shrug it off, he finished dressing. He needed to get over to Layna's; he couldn't waste too much time here.

Paul grabbed his jacket, his weapon, and his car keys. He got behind the wheel and headed directly for Layna's house. Using the keys she gave him, Paul entered the home. He took note that both locks were engaged, as expected. He would've been concerned if they were not. He stood still in the foyer, looked, and listened. He didn't see anything that appeared out of place. He didn't hear anything at all. He reached for his weapon and made sure that the strap on his holster was free. He moved into the living room, then the dining room, finally the kitchen. Everything looked to be in place. Everything looked the way it did when he stayed for the weekend. Layna's neighbor complained about a lot of noise coming from the house. If a lot of ruckus took place in here it must have taken place upstairs, because everything was perfectly fine downstairs.

Paul used the main hallway to exit from the kitchen and to re-enter the foyer where the main stairs were. He relieved his weapon of its holster and slowly took the stairs, one at a time, back up against the wall, and weapon out in front; he was poised for any eventuality. He reached the second floor and again he stopped, looked, and listened. Again, nothing. There were three bedrooms and a main bathroom on this floor. Paul decided to start from the rear and move forward.

The rear bedroom was a guest room. It was neatly furnished with a queen-sized bed, two nightstands, a dresser, and a small television. There were a few knickknacks that were spread throughout the room to give it some character. From the look of the room, it was rarely used. Paul could see nothing that was obviously out of place. He headed for the next bedroom.

Layna used the middle bedroom as a hobby room. She liked to knit, crochet, and sew. All of the materials and utensils she used for each of those vocations could be found in this room. She had swath upon swath of materials, a multitude of threads, pattern books, and clip-outs. There were so many small items in the room that Paul wanted to make sure that he made a thorough visual sweep. He entered, looked around carefully, slowly. He saw nothing that gave rise to concern.

The next room was a full bathroom. Paul looked in and gave it a quick once-over. Again, he saw nothing but an immaculately kept room with everything seemingly in place.

The front room on this floor was Layna's bedroom. It was the biggest bedroom in the house. It was warmly furnished; Paul recalled the first night he spent in the room. The canopy bed, the sitting area in the alcove by the bay window, all of the matching mahogany furniture that he thought probably cost more than all of the furnishings he had in his entire unit. On the night Paul first entered this room, he felt as though he had travelled back in time and was about to spend the night in the bedroom of Queen Elizabeth II. Everything in this room was impressive, well kept, and well cared for. Paul took his time scanning the entire space. Everything was as he recalled. Nothing moved. Nothing changed. He looked at Layna's bed and imagined where the ring and the note might have been positioned on the bed. A swell of anger began to grow. He turned and left the room.

He looked up the stairs toward the third floor. There were two more bedrooms and yet another bathroom up there. Again, he placed his back securely against the wall, pulled his weapon into position, and slowly took the stairs one at a time. After thirteen steps he reached the third-floor landing. Again, he decided to start in the rear. He entered the rear bedroom; it was a room that was generally used for storage. Inside, there were some boxes and some bags neatly arranged. Paul looked at each item closely. He wondered if he should go through the contents of each box. He didn't want to take that time without first making sure the entire residence was clear.

He left the room and entered the bathroom. This bathroom was slightly smaller than the one on the second floor, but it was just as clean. Layna was an exceptional housekeeper; every room was well kept, well furnished, and equally inviting.

The front bedroom was another guest room. Like the guest room on the second floor, this bedroom was modestly, but practically furnished. All of the items therein were well coordinated. The matching cherry bedroom set looked cozy, although not frequently used. Paul looked through the room thoroughly and concluded that the room was relatively undisturbed.

Paul replaced his gun in its holster. He stood erect in the center of the room and took a deep breath. He didn't find anything that would lead him to believe that the unsub had been in the house or had done anything to create all of the noise that was claimed to have been made. It belied the fact however, that he *had* been in the house. The ring and the note were evidence of that. Paul had to take a moment to reflect upon his own actions—how he prepared and did his research. Before all of his kills, Paul had done extensive preparatory work. He had scoped the living spaces of all his victims, unbeknownst to them. He was able to learn a great deal about his victims as he foraged through their personal items, but replaced everything so neatly, so perfectly, that everything seemed perfectly undisturbed. He had every reason to believe that the very same thing occurred here. Whatever secrets this home held with regard to Layna, the unsub had uncovered them.

Paul calmly left the bedroom and started to head back downstairs when he suddenly banged up against the wall as if he had been shot from the side. He had just realized what had been amiss at his home. He had just realized what was wrong, what was *missing*. Before Paul left for Kansas he had gone home to collect his travel kit. Since he had just cut his hand earlier in the morning, he changed his bandage to keep it fresh. He tossed the old bandage in the wastebasket. But when he returned home from Kansas the wastebasket was empty. It should not have been. He didn't previously empty that basket, so the bandage should have still been there.

"Damn it!" he cried aloud. The unsub had been in his home. He had taken the bandage and now, he had Paul's DNA. Paul's anger was getting the best of him. He was behind this guy at every turn, but nothing he seemed to do was enough to catch up.

"Oh, shit!" Paul stopped again at another realization. If the unsub had managed to enter his condo and take something that could easily implicate him in another murder, there was no telling what he might have actually planted there as well.

Paul started down the stairs taking two at a time. He reached the bottom landing and just before he swung the door wide his cell phone rang. He looked at the number: Maryland area code. It was Layna.

"Layna, what's up?"

There was a small silence on the other end of the line.

"Hello?" Paul spoke again. "Layna?" He heard breathing on the other end of the line. In the background Paul could faintly, but assuredly hear Layna's voice ask someone if they would like a cup of coffee. He then heard, with a little more clarity, a raspy male voice decline the offer. Then that same male voice spoke into the phone.

"I told you she was mine. Now, *she* will pay."

Paul could hear Layna's voice grow louder as she asked the man if he preferred tea instead.

"*Layna!*" he screamed into the phone, but the line was suddenly dead. Paul was in complete panic. *He* was there. Paul rushed out of the house and into his car before he realized that he didn't know where Michele actually lived. He tried to search his memory of any mention of where Layna was staying but nothing came to mind. He had Michele's phone number, but not the address. He was so anxious to get moving that he was actually trembling. He was experiencing fear and rage at the same time. It was an emotional mix that did not blend well. With difficulty, he dialed assistance on his cell phone and using his credentials, he requested a reverse directory to ascertain Michele's address. After a few moments, he got the information he needed, cranked the car, and headed for Maryland throwing caution and traffic laws to the wind along the way.

Chapter Twenty-Seven

Back in Kansas City, a few significant turns had dramatically changed the direction of the investigation. Over the course of the previous few hours, Agent Jordan had received some of the information she requested with regard to possible links between the current case and absentee agent Paul Andersen. Jordan had already been able to establish that, via various events, Paul was in the area during three of the seven identified murders. Jordan requested that Agent Terry Carter, her right-hand man, look into all of the assignments Paul had received since joining the Bureau and cross-reference them with any cases that might possibly be connected to the present investigation.

It did not take long before Terry found a hit. As recently as the previous week, while they were in Minneapolis, a promising young lady, a nurse, was found brutally murdered in her own home. It was an extremely bloody scene; the victim, Amy Brandenburg, died from a slit throat. According to some of her family and friends, there was an item taken from Amy's person, a pendant that she allegedly wore everywhere. It was something small, yet significant. Just the type of item that the killer would take as a souvenir. Just the type of item he would enjoy placing around the neck of another victim. The worst thing, at least where Paul was concerned, was that there was video. Paul was actually recorded leaving the complex—then returning and leaving and returning and leaving again.

In the video conference room of the Detectives Division, Agents Jordan, Carter, and Nance-Roberge sat and viewed the video. Agents Torres and Lynch, and Dr. Hermanski were away on assignment but en route to return to KCK, to regroup and address these new developments.

"I just can't believe this," Leisa Nance-Roberge said, shaking her head as she sat with her gaze glued to the monitor.

"None of us can." Terry stood in front of the desk he'd been sitting on and began to pace around the room.

"I knew he was acting strangely." Jordan was actually talking to herself despite the fact that everyone else in the room could hear. "I *knew* he was acting strangely, but this? I really didn't think . . . it was like this."

Terry turned back to the front of the room.

"So, this is what we have. We know he had opportunity during the Susan White, Katana Lopez, and Paige Traxler murders. He was in each of those vicinities during the times those ladies were killed. We also know that he was available during the Brandenburg murder because we were all there last week when that happened. Now, personally, knowing what I know of Paul I would still need more than this before I'm ready to pin a murder on him, but this video hurts. It gives us the time, and it shows that he was definitely there."

He turned to Jordan. "There's no way around this. We've got to bring him in. If he's got any brains whatsoever, he knows that sooner or later we were gonna catch up to him. He has to know this."

"Maybe this is why he asked for leave?" Jordan asked.

"Maybe. We can't be sure. But we have to talk to him. You need to make a call, Connie. You gotta bring him in. You gotta hold him."

"You're right. I've already called his cell a couple of times, but I've been unable to reach him."

"Call HQ." Terry was firm but insistent. "We have to go get him, Connie."

"Wait a minute, wait a minute," Leisa chimed in with more than a hint of confusion in her voice. "What about the descriptions we

265

have? They've all been pretty consistent and they definitely do not match Paul."

"I'm inclined to agree," Jordan said softly, trying to overcome the empty feeling that had invaded her body. "But, it's possible that Paul and this guy might be working together. I'm thinking that maybe they take turns doing the actual killings. That Paul might have been using some of the resources that we have available to us to research all of these victims and then pass that information on to our unsub—or something along those lines. I mean, I know we can't tie all of these killings to Paul, but we can establish that these cases are linked by virtue of the souvenirs. They had to be transferred to these other victims some way. These guys are working together."

"All this time?" Leisa was in disbelief.

"All this time," Terry said with conviction. "I looked at his assignment record and did some research and while there weren't murders in all of his travel assignments, there were enough to make me believe that a conversation was in order. And I'm talking about going back all of his six-plus years with the Bureau."

"Well, it might go back even further than that," Jordan offered. "Some field work will be required, but I believe that Paul might have started his activities before he joined the Bureau. Maybe even as far back as his college days. I can't be sure, but there are a few mysterious deaths there that might require a closer look."

"Then you know what we need to do." Terry continued to be firm.

Jordan reached for her cell phone to call Quantico. She activated the speed dial function on her phone and pressed the number 1.

"What is he doing?" Agent Roberge called everyone's attention back to the video. "What's wrong with him?"

S. E. Robinson

By virtue of technology, they were emailed the video stream from Lieutenant Brennan and the Minneapolis Police Department. It was then a simple matter to patch the video into the video conference room. As they continued to scan the video, they were able to see Paul first leave the courtyard in a calm and relaxed fashion. But his subsequent arrivals and departures grew increasing more frantic. It looked as if he was losing his mind every time they actually saw him on the video.

"I don't know," Jordan said honestly. "I wondered about that too. He looks worse and worse every time you see him on the video. And this last time . . ." Jordan walked closer to the monitor. "The last time, he's almost limping to the truck and he pulls away like he's wounded or something." Jordan looked at the end of the video clip again. "It's all just very strange."

"We just need to talk to him." Terry was unrelenting.

Jordan pulled out her cell phone again and this time followed through with the call. She spoke with her special agent in charge and shared the key points of her investigation with him. She did not speak in a definite terms, but she impressed upon the SAC the necessity of detaining her subordinate agent. While he was hesitant, at least in his voice, he agreed that Paul was due for a conversation. He agreed to dispatch a couple of agents to secure Paul for the team's return to Virginia.

"Done." Jordan closed her cell phone and turned back to the room. "Leisa, our wayward team members are due within the hour, correct?"

"Yes, in approximately fifty minutes," she said, looking at her watch.

"This is what I want to do. When they get back here I want you guys to continue to work the case. Terry, I want you with me. We're going back to Virginia. We're going to have that conversation with Paul."

Jordan turned to Leisa. "Please make the arrangements to get the plane prepped and ready. I want to head out as soon as possible."

"No problem. I'll get right on it."

"Terry, let's get this video burned to disc. I want to bring a copy with us back to VA. I want it handy when we sit down and chat with Paul."

"Sure thing," Terry said, and immediately left the office to look for a tech.

Jordan and Leisa shared a worried glance. Neither of them wanted to believe what they had seen, but they knew what needed to be done. Paul was clearly involved. To what extent, they couldn't be certain—but they needed to get to the bottom of it, and more importantly, get this unsub off the street. This was the most dangerous perpetrator this team had ever pursued. The sooner they could get him behind bars, the better.

Leisa left the room, leaving Jordan to stare at a repeat of the video. While the quality of the video was pretty good, it wasn't as if they could see all of the features of Paul's face. However, due to his overall build, the way he moved, and they way he was dressed, they were completely confident that the man in the video was Paul. As Jordan continued watching, even after the last time Paul left the scene, she saw a man walk out of the courtyard. There was nothing significant about the man save for the fact that he appeared to look directly at the camera. Jordan stopped the feed, rewound it a bit, and watched the man again. The man seemed a bit out of place, but not much more than that.

"But that could be anybody," she wondered aloud. "I wouldn't be surprised if a lot of the residents did that with the newly installed system." It was almost natural, she thought. She shrugged as the clip came to an end.

Whenever the B.A.U. came close to apprehending a suspect, there was a certain type of excitement that permeated throughout the entire team. It was more than a feeling of accomplishment. It was more than a feeling of relief. It was a satisfaction that encompassed myriad feelings, not the least of which included making the streets a little safer than they were the day before. This feeling, however, was different. This feeling included a great deal of conflict. This feeling included a hint of regret and almost a tinge of guilt. It was uncomfortable. It was uneasy. Jordan needed to get rid of this feeling as soon as possible, but the only way to do that was to sit down and have a nice long chat with Paul.

She couldn't wait.

Chapter Twenty-Eight

Paul used the GPS system in his BMW to get directions to Michele's house. He was unfamiliar with the area and he didn't need any distractions that would prevent him from getting there as soon as possible. The caveat, however, was that when using a GPS, especially in rural areas, the directions weren't always exact. Paul decided that the directions didn't need to be exact. He simply needed to be in the area. Once in the area, he would try to find Layna's car and that would lead him to Michele's house.

Paul wasted no time leaving DC and heading into Maryland. According to his information, Michele lived approximately forty minutes away. Putting the pedal to the metal, Paul made it in less than thirty.

Michele and Chad Finley lived in a non-traditional cul de sac. It was circular as one would expect, but very large in circumference; nearly a hundred and fifty feet. There was a center island that had an array of bushes and flowers that gave the area an almost tropical feel. There were only three houses in the area, one on either side of the drive, with the third one at the rear. They were large homes, each boasting a significant amount of land that was well maintained and led back behind the houses to a more wooded area that truly added to the feel of being in the "sticks." As for isolation, the next set of neighbors was nearly a mile away.

The Finleys lived at the house at the far end of the drive. Paul turned off his headlights and could see that the house was completely dark. He could not see any movement. All the window shades and curtains were drawn, and there didn't appear to be any activity taking place behind them; but he could see Layna's car parked behind two others in the side driveway. Paul slowly pulled up to the front of the house. He pulled out his phone and used the call back feature to dial the Finley home. The phone rang—no movement, no pick up. He dialed Layna's cell and the call went straight to voicemail. Nothing there either.

He parked the car and killed the engine. He exited his car with his weapon drawn and the safety off. The first thing he intended to do was make a perimeter sweep of the house. Slowly, steadily, and with extreme caution, Paul completely circled the house. Each time he passed a window he ducked down to remain completely out of view. He did not want to be seen. He didn't know if anyone would be peeking from behind those curtains. He didn't want anyone to know he was there—at least not yet.

Once satisfied that the perimeter was clear, Paul decided he would try to enter. Along the left side of the house was the driveway where the three vehicles were parked. There was a door on that side of the house. Paul presumed that this was probably the main entry and decided to give the door a try.

Paul moved cautiously, walking closely beside the house. He peered into each vehicle as he passed by just to make sure that they were empty. He reached the door, crouched down, and listened. He didn't hear a thing: no talking, no television, no music, nothing. He didn't like the sound of it. He reached for the screened security door and pulled it open. It was not locked. He pulled the retracting door behind him so that it came to rest up against his rear, and while still crouching, reached for the main door to try the handle. It too was unlocked. Paul turned the handle and the mechanism worked free. He gave the door a small push, and it smoothly opened at a slow but steady rate. As the door continued to open, Paul eased into the home, gun first and ready.

He quickly and quietly pressed his back against the wall to his right. From the configuration of the house, the living room was off to the right and he wanted to check that area first. It was dark inside. Too dark, he thought. The street lighting from the cul de sac should be spilling into this room, but with the shades and curtains drawn no light was seeping through. He felt around the wall for a light switch. Normally, one could be found at the entry of every room. Nothing. He was only able to find what felt like the main pad for a security system for the house. He stopped and listened again. Again, nothing.

He reached into his pocket and pulled free a mini flashlight. He slowly scanned the living space and almost immediately found the bodies of Chad and Michele Finley in the middle of the room. They were bound and positioned in two chairs opposite each other. He moved the light slowly over their bodies and shuddered at the sight. Their bodies were slashed to such a degree that Paul revulsed involuntarily. It was as if they had been carved with a Katana. The flesh was just hanging from bone. Regaining his composure, he squinted and continued to scan the room until he came across the bodies of two children, lying on their backs on the floor just beneath the front window. Even from this vantage point, Paul could see that each child had been stabbed repeatedly, presumably with the same weapon. They were positioned in such a manner that the crown of each child's head was touching. Paul's legs began to grow weak. He leaned against the nearest wall for support, struggling to to keep himself together. He gathered his strength and scanned the room again. He kept looking until he finally found her. Layna was stretched out on the sofa against the far wall.

"Layna!" he cried out to her as he rushed over to her side, however as he took his third step into the room, his foot found something wet that, against the ceramic tile floor, caused his right leg to fly out from underneath him and caused him to slam hard against the floor, dropping his weapon and flashlight in the process. He felt around for his gun but couldn't find it. He scrambled to get to his feet but found it difficult to do so, on the wet floor. He crawled over to the flashlight, grabbed it and to the best of his ability made his way over to the sofa.

"Nooo, damn it!" He screamed as he knelt down beside her. "Layna, baby! Wake up, baby! It's me! It's Paul! Come on, baby, please wake up!" Paul tried desperately to wake her but she was lying still, so still. She had no visible trauma on her body save for a single stab wound to her heart. Paul cried, the tears flowing freely from his eyes.

Paul reached out to touch Layna but withdrew. He wanted his touch to remember her warm and lively, not cold and dead. He used the flashlight to look down at his person. He could see that he was covered in blood. Using the flashlight he looked around the room again and he could see that there was blood everywhere. He moved over to the lamp that sat upon an end table to the left of the sofa, found a button on its base and depressed it.

As the light filled the room, Paul could see that the scene was much more horrific than he had imagined. There was blood on every piece of furniture, on every corner of the floor. But the walls, the walls were worst of all. Written all over each wall, in different sizes and in different shapes, were three godforsaken words:

'THEY'RE ALL MINE!'

Paul first stumbled backwards; the air had been knocked from his lungs. He desperately fought the urge to vomit as he realized that those three words were actually written everywhere. He looked closely and could see that they were written on the furniture, on the television, on the lampshades, even on the back of the window treatments. The bastard had used every available surface he could find to send his message. A message that was repeated no less than thirty times throughout the room. Paul dropped to his knees. He was weak; he was defeated. Everything that he had once known had been destroyed. Everything that he had truly stood for had been shattered, and he didn't have anything left with which he could use to pick up the pieces. Layna had been the last piece of sanity he had during this entire ordeal. She was the glue that had been keeping him together. It was just as she said; the potential had been incredible. There was so much that they could have shared together—should have shared together. Now, it was lost. All was lost.

Paul was overwhelmed by a feeling of hopelessness as he realized, definitively, that it was over. There would be no catching this unsub. There would be no setting things straight—no shit for him to settle. He was done; and what he needed to do was drop his tail between his legs and run. Run like the defeated dog that he was. Run like all hell and just get away.

Paul heard a soft sound just behind him. He took a moment to stand as still as possible in order to hear more. He began to curse under his breath because he realized that he did not properly secure the entire premises. He came into the living room, was confronted by the present scene, and completely neglected the rest of the home. He knew better. He'd been trained better. The killer could still be in the house; Paul should have checked every room.

There. He heard it again. This time it sounded nearer. Paul slowly turned to direction of the sound and was startled as he was greeted with a voice and a chloroform-soaked rag.

"Hello, Paul." Although he could barely hear it, Paul recognized the raspy voice, but only just before he quickly faded into a black pool of emptiness that claimed his consciousness. He fell to the floor.

Chapter Twenty-Nine

It was the soft intermittent tapping that actually woke him up. A singular kind of tap. Like the cap of a ballpoint pen against a linoleum surface. The kind of sound that annoyed most people. An annoyance that might start with a few dirty looks but, given enough time and dogged persistence, could lead to a brisk discussion and, on occasion, even violence. Paul was not particularly fond of the sound, at least not on most days. Today was different however—different from any other day Paul had ever known, and quite frankly, right here, right now . . . Paul welcomed it.

"Hello, Paul." There it was again—the raspy voice from the phone. "Did you enjoy your little nap?"

Paul was blindfolded. He could not see his adversary, but he could listen. The area was quiet. There were no identifying sounds that Paul could hone in on, at least not yet.

Paul knew immediately that he was tied down. He was in a seated position and securely bound to a chair. Try as he might, Paul knew there was no chance of freeing himself. His adversary had secured him properly, effectively.

"Who are you?" Paul managed to say with a raspy voice of his own. His voice however was a result of his extremely dry throat. "Why are you doing this to me?"

"Why am I doing what to you, Paul?" the other man chuckled. "What am I doing to you?"

"Fucking with me!" Paul's voice grew stronger as he made no effort to disguise his contempt. "Why are you fucking with me? What in the world have I done to you?"

The other man began to walk around the room. As he got nearer, Paul listened to the footsteps. He stopped just behind Paul, leaned forward, and whispered in his ear.

"Honestly, Paul. Don't you know who I am?"

"No, I don't know who you are!" Paul was shouting. "Other than some sick fuck, I have no idea who you are! Take the blindfold off! Let me see you, you crazy bastard!"

The man stood up. H.e reached down and relieved Paul of the blindfold. Paul took a moment and worked his eyelids open and closed to adjust to the lighting of the room. It was a relatively dark, small room. There was a table just in front of him and beyond that, another chair. The light in the room came from behind Paul, so he could not identify the source. He waited as his adversary came into view, sitting in the opposite chair.

Paul looked at the man. He could not get a great look; he was still a little groggy. The lighting was not good, and his eyes were not quite focused—not just yet. But, from what he could see, the man fit the general description of the man that all of the witnesses described: fairly tall, well-built, neat, clean shaven. This was definitely the bastard that had been killing those women.

The man simply stared at Paul. He fished a quarter out of his breast pocket and began tapping it on the table. He looked to Paul for any kind of reaction.

"*Who the fuck are you*?" Paul's chair rattled, nearly breaking free from the bolts that were bracing it to the floor, as he screamed at the top of his lungs.

"You really don't know do you?" The man seemed genuinely surprised. "You really don't remember."

"Remember what? Remember you? No, I don't fucking remember you!"

The man shook his head. "Such a shame. It really is."

276

Paul glared at his adversary. He was seething with hate and wanted no less than to be free of his binds. There were so many things he wanted to do to this man. If only he could just get free.

"Well, Paul let me tell you. I'm surprised that you don't recognize my face, hurt even. But then again, it was many years ago, many lives ago." The man paused for a moment. He looked down at his hands and began to systematically crack each knuckle. He had to steal his glance away from his hands to look at Paul.

"Do you remember Lucy Mallon, Paul?"

Paul sat up straight in his chair and offered a look of indignation in response.

"Do you, Paul? Do you remember Lucy Mallon?"

This time Paul took a moment to actually consider the question. No one and nothing came to mind. "No," he responded. "I don't know a Lucy Mallon."

"Ahh, but you did, Paul." He leaned back into his chair and waved a finger in Paul's face. "You did know her. You knew her quite well as a matter of fact—at least for a brief moment in time, you knew her intimately well."

Paul shook his head and tried again to wrench himself free. "What are you talking about?" Paul looked around the room. He was searching for anything that might aid in his escape.

"Look at me!" The man was growing impatient.

Paul ignored the request and continued to look around the apparently empty room.

"I said look at me, damn it!" the man shouted as he pounded on the table.

Paul was immediately taken aback by the ferocity of the action. His captor had been cool and relatively reserved one moment and instantly agitated and hostile the next. He seemed to go from zero to sixty in no time at all. As a result, he had attained Paul's complete and undivided attention.

"That's better." he said, regaining his composure quickly. He eased back into his chair and gave Paul a long appreciative look. "Let me tell you a story, Paul." He spoke in a thoughtful tone. "A childhood story. A tale of one's childhood. A mere reminiscence."

Paul squirmed a bit more in his seat, but he was listening intently.

"Let's go back, Paul. Let's go back about eighteen years. Let's see." The man paused for a moment. "Eighteen years ago—that would have made you—what? Fourteen years old? Is that right, Paul?"

"Yeah, that's right. I would've been fourteen. But you know that. So what?"

"Well, see. I remember you when you were fourteen, Paul. You were this hot little shit in the neighborhood. Don't you remember? All the parents thought you were such a great kid. Great in school, great in sports. Everybody loved Paul Andersen. All the girls in the neighborhood wanted to spend some quality time with Paul Andersen. But I've got to give you some credit. You didn't let a lot of that nonsense go to your head. You kept to yourself. You really didn't bother with anybody. You could've been a real prick, but you weren't."

"So, what are you saying?" Paul was still a little confused. "You're from my neighborhood. You're from Tulsa?"

"Yes, Paul. I'm from the neighborhood. I'm from Tulsa, and I remember you quite well. And by the time I'm finished this story, you will remember me as well."

Paul glared at the man. His eyes had adjusted to the light, and he was able to ascertain his adversary's facial features. There was a hint of recognition there, but still not enough to place the man.

"Do you remember playing baseball, Paul?"

"What?"

"In junior high school, do you remember playing baseball?"

"Uh, yeah. I remember. What's that got to do with anything?"

"You played for the Lincoln Junior High Hawkeyes. You were a pitcher, I believe—a pitcher and third baseman."

"*What's that got to do with anything?*" Paul was at his wit's end.

"It has to do with everything!" The man slammed his fist down hard on the table once again. His composure was completely gone. "It has to do with everything, damn it!"

"April, eighteen years ago!" He was still shouting. "You were coming back from baseball practice! You cut through Willow Creek Park as you always did! But this time was different," he started to lower his tone. "This time was very different, because this time you came across Lucy Mallon.

"Beautiful Lucy Mallon. She was seventeen at the time. She was lovely, full-figured even at that age. She was smart. She was a prize. She was my prize. I had lusted for Lucy for four years, and on this particular day, I planned to have her. She was sitting in the park having a picnic for one. That was one of her favorite things to do. She'd make herself a sandwich, maybe have some cheese and crackers and a few pieces of fruit and sit and read, all by herself, for hours. That's what she'd do all alone, there in the park, away from everybody.

"Every kid in the neighborhood wanted Lucy Mallon. Everybody wanted a piece of that ass. Eighteen years ago, I was gonna have that ass even if that meant I had to take it. But then, out of the blue, guess who comes strolling along out of nowhere?"

Paul's eyes squinted and his brow furrowed as he tried to remember.

"Yes, that's right. You come up out of nowhere. You startled Lucy as she didn't expect to see anyone and she startled you for the same reason. You two fucks laugh it off and she invites you to join her for a while."

Paul still struggled to draw the memory.

"I was there. I saw the whole thing. I saw how she went on to tell you how much she liked you. I heard her when she told you how all these other guys wanted her company, but that she really wanted to be with you. And you! You, with your dumb ass, never really paid her any mind. But not on this day. On this day, you paid her all the mind she wanted, because it didn't take her long to ease her shirt off to show you her beauties.

"See, I had to watch as she gave herself to you. I had to watch as you, with your virgin ass, fumbled your way though something that should have by rights been mine. You didn't deserve her, Paul. You didn't even really know who she was. I knew who she was. I loved her. I wanted her. I needed her, Paul, but she gave herself to you! But I fixed you. I fixed you both!"

Paul did his best to recall. His mind, for whatever reason, had blocked out the entire episode. Images began to break through, but they were hazy and disjointed at best. He still could not quite grasp it.

"What do you mean you 'fixed' me?"

"Wow," the man said, genuinely amazed. "You still don't remember."

"Well, Paul, after you two finished—after you robbed me of what was rightfully mine, I walked up on the two of you as you slept half naked in each other's arms. I grabbed you, suffocated you and made sure you stayed passed out. Her, on the other hand—I did much worse to her. Come on, Paul. Don't you remember?"

Paul did his best to recall.

"Don't you remember, waking up in all that blood—Lucy's blood?"

The image became vivid in Paul's mind's eye. Technicolor flashes began to bombard his psyche as the mental iron gate that had so capably hidden these memories away began to crumble.

"Don't you remember how I carved off her gorgeous tits?"

An image of being blood-soaked filled his mind. He recalled reaching out to her. She was awash in red, awash in blood. He remembered holding her severed flesh and wondering what it was he was holding.

"How I sliced her face so badly that they needed her dental records to identify the body?"

Paul remembered, running his hand over her face. It was a face he had known to be smooth just an hour before becoming so rife with slices and cuts that he wasn't sure that it was still human. Then, Paul remembered . . .

"Her stomach . . . ," he uttered.

"Ahh." The man actually mustered a smile. "So, you do remember. Tell me, Paul. Tell me about her stomach."

"You carved up her stomach."

The man stood up and gleamed as Paul began to relay his memory.

"Words. You carved words into her stomach."

He began to walk around the room, again standing behind Paul.

"She was mine?" Paul trembled as he recalled the memory. He could not control himself as his bladder relieved itself, creating a pool under his seat.

"You carved *'She was mine!'* into her stomach."

The man leaned over Paul's shoulder and whispered into his ear. "Do you remember me now, Paul?"

MINE!

Paul remembered that there was one person who was completely obsessed with Lucy Mallon. He was the neighborhood bully, a troublemaker, a psychopath. With the voice of a frightened child, Paul answered, "Barry?"

In an instant, Paul's nose and mouth were once again covered with the chloroform-doused rag and Paul, once again, lost consciousness.

Chapter Thirty

When Paul came to, he was back home in Alexandria. He tried to piece together everything that just happened. He remembered now. He remembered waking up to the horrific sight after making love for his very first time. He remembered being covered in Lucy's blood. He remembered the sliced flesh and the grotesque engraving of her stomach. He remembered the ordeal that followed afterward: the police investigation had been a nightmare. The medical examination saved him. The doctors were able to determine that he was attacked as well: that given the evidence, he was not the perpetrator. But, the police were certain that he knew his assailant. But he had never seen him. Paul truly never knew what hit him. He had made love to Lucy and woke up to a horrific mess. There really hadn't been much he could offer by way of evidence. He just didn't know.

That didn't assuage his neighbors, however. For the longest time, he was a pariah. He became much more of a loner than he already had been. It was then that Paul truly began to withdraw into himself. It was then that he began to see life differently. As terrified as he was to wake up next to Lucy's bloody corpse, he was also intrigued at the same time. There was a small fascination that accompanied his fright. It was a fascination that left him morose, but curious—curious enough to be eager for more. It was then that Paul began to sense what his true calling was, although his mind was not strong enough to hold on to the event. All things considered, Lucy's slaughter was too much to handle. Yet it was the impetus for *his* becoming.

As Paul began to regain his senses—recognize that he actually *was* home, he intended to grab a few things and just leave—grab a few of his essentials, perhaps his travel bag and a couple of other things and be gone. Never to be seen or heard from again. Unfortunately, like the rest of this evening, things would not turn out as well as he had hoped.

As he started to make his way around the condo, he could see that there was a small trail of blood that led from the door to his bathroom and eventually to his bedroom. He followed the trail. First to his bathroom where it appeared that he tried to clean up after himself. Then to his bedroom where it looked like he changed clothes; there was a set of bloody items tossed off to the side of his bed. There was a suitcase on his bed that was partially packed; his dresser drawers were opened in a peculiar fashion as if someone had been rummaging through them in a hurry. The staging was perfect. He turned and looked at the suitcase. Inside, there was another, smaller bag he had never seen before. He reached for the bag and began to open it but decided against it. He just needed to get the hell out of there as soon as possible.

Paul looked around the room one last time and shook his head. He backed out of the bedroom and whirled to head out of the front door when he was met by four other agents, including Special Agent in Charge Charles.

"Paul . . ." SAC Charles held out his right hand to motion Paul to stop. He complied. He carefully reached for his weapon and sat it on the floor and kicked it over to the agents.

"Do you have a back-up, Paul?"

Paul shook his head no. He had never been interested in carrying a secondary weapon. Remaining completely quiet, Paul turned and extended his arms out behind him. He knew the routine as well as anyone. He waited for the cuffs to be clamped against his wrists and then, respectfully, he was led from his home, into a waiting vehicle and back to Quantico.

Chapter Thirty-One

For nearly two hours, Paul sat in a guarded conference room, quietly waiting to be questioned. He took the time to recount everything that had happened over the past two weeks. He marveled at how completely things could change in a relatively short span of time. He tried to assess his situation. He wondered what evidence, if any, that they could actually have against him. He knew they had the blood on his clothes, which had already been confiscated from him. He was presently wearing an assortment of clothes that were provided to him by some of his similarly built coworkers. He knew that his prints and DNA were on the scene. He was also aware that there might be a great deal of evidence that might have been planted in his condo, but just how much and with regard to which victims, he could not be sure.

Paul imagined several scenarios. He tried to imagine every contingency as he prepared for the questioning that would inevitably ensue. Because the wait was so long, he assumed that Connie Jordan et al were probably en route to conduct the interview. It made logical sense. First and foremost, Connie was good. Very good. So, from a productivity standpoint, it made sense. Second, Connie was his supervisor, his boss, his mentor. For what it was worth, no one knew him better than she. Of course, that wasn't saying but so much, because she really did not know him all that well; but she was as close as it got. Terry, Paul thought, would probably be in on the interview as well. Interrogation was his strength, his forte. If anyone could get Paul to talk, to crack if you will, it would be Terry. Of course, Paul had seen Terry work innumerable times over the years, so he was intimately familiar with the drill. He knew the mood swings, the clever dialect, the mind games that Terry tried to execute whenever he needed to during an interview. It had proved to be very effective over the years, but Paul knew better. He knew to just keep quiet; keep his mouth shut. He would listen to whatever they had to say, take it all in and when it was time to confer with his attorney, he would be able to share all that he had heard and everything they tried to do, during their little "chat".

Paul sat quietly and waited. His attention was drawn to a little commotion outside of the conference room and he concluded that his colleagues had finally arrived. As he suspected, Connie Jordan and Terry Carter walked into the room soon after. They both had very stern looks on their faces. They had stern faces that were accompanied by exhaustion and regret; especially on Jordan's face, not so much with Terry. Paul could only imagine the multitude of thoughts they might have entertained on their flight back east. He could only guess at the types of conversations that they might have shared. He was sure that disappointment was present. If not in the actual words, he was sure that disappointment was present in their tones.

Jordan walked into the office first. Terry was close behind. She took the seat opposite the table from Paul while Terry stood in the corner near the door. Neither of them said a word. They simply sat or stood, and stared at Paul. They tried to hide their emotions behind their faces, but neither was particularly successful. At least not to Paul's discerning eye. He could read emotions. He did so extremely well. Their faces were like an open book to Paul.

After a few moments of silence, they were interrupted by one of the tech guys as he wheeled in an all-in-one monitor. It was a monitor that could be used with a computer to play a DVD or to connect to an input cable for any assortment of source feeds; it served a variety of purposes. Paul presumed they either wanted to record their session or that they had something that they wanted him to see.

As soon as the tech finished his set-up, he left the room. Paul turned his attention back to his visitors. He wondered where they would start. Would it be Layna? Would it be any of the three ladies that were pinned to the board back in KCK? Would it be Lorri Massey? Had they finally traced that change purse all the way back to its owner, and were they now questioning the validity of her "accidental death"? Connie was the first to speak.

"Paul," she took a moment to clear her throat after speaking his name. "What can you tell me about the night of April twentieth and the morning of the twenty-first?"

Paul could not hide the surprise on his face. It was the last question he thought they would have.

"I don't understand." He did his best to look and sound confused. "I was in Minneapolis with you. Working on the Konetchy case. You know that."

"Yes, I know. But what did you do after dinner? After we broke for the night?"

"I went to my room. I was bushed." He tried to sound as nonchalant as possible.

"No, you didn't." Terry said from the back.

"Sure, I did." Paul was confident.

"No, you didn't Paul, because Milly and I saw you when you got in. It was after four and you looked like hell."

Paul had to switch gears quickly. He had no idea he had been seen.

"Oh, yeah. That's right," he said as if he had completely forgotten. "I did come in after dinner, but went out later. I went to get some drinks, blow off some steam. I told you, Connie, I'm dealing with some personal problems. I got so loaded, I almost completely forgot all about it. You guys have to know that that's not something I do very often."

"Okay," Jordan conceded. "Where did you go?"

"Oh, I don't know the name of the place. I just found someplace nearby and tried to drown my sorrows. That's all."

"That's all?" Jordan asked. "Are you sure?"

"Absolutely."

Jordan paused for a moment. She simply looked at Paul—read his expression.

"Have you ever been to the Santa Fe Courts?" Jordan spoke in a manner that was calm and plain. She was very matter-of-fact in her tone and her mannerisms.

"What do you mean? Like in New Mexico?" Again, Paul feigned any understanding of the line of questioning.

"No, Paul. The Santa Fe Courts is a residential complex in Minneapolis. I think you know this. Have you ever been there?"

"I don't know, I mean . . . I don't think so. I might have passed by them without my knowledge. I really couldn't tell you."

"Really? You have no recollection of spending time at the Santa Fe Courts?"

"None." Paul was confident and convicted in his responses.

"Well, maybe we can help trigger that memory for you a little bit." Jordan turned to Terry who activated the monitor and began play of a DVD.

Paul was more than curious to see what they had to play. He wondered how it all tied in with Minneapolis. After a few moments of nothing, Paul was able see a view of East Franklin Street from up above. Presumably, from the angle, the camera was poised at the entry of the courtyard just along the edge. It was positioned in such a manner that it would show anyone who entered or exited the courtyard from the East Franklin side and although the distance was from approximately a hundred feet, the clarity was good enough to get a decent look at whomever was moving in and out. Paul hid his surprise and his despair very well, but his insides were twisting.

They watched for a moment and just as he expected, he could see himself walking out of the courtyard and toward the truck, which was parked on Fourteenth Street South at the time. They sped up the footage and showed him returning for the pendant, then, leaving in a state of panic. The footage showed him returning, yet again, before leaving for a third time, but just barely, as he almost didn't make it back to the vehicle due to his disheveled and weakened state.

"So what do you say, Paul?" Terry stepped forward. "Do you want to change anything about your story?"

Paul was speechless.

"See, the way I figured it. It was like this." Terry grabbed a free chair, and spun it around sitting on it backwards. He leaned on the back of the chair and spoke frankly with Paul.

"We were in the Minneapolis area a few months ago, before the Konetchy killing. You probably used that time to scope the area out, get a feel for the place—all that good ol' serial killer, stalk-your-victim type of stuff."

Paul sat quietly. He couldn't look directly at Terry. He didn't dare to. He continued to look at the video as it looped it back to the beginning.

"You probably did a half-way decent job of it too." Terry continued without missing a beat. "You're very thorough Paul. We know your work. You pay attention to every little detail. That's what makes you such a damn good profiler. But here's the problem. Here's where you fucked up. See, when we were there three months ago, those cameras weren't there. There was no surveillance. So, you figured you'd be able to do your dirt and get away with it unnoticed. But two weeks before the Konetchy case, they installed a complete, state-of-the-art, surveillance system at the behest of the residents. You see, Paul, there are quite a few single women who live in that complex. So, with their H.O.A. fees, they decided to add the cameras with the hope that it would make it a little safer for them, especially at night."

Terry leaned back a little in his chair. "Now, that didn't help Amy Brandenburg too much, did it Paul? Did you actually know her, Paul? Did you actually know Amy Brandenburg or was she just one of those random kills? One of those random marks? Which was she, Paul?"

Paul continued to sit quietly. Of all the things he had going against him, Amy Brandenburg's murder was going to be the toughest to deal with. He felt sure of that, if for no other reason than that the entire team was present when that murder took place.

"You see, Paul. All this footage really does, is tell us that you were at the location during the time of the murder. This footage doesn't actually put you in Brandenburg's townhome. But, do you know what *does* put you into her townhome, Paul? Any idea? Come on, give me a guess. Nothing? Well, let me answer that for you."

Terry reached into his pocket and pulled free a plastic evidence bag. Into his pocket again, he pulled free a pair of latex gloves and slipped them on with rehearsed ease. "This! This puts you in her townhome, Paul."

He opened the evidence bag and carefully extracted a wonderfully made platinum Aesculapius. *The little item that started it all*, Paul thought. He tried to maintain his composure but he could feel himself cracking up inside. He only glanced at the pendant. He tried to keep his focus on the monitor screen. Terry had set the player on repeat so it could play incessantly while they talked.

"You see, Paul, we found this little baby in the bag you were trying to pack before you were picked up by your illustrious colleagues. By the way, . . ." Terry began, carefully laying the gorgeous pendant on top of the evidence bag so no part of it actually touched the table. He looked directly at Paul who refused to return the glare. "Where were you going, Paul? We didn't find an airline ticket anywhere. Were you just going to drive, Paul? Were you headed back to Tulsa?"

Paul remained quiet. Jordan decided to take a turn.

"Talk to us, Paul. Talk to me. Look, we know you didn't do all of these murders by yourself. It wasn't possible. We know you were working with someone else."

At this point, Paul finally looked away from the monitor and directly at Jordan. *They can't be serious,* he thought. *They actually thinking I was working* with *this guy?*

Jordan saw the change in his expression.

"What, Paul? What is it? Talk to me—who is it, Paul? Who were you working with?"

Paul just could not believe it. With everything that he'd had to deal with over the previous couple of weeks, they actually thought that he was working with this guy. The bastard who totally, and quite effectively, ruined his life. He'd killed Layna, the only woman Paul would even remotely consider as a love interest. They thought he was working with *that* guy. Barry. Barry-fucking-Linden! Again, Paul was beyond words.

He stared back toward the monitor, and this time he saw a little bit of footage he had not seen before. This time, Terry let the video play a little longer than he had before, and for the first time, Paul could see the man that left the courtyard not long after his last departure. The man, whom he could not quite make out, walked out of the courtyard, and to Paul's disbelief stared directly at the camera. He stared directly into the camera and right at Paul.

"That's it! That's him! He's the one you need to catch!" Paul exploded as he jumped out of his seat and pointed at the monitor. Jordan instinctively pushed her chair back from the table, and Terry nearly fell out of his.

"Paul?" Jordan was exasperated. She had no clue what was going on. "What are you talking about?"

"*Him*! That mutherfucker, right there! He's the one you should be going after!"

Jordan and Terry both turned to look at the monitor. They took note of the strange man leaving the courtyard.

"Paul, look," Jordan said, trying to regain control of the situation. "You really need to calm down. Tell us what the hell you're talking about."

Paul was still agitated, still angry over the fact that the guy was still mocking him. Even now, behind these walls, the guy could still get to Paul.

"Okay, look. It's like this." Paul sat back down in his seat, but he was still clearly excited. "This guy," he turned to the monitor. "That guy," he said, pointing, "his name is Barry. Um. Barry Linden. And he has apparently been fucking with me for years." Paul took a moment to swallow and clear his throat.

"Okay, yes, I admit it. I've killed a few of those women." Once, stern and stoic, Paul now seemed more than willing to allocute everything. "But, Barry Linden is the bastard you should be looking for."

"Barry Linden?" Jordan was perplexed. "Do you mean SAC Barry Linden?"

"*SAC* Barry Linden? That mutha-, . . ." Paul took a moment. "That bastard works for the Bureau?"

"Yes, Paul. Barry Linden is an SAC out of the KCK office."

"Really?" Paul was putting everything together. "Well, that actually makes sense," he muttered to himself. "Can't you see? That's how he was able to do it. He was able to use the Bureau to find these girls . . . learn about them."

"You mean, like you, Paul." Jordan held up her hand to stop him. "Listen, before we go any further, I need to read you your rights."

"Come on, Connie. I know my rights. I waive them. I know you're recording this. I waive my rights. Just let me finish."

Jordan leaned back in her seat and waved her hand in a manner that suggested he continue.

"Okay, yes. I did kill the Brandenburg girl. I killed three of the girls that Chen had on his board. I admit to that. I do. I'll tell you what I did. I'll tell you everything. But this guy—this guy . . ." He pointed to the monitor again. "*Him*! Barry! The same guy that all the witnesses are talking about has been fucking with me. He's been planting evidence in cases that I had nothing to do with. He's been doing all kinds of shit. I never took a souvenir from my victims. Never. Not once. Let alone take something from one scene and leave it on the scene of another. That's crazy. I never did anything like that."

"Come on, Paul." Terry was not moved.

"Terry, I'm telling you. I never worked with anybody. But Barry is the guy that everybody's describing. He's been after me ever since childhood. Apparently I fucked a girl he really liked and he's never gotten over it. He slaughtered that girl. Look it up, eighteen years ago. Lucy Mallon, she was slaughtered, and I was a suspect for a little while but was cleared early on because I was attacked too. There was medical evidence that cleared me. But Barry...he was a predator in the making. He really liked Lucy, everybody knew it, but she wouldn't give him the time of day. Nobody would bother with him. Now, he's with the Bureau." Paul was still in disbelief.

Paul's voice began to grow soft, almost reflective. "Listen to me. All I know is that Barry is the guy you need to be looking at. He's out there and he's dangerous. He's a helluva lot more dangerous than I ever was, and you guys need to stop him."

"What about this?" Terry lifted the pendant.

"That! That fucking thing is where this whole thing came to a head. Listen, after I killed the girl, I went back to get that pendant. I don't know why so don't ask me. For some odd reason that thing was just calling me, and I figured that since I had never taken anything else, that it wouldn't be too big of a deal. That was the first time you see me return on the video. But when I got there . . . when I got there that pendant was pinned to her front door along with a note saying '*She was mine!*'"

They looked at Paul.

He held up his right hand. "I kid you not. I swear to God that's what happened. You can see how I look on the video. You can see that something was wrong. That shit rocked me, so I left. Halfway back to the hotel, I figured that I just couldn't leave that thing pinned on the door like that. Someone might see it. So, I went back to get both the note and the pendant. But when I got there." Paul was almost out of breath. "When I came back again the pendant and the note were gone. I was done. I didn't know what to do. But ever since then, this guy, Barry, has been fucking with me and fucking with me. I just couldn't . . . I mean, it wasn't like I could tell anybody about it. I mean, what could I do?"

"Are you kidding me?" Terry was taken completely aback by the question. "You're not seriously asking that question, are you?"

"Terry, listen to me." Paul was very calm and firm in his statements. "Yes, I killed some of these women. I will tell you who, how, when, and where. But you, and you too, Connie," he said turning back to her. "You all have to believe me when I say that Barry Linden is out there killing women, and he's a helluva lot better at it than me. For Christ's sake, he carved '*She was MINE!*' into Lucy's chest way back then. Dig up the case, you'll find it. You'll find I'm right. He did that shit and he's been on my ass, turning my life upside down ever since. I don't know what to tell you, except for the fact that you have to take a real good look at this guy. You have to get this guy off the streets. He's not gonna stop killing. He loves it too much, and he's too damn good at it to stop now."

"Paul, Barry is a well respected SAC. There's no way that he's the man that you're describing." Jordan was unapologetic with her response. "I don't know what you're trying to pull, but it's not going to fly. Not to me or anybody else are you gonna sell that bullshit. But I'll tell you what . . ."

Jordan leaned back and whispered a few things into Terry's ear. Terry collected the pendant and placed it back into the evidence bag. He stood up and then Jordan stood up. She walked over to a cabinet off to the side in the room. She rummaged through the drawers until she found a pen and a pad. She tossed both items onto the table and at Paul.

"Write it down."

Paul picked up both items. "Write what down?"

"All of it."

"Okay, okay. No problem. But you believe me, right?"

The two agents began to make their way out of the room.

"You believe me, right?" Paul raised his voice as they left the room and headed toward the B.A.U. "You have to believe me! This guy is still out there. It's Barry Linden! He's the real monster! *You have to get this guy!"*

Terry and Paul were out of earshot. They exchanged looks, but no words. They both had seen the man on the video and the odd way he looked into the camera. And they conceded that there was a consistent description of someone else who might be involved. They both also knew Barry Linden. They had worked with him on a few occasions and found him to be an outstanding agent and a superior SAC. But Paul had been highly regarded, as well. It just seemed to be too much to take in at one time. Two FBI agents going rogue?

Jordan's mind found it hard to lose the thought. Neither she nor Carter was willing to believe Paul's story of being set up. There was too much evidence against him, and it was still coming in. Shortly, they would learn of the murders committed at the Finley household and with Paul's DNA and prints present in the blood, it would simply serve as another nail in his coffin.

Paul continued to shout in the conference room. Even as he returned to his seat and began to write everything that had occurred over the previous few weeks, he would occasionally restate, at the top of his lungs, his point, that there was true evil loose in the country. He needed to make sure they would not simply stop with him, that they would keep looking, that he wouldn't take the fall for a series of murders that he had absolutely nothing to do with. He had to make them see. He had to make them see or die trying.

Epilogue

Four and a half years passed. Paul Kenneth Andersen was tried and convicted for the murders of Amy Brandenburg in Minnesota; and Layna Mincher, Michele Finley, Chad Finley, and their children, Phoebe and Chase, in Maryland. He was still awaiting trial for the murders of Susan White in Wisconsin, Katana Lopez in Illinois, and Paige Traxler in Nebraska. With this many convictions he would never again embrace freedom. To his knowledge, the authorities were still trying to pin at least seven more murders on him. There wasn't enough evidence to charge him with the murder of Lorri Massey. Her accidental death was still officially ruled an accident.

Currently, Paul was back in Kansas—Leavenworth Prison to be exact. Leavenworth had become his "home away from home" as he awaited the various arraignments and trials that were to be the main focus of his life over the next decade or so. By virtue of his confession and convictions, Paul had managed to become one of the most prolific serial killers caught since Gary Ridgway, the Green River Killer—a feat of which he was not proud.

Next up for Paul—a trip to Chicago. He was awaiting extradition in order to be arraigned for the murder of Katana Lopez. It would be a quick procedure. He had already confessed to killing Ms. Lopez while he was detained in the B.A.U., a millennium before, it seemed. It was just a matter of going through the motions. The drill had become second nature to him.

For the first couple of years, he tried earnestly to convince anyone that would listen that there was still someone out there that needed to be caught. That he had not killed everyone he would eventually be charged with, that there was still a monster on the loose. Originally, he thought he had the ear of the authorities, but, subsequently, their actions proved otherwise. It appeared to Paul that everyone was really only interested in pinning the most murders on him that they possibly could. Never mind about the other guy. Never mind about *him*. Paul continued to plead his case until he was convinced that no one was listening. It took a couple of years, but he finally got it. They were very convincing.

By virtue of his actions, and his extremely long fall from grace, Paul had attained a degree of fame and had become somewhat of a celebrity. He received a great deal of fan mail. It ranged from those who expressed sympathy to those who wanted him crucified. There were women who wanted to marry him. There were men who wanted to marry him. There were those who even wanted to continue his work. There were those who wanted to vilify him for his work. And then there were those that were so perverse that he couldn't stand to touch the paper upon which such filth was written.

Occasionally, Paul would receive something that actually interested him. It might be a letter that held a ring of sincerity; some people sent him prayers in order to help save his soul. He wasn't sure if he believed in such things, but in some of them, he would read something that actually moved him, touched his spirit. He appreciated those letters more than most. Other times, people would send him things: photos, greeting cards, hand-drawn pictures—some people even sent him some money.

Every once in a while, he would receive newspaper clippings. These he truly appreciated because it kept him in touch with some of the things that were taking place in the outside world. He couldn't always discern exactly why a particular clipping was sent to him but he really didn't care. It gave him something to read. It kept him up to speed with at least on some of the events that were happening throughout the U.S.

On this particular day, he received another news clipping. The envelope was already opened and the contents were already read; that was the usual case. There was no return address and no indication of where the clipping came from; that too was common with some of the things he had received. He sat on his bunk and played with the envelope for a few moments. He wasn't accomplishing anything, but there was no rush. He had all the time in the world.

He pulled the clipping from the envelope and looked at the paper. The source paper was the Madison Gazette, a Wisconsin-based newspaper. He looked over both sides of the sheet, which held numerous articles on both sides. He saw that one side of the paper was the obituary page. It listed the recent deaths of nine people; but it was the feature article that drew Paul's attention. The headline read:

School Teacher Found Slain In School

It was circled in highlighter suggesting that Paul read the article, and he did. The article carried the report of a Rita McAllister who had been found dead, suffocated in her classroom after hours, choked by a chalkboard eraser of all things. The article discussed how Mrs. McAllister had been an award-winning teacher, how devoted she'd been to her students, how well liked she'd been by her students and her colleagues. The article was truly a glowing memoriam to a woman who had apparently made a difference in her community.

As Paul continued to read the article, the text turned from her professional life to her personal life: a married mother of four, who liked camping, fishing, shopping, and spending time with her family. As Paul continued to read, he learned that Rita's maiden name was Frisk and that she was born and raised in Tulsa, Oklahoma.

"Rita Frisk?" Paul lowered the paper and turned his gaze upward as he tried to remember. "Rita Frisk . . . yeah . . . I think I remember her." His memory became stronger. "Yeah, Rita!"

Rita was another childhood friend. She was another young lady that had made no secret of her affection for Paul. But unlike with Lucy, Paul and Rita had never had relations. They never got together or shared any special time in one another's company. She was just a girl that had liked Paul. Now, she's dead. Paul continued to read the story and learned that the killer used the board erasers to dab *"MINE!"* onto the board.

Paul jumped up from his bunk and started screaming for the guard. "C-O!" he screamed. "C-O! On the gate! I need to talk to somebody! C-O! Anybody! I need to get the warden down here. C-O!"

Paul's cries would go unanswered, though not unheard. He would be unrelenting in his attempts, regardless of the results, because he knew that his tormenter, his adversary, his nemesis, Barry Linden was still out there—and still a monster. He would be unrelenting because someone needed to understand that the man needed to be stopped. Unfortunately, there was only so much that he could do from behind bars. So he screamed and screamed and screamed some more. He screamed so much that it became clear to certain authorities that he was no longer capable of aiding his own defense.

***

Two days after agent Jordan learned of Paul Andersen's suicide, she still found it difficult to leave her office. Her relationship with Paul had deteriorated so deeply, so quickly, that she was still trying to fully come to grips with all that had occurred.

"Agent Jordan . . ." She was startled by the sound of her name. She looked up to see the mail clerk standing at her door.

"Agent Jordan, sorry to startle you—I have a letter for you. Believe it or not, it looks like it's from Agent Andersen."

The clerk placed the letter on Jordan's desk and left her to stare at it. She had no desire to open it—but since it was the only thing that Paul had sent since this entire business unfolded, she felt she had to. She reached for the letter and turned it around a few times. She could clearly see that it came from Paul. She closed her eyes and opened the envelope without looking. Relieving the envelope of its contents Jordan dared to open her eyes. It was a news clipping. She read it once. She read it twice. After the third time, she reached for her cell phone. She dialed a familiar number, and when the phone was answered, heard a familiar voice.

"Mickey . . ." Jordan's voice was slightly weak.

"Connie, hey, I'm really sorry to hear about Paul." He was sincere.

"Yeah, it's been a little rough going." Jordan paused. "Listen, I need you to do me another favor."

"You're kidding." There was a hint of trepidation in his voice.

"Unfortunately, no." Jordan paused yet again. "Hold on—let me close my door."

###

About the author

Truly a writer of versatility and imagination, S.E. Robinson has developed a strong devotion to the craft. Through the years, Robinson has been enthralled and inspired by the writings of Stephen King, Dean R. Koontz, Edgar Allen Poe, Richard Matheson and Daphne Du Maurier. However, the greatest respect is for the works of Michael Crichton. Primarily a creator of thriller, suspense and horror novels, Robinson has scores of working titles, which range from comedy to gothic literature. With a plethora of ideas, S. E. Robinson hopes to author stories that are diverse and dynamic and that people from all walks and tastes will take pleasure in reading.

Robinson strives to be unique and daring within the realm of dark and suspense literature. The expectation is to give readers something new and interesting to think about with each chapter. Whimsically, Robinson believes that, "if you could put Salvador Dali's work to words, you'd find me".

S.E. Robinson currently resides in Chester, Pennsylvania with canine companions Bella and Nefertiti.

S. E. Robinson

Also by S. E. Robinson:
Glints of Fascination, Vol. I

And look out for these upcoming titles:
Strange Behaviour 2020
Dead By Dawn 2021
Widow's Web 2021

S. E. Robinson

MINE!

S. E. Robinson

Made in the USA
Middletown, DE
19 April 2021

37950404R00182